MURDER
in
PARIS

BOOKS BY HELENA DIXON

MISS UNDERHAY MYSTERY SERIES

Murder at the Dolphin Hotel

Murder at Enderley Hall

Murder at the Playhouse

Murder on the Dance Floor

Murder in the Belltower

Murder at Elm House

Murder at the Wedding

Murder in First Class

Murder at the Country Club

Murder on Board

Murder at the Charity Ball

Murder at the Beauty Pageant

Murder at the Village Fair

Murder at the Highland Castle

Murder at the Island Hotel

Murder on the French Riviera

Murder in the Countryside

Murder in New York

Murder on the Cornish Coast

Murder at the English Manor

The Secret Detective Agency series

The Secret Detective Agency

The Seaside Murders

HELENA DIXON

MURDER
in
PARIS

bookouture

Published by Bookouture in 2025

An imprint of Storyfire Ltd.
Carmelite House
50 Victoria Embankment
London EC4Y 0DZ

www.bookouture.com

The authorised representative in the EEA is Hachette Ireland
8 Castlecourt Centre
Dublin 15 D15 XTP3
Ireland
(email: info@hbgi.ie)

Copyright © Helena Dixon, 2025

Helena Dixon has asserted her right to be identified as the author of this work.

All rights reserved. No part of this publication may be reproduced, stored in any retrieval system, or transmitted, in any form or by any means, electronic, mechanical, photocopying, recording or otherwise, without the prior written permission of the publishers.

ISBN: 978-1-83525-779-1
eBook ISBN: 978-1-83525-778-4

This book is a work of fiction. Names, characters, businesses, organizations, places and events other than those clearly in the public domain, are either the product of the author's imagination or are used fictitiously. Any resemblance to actual persons, living or dead, events or locales is entirely coincidental.

For my gorgeous second grandson, Ezra Reuben Griffin, born while I was writing this book.

PROLOGUE

Torbay Herald June 1937

News

Duke Forgets His Wedding Kiss

His Royal Highness the Duke of Windsor and Her Grace the Duchess were married at the turreted Château de Candé, France, yesterday in a couple of simple ceremonies. Charles Mercier, the Mayor of Monts, read the civil service, and Reverend R. Anderson Jardine performed the Anglican service. The Duke, however, omitted the traditional kiss for his blushing bride. After making a plea for privacy the couple left for an Austrian honeymoon.

Announcements

The engagement is announced between Mr Robert Potter, only son of Mr Reginald Potter and Mrs May Potter of Dartmouth, and Miss Alice Mary Miller, eldest daughter of Mr Elijah Miller and Mrs Mary Miller also of Dartmouth.

Mr Robert Potter is the proprietor of Potter's Excursions, the popular local touring bus company, while Miss Miller is the owner of a successful tailoring and drapery business based in Winner Street in Paignton.

Advertisement

Springtime in Paris! Marvel at the Eiffel Tower, stroll along the banks of the Seine, enjoy the marvels and gaiety of shopping in the exclusive boutiques. Visit the many galleries and enjoy the delights of Notre-Dame and Montmartre. Contact Paris Travel, Fleet Street, Torquay, to plan your holiday with our experts today. Tel Torquay 371

CHAPTER ONE

Kitty parked her red touring car on the embankment near the ancient Dolphin Hotel in Dartmouth, Devon. The summer sun was warm on her back as she made her way along the busy pathway beside the river towards the imposing black and white half-timbered building.

The hotel had been in her family for centuries and her beloved grandmother still resided in the building in a spacious apartment that afforded her a view of the riverbank. Although retired, her grams still liked to keep an eye on the business. This was despite them having employed a charming and very capable manager.

Kitty still oversaw the hotel accounts and had regular meetings with the hotel staff, even though she had her own business to manage. She and her husband Matt were partners in Torbay Private Investigative Services. They had been kept very busy of late with an influx of all kinds of problems. Their last big case had started as a missing person's investigation but had culminated in murder.

Her grandmother's oldest friend, Mrs Craven, had been personally involved. She was still away from home on Dartmoor as a result of everything that had happened. While Mrs Craven had never been one of Kitty's favourite people she did feel very sorry for what had happened on the moor.

After Kitty and Matt had returned home her grandmother had been taken seriously ill with pneumonia. For a few days it had been touch and go and Kitty had resided at the hotel to care for her grandmother. The last week or so had finally seen her improving, however, and Kitty had returned to her home just across the River Dart in Churston.

Although her grandmother seemed to physically be making a good recovery, Kitty was still concerned about the older woman's low spirits. Her grandmother had been unusually listless and depressed. She had not even seemed excited by the news of Kitty's friend Alice's engagement. Something that normally she would have been eager to discuss.

Kitty paused on the pavement outside the oak and glass door that led into the hotel lobby. She gave herself a mental shake and squared her shoulders before entering, hoping that her grandmother was in better spirits this morning.

'Good morning, Kitty, your grandmother is waiting for you today,' Mary, the hotel receptionist, said as soon as Kitty drew near to the polished mahogany desk.

'Oh, is everything all right? She isn't feeling ill again?' A frisson of alarm swept through Kitty at Mary's greeting.

Mary smiled sympathetically. 'No, quite the opposite I should say. I think she had something come in the post this morning and she's been calling down every fifteen minutes or so to see if you've arrived yet. All perked up, she is.'

Kitty frowned. 'I wonder what she's up to. At least if she's taking an interest in something at last that must be a good thing.'

As she spoke, the black Bakelite telephone on the desk gave a short ring signalling an internal call. Mary's neatly pencilled brows lifted, and she picked up the receiver. 'Yes, Mrs Treadwell, Miss Kitty's just come in.' She grinned at

Kitty who started towards the broad oak staircase that led to the upper floors of the hotel. 'She's on her way up to you now.'

Kitty hurried up the stairs wondering what her grandmother could have received that had effected such a miraculous change in her spirits. She hoped it was something good and not something troubling. She knocked on her grandmother's door and let herself in on hearing her grandmother call out to her to enter.

The spacious salon of the apartment was flooded with sunshine through the diamond leaded-pane bay window and the air was scented from the large Delft bowl of pink roses on the table. Her grandmother was in her customary favourite chair next to the Portland stone fireplace. A letter lay open in her lap and her cheeks held a pink tinge that had been missing for the last couple of weeks.

'Kitty, darling, at last.' Her grandmother tilted her head to accept Kitty's kiss on her powdered cheek. 'I've been simply longing for you to get here this morning, ever since this arrived.' Her grandmother shook the letter in her lap.

Kitty took a seat on the sofa closest to her grandmother and drew off her pale-pink cotton summer driving gloves, stowing them in her handbag. 'Why? Whatever is it?'

She didn't think it was something bad judging by the smile on her grandmother's face, but it was obviously something out of the ordinary. There was another knock on the door and one of the hotel maids wheeled in a trolley laden with tea things. She parked it next to Kitty's grandmother, bobbed a shy small curtsy and left.

'Do pour the tea, darling,' her grandmother instructed.

Kitty set out the floral-patterned china cups on their saucers. 'Well? What is this terribly exciting letter? Who is it from?'

'It's from Eliza DeTourner.' Her grandmother watched as

Kitty placed the metal tea strainer over the top of the cup, before inspecting the contents of the teapot.

'My godmother? You haven't heard much from her lately, not since her husband passed away. Is she still living in France? I know you told me she was thinking of returning to England.' Kitty's curiosity was roused.

Eliza DeTourner had been one of her grandmother's closest friends some years ago, but Eliza had married a Frenchman much older than her around the time Kitty was born. Since then the couple had lived in France and although her grandmother had met her friend a few times since, their contact had mainly been via Christmas and birthday greetings.

Monsieur DeTourner had died a year ago, leaving Eliza widowed and living with her son, Julian. He had been a late blessing to the DeTourners and was a little younger than Kitty. Since Monsieur DeTourner's death her grandmother had only heard from Eliza a few times and the last time she had received a letter, Eliza had been thinking of selling her apartment and leaving France.

'I know, my dear. I spoke to her just over a month ago on the telephone while you were on Dartmoor. She was very undecided about what she should do about relocating as it's taken quite a while to settle her husband's affairs. Then, of course, she had Julian to consider.' Her grandmother paused to accept a cup of tea from Kitty.

'So, has she decided then? Is that what she says in her letter?' Kitty asked, offering her grandmother one of the dainty biscuits the hotel cooks had prepared for their mid-morning refreshments.

'I think so, but it seems that she still has a few loose ends to tie up and instead has suggested that I come to visit her in Paris. A final fling, so to speak, for us to revisit the places of our youth.' Her grandmother took a biscuit from the plate.

'That sounds lovely. You've always enjoyed Paris and it's

been years since you were there last.' Kitty helped herself to biscuits and tried not to shudder at the memory of her own previous visit to Paris.

The last time she and Matt had been in France had been at the behest of the British Government. That had seen them on a dangerous mission in Nice on the French Riviera. It was a mission that had almost killed both of them.

Her grandmother sighed and set the letter down.

'I don't know, Kitty. She is suggesting I come as soon as possible before the heat in Paris becomes too much and everyone disappears off to the coast in August. She is packing and looking for a house to rent in England so won't be there for much longer,' her grandmother said.

'Do you feel well enough to travel?' Kitty asked with some concern.

'I don't know, darling. I should love to go, and it would be wonderful to see Eliza and Julian. She talks of visiting some of the places we enjoyed in our younger years. There is even the possibility that I could attend a small private fashion show.' Her grandmother heaved a gusty sigh.

Kitty sensed that she was about to be manipulated into something. She knew it had been a lifelong dream of her grandmother's to attend a couture show in Paris. Grams had never thought she would be able to afford to buy from one of the designer houses, but she had always wanted to see where they were made.

'That does sound very tempting,' Kitty agreed cautiously.

'She also mentions a young lady that she thinks Julian wishes to marry. It is what she doesn't say about the girl, this Simone Belliste, that's interesting. I don't suppose that you and Matt? But, no, it's too much to ask, I know how busy you both are at this time of year.' Her grandmother looked at her.

Kitty sipped her tea and refrained from speaking. She knew what her grandmother was hinting at. Ordinarily, a short trip to

Paris would have been delightful but they were very busy. She was also concerned the journey might be too much for her grandmother after her recent illness.

'I'm sure if I had someone with me and I took plenty of rest the trip would do me the world of good,' her grandmother added in a meaningful tone. 'I'd have suggested that Millicent Craven could come with me, but she is still with the Favershams. With Sir Henry's funeral and then only a couple of weeks now until Sebastian's wedding, well, Lady Sarah needs her support.'

'Yes, there is a lot happening,' Kitty responded diplomatically. She and Matt had been invited to the wedding, now a quieter affair after the recent demise of the late Sir Henry Faversham. However, she had not been inclined to attend, fearing their presence might take attention from the bride and stir up bad memories after recent events there.

'Are you and Matthew terribly busy at present?' her grandmother asked before nibbling on her biscuit.

'Well, Matt is seeing Chief Inspector Greville this morning about the Redvers Palmerston case. I told you about that poor woman who came forward after he had married her bigamously and then absconded with her money a few months ago?' Kitty said. She had discussed the case with her grandmother during her illness, hoping to stir some interest.

Redvers had been a brother officer of Matt's during the Great War. He had faked his own death whilst convalescing at a requisitioned stately home acting as a temporary hospital in England. Something Matt had only recently discovered when he had sighted Redvers in January at the docks in Plymouth and had thought he had seen a ghost. Back in 1917, he had assumed Redvers had succumbed to an infection and had even attended the man's funeral.

Now it seemed that Redvers was making his living from taking on various fraudulent identities and conning vulnerable women out of their life savings. More and more evidence was coming to light about crimes the man had committed. They had been tracking him since January and Matt had gone to meet the chief inspector to see what could be done.

'Ah, yes, I know you said the whole affair had upset Matthew terribly. Perhaps then just a very short break in the sunshine, a change of scenery, might be just the ticket?' Her grandmother gave her a sly glance.

'Grams!' Kitty protested. 'Look, I don't know. I'd have to speak to Matt and then I'd have to make arrangements for Bertie and Rascal.'

At that moment, Rascal lay purring contentedly near her grandmother's feet. The company of the cat had been the only thing that had seemed to cheer her grandmother up while she had been so ill.

Bertie, her roan cocker spaniel, was at home with Mrs Smith, Kitty's housekeeper. He had been out in the back garden when Kitty had left that morning. She suspected that by the time she returned home another hole would have miraculously appeared near the raspberry canes at the side of the garden.

'Of course you must consult with Matthew. It's just, well, I'm not getting any younger, my dear, and this may be my last chance to fulfil a lifetime's ambition. And if Eliza has decided to return to England to live, then she will probably not go back to Paris for some time.' Her grandmother's expression took on a wistful air. 'Mickey would always have Bertie you know for a few days and I'm sure Rascal could stay with Mrs Smith. Just for a short holiday.'

Kitty suppressed a sigh. Her grandmother still looked unwell. The illness had taken its toll on her and she knew that Grams was right. She might not get this chance again. Especially if Eliza did decide to return to England in the next few months. She knew too that Mickey, the hotel maintenance man, would probably agree to look after Bertie.

'I'll speak to Matt when he gets home. We would have to

look at what cases we have open to see if we can manage something. I can't promise right now,' Kitty warned.

'Of course, darling. I wouldn't want to be a bother to you. Paris in the sunshine, a couture show, it does sound so lovely,' her grandmother murmured wistfully.

Kitty finished her tea and placed her empty cup and saucer down on the trolley. 'Where in Paris does Eliza live exactly?' she asked.

'Oh, it's in one of the nicer areas. What do they call them? Arrondissements? Passy near the Bois de Boulogne. Her husband was very wealthy, so she is quite comfortable. Julian has some kind of job in the city, I believe, managing investments. He seems such a nice young man. I have a recent photograph somewhere. Look in my bureau, Kitty, dear, the bottom drawer.'

Kitty jumped up and went to the small oak bureau where her grandmother kept her correspondence and most of her important documents. It was unlocked so she opened the drawer as instructed.

'There is a bundle of pictures just on the left there. Bring them over to me, darling,' her grandmother directed.

Kitty spotted the pictures and took them to her grandmother before resuming her position on the sofa.

'Now then.' Grams donned a small pair of gold-framed spectacles and began to sort through the small pile of pictures. 'Ah, here we are. This is one of Julian.' She passed the picture to Kitty.

Kitty saw a tall, good-looking, confident young man in smart attire and a straw boater standing beside a stone fountain.

'And here is a recent one of Eliza.' Her grandmother passed her another picture.

This one showed the man from the previous image with a shorter older woman dressed in very chic clothing, her arm linked with his and a sable stole around her shoulders. She recognised her godmother straight away.

'Lovely pictures.' Kitty passed them back to her grandmother.

'They were taken around Julian's birthday. Her husband was very ill at the time, and she was putting on a brave face for her son.' Grams studied the picture more closely. 'Eliza was always good at hiding her feelings, but I think you can see the worry in her eyes. I should like to see her to make sure she is doing as well as she says. I'd love to know more about this Simone who she says Julian is smitten with. I suspect she would like my opinion on the matter, as well as advice on finding a good property in England to rent.'

Kitty again said nothing to this. She suspected that she and Matt would be packing for a Parisian holiday very soon, however.

CHAPTER TWO

The sound of Bertie's enthusiastic barking alerted Matt to Kitty's return home. She emerged through the open French windows onto their small stone-paved patio and came to join him. He was enjoying a cold glass of cider outside in the summer sunshine admiring the garden. Bertie bounced happily at Kitty's side, clearly pleased that his mistress was home.

'Hello, darling, how was your grandmother today?' Matt rose to greet his wife with a kiss on the cheek. He could see from her face that something had gone on.

Kitty had never been very good at hiding her feelings. He hoped her grandmother had not taken a turn for the worse. When he had visited a couple of days ago he had noticed how frail she had become due to the pneumonia. Mrs Treadwell had always been a strong, determined woman despite her refined, petite exterior and it had been distressing to see her so unwell.

He knew Kitty was alarmed that she had seemed in such poor spirits, despite having seemingly turned the corner physically.

'Oh, she is much better in herself,' Kitty remarked as she

took a seat on one of the rattan garden chairs. She placed her handbag on the table and bent to throw a tennis ball for Bertie.

'Why do I sense there is a but coming?' Matt asked as he retook his own seat beside her.

'She received a letter this morning from an old friend of hers inviting her on holiday. Eliza DeTourner is actually one of my godmothers.' Kitty explained the connection, and told him of the contents of the letter.

'Grams suggested we might accompany her so she could go to Paris,' Kitty said as Bertie returned bearing his ball in his mouth, tail wagging proudly.

Matt grinned. He knew Kitty's grandmother all too well and he could imagine how the conversation would have gone and the hints both subtle and unsubtle that would have been dropped.

'And would you like to go to Paris? To see your godmother and her son? And, of course, the mysterious Simone?' he asked.

Bertie flopped down at Kitty's feet and dropped the tennis ball.

She sighed and fiddled with the strap of her cream-leather summer handbag. 'It just seems to mean so much to Grams. If this invitation had come when she had been well, then it wouldn't have been a problem. No doubt one of her other friends would have accompanied her as Mrs Craven isn't free. She still looks so frail though, Matt. This chance too, that Eliza mentioned, of attending an exclusive private couture show. It's been a dream of hers for years.' Kitty looked at him.

'Your grandmother has been very ill, and I know she is missing Mrs Craven's company,' Matt said.

'She is. Although I don't know how anyone could miss Mrs Craven, but they have been friends for such a long time.' Kitty gave him a wry smile.

'We do have a few days free before we take up our next commission.' Matt knew they were going to end up in Paris.

Kitty's expression brightened. 'What about the Redvers Palmerston case?' she asked.

'I'll tell you all about that in a minute. For now, let's decide if we are to accompany your grandmother to Paris or not.' Matt took a sip of his cider.

'If you think we could swing it?' Kitty asked in a hopeful tone.

'I think so.' He was prevented from saying much more as she enveloped him in a hug which made Bertie start barking with excitement.

'Thank you, Matt. Grams will be so thrilled. She looked so much perkier when she was talking about seeing Eliza again. I'll go and telephone her right away.' She suited her actions to her words and disappeared back inside the house to telephone the Dolphin.

Matt finished his drink while Bertie settled back at his feet with a disappointed huff at being left behind. Kitty re-emerged onto the patio a few minutes later, a beaming smile on her face.

'Grams is so excited. She said to thank you,' she said as she retook her seat.

'I'll sort out the arrangements. Will we need a hotel?' Matt asked.

'I think so. Grams said that Eliza would have offered for us to stay with her, but she is rather upside down at present as she's been clearing and packing. She has the decorators at her apartment too.' Kitty smiled at him.

'Very well, I'll sort something out. Now, I suppose you want to know about my meeting with Chief Inspector Greville?' Matt looked at Kitty.

'Yes, what did he say?' Kitty asked as she leaned her elbows on the table, giving him her full attention.

'I brought him up to where we were at in the case. That we had confirmed that Redvers had indeed faked his own death back in 1917. I told him about Redvers's wife having seen him and the burglary at his son's house,' Matt said.

'The one where we think Redvers stole back his family ring and his watch?' Kitty said.

'Yes, and then about this latest letter we received with the photograph of that poor woman, Mrs Weston, that he had married bigamously under a false name,' Matt continued.

'That poor lady. She was so lovely when we went to see her. I can't believe Redvers had robbed her of all her jewellery and emptied their bank account.' Kitty looked indignant.

'She was dreadfully upset and embarrassed when she realised she had been taken in,' Matt agreed.

'Did the chief inspector say what he intended to do? I don't know if we can track him any further on our own without the help of the police. I mean, he could be anywhere in the country by now.' Kitty frowned as she spoke.

'I gave the chief inspector all the information we had gathered, and he is going to alert his colleagues in the other forces. He will have a copy made and circulated of that wedding picture Mrs Weston gave us. He will also alert them to the aliases which we think he may be using.' Matt knew Chief Inspector Greville would do his utmost to try and locate the missing conman.

'That's good. I don't know that there is much more we can do then at the moment until he surfaces again,' Kitty said.

'I agree. It will take a few days for everything to get circulated to the various police stations. The chief inspector thinks that Redvers will probably stay within the West Country. He believes most of the contacts Redvers may have will be in this area and he will need some assistance.' Matt traced the tip of his forefinger down the outside of his empty cider glass.

'That does make sense. We know that Redvers has had help before to pull off his death as well as to probably establish himself under the various names,' Kitty said.

'The chief inspector is still somewhat short of staff.' Matt grinned at Kitty as he watched her instantly perk up at this piece of gossip.

'Oh? Is our friend Inspector Lewis not back from his secondment to the station in Exeter?' Kitty asked.

There was little love lost between Inspector Lewis and Kitty and Matt. The inspector had made it clear from their very first meeting that he disliked private investigators, and he especially disliked female private investigators. This had not gone down well with Kitty.

They had since had a number of cases which had forced them to work together. Although it was more that they were engaged on the same cases with minimal co-operation from Inspector Lewis. The last case on Dartmoor which had involved the Faversham family had once more involved them becoming a thorn in Inspector Lewis's side.

The inspector had been trying hard to secure a promotion to chief inspector and had undertaken a few secondments to other police stations in an attempt to secure this aim. Kitty had hoped that this would mean he would not return to Torquay.

'No, it seems that Exeter have even less manpower than Torquay at present.' Matt's smile widened at the look of glee on his wife's face.

'What a shame.' Kitty was unable to suppress her gurgle of mirth.

'Indeed. Now, are you upset about going to Paris when we could be working unfettered by Inspector Lewis?' Matt teased her.

'It does rather take the shine off it.' Kitty smiled back at him. 'I shall have plenty of news to tell Alice when we meet for our cinema visit tonight.'

'I'll go and telephone the travel agent and get our tickets booked and the arrangements made. I presume your grandmother will ask Mickey to look after Bertie?' Matt ruffled the tuft of fur on top of the dog's head.

He knew the Dolphin's maintenance man was very fond of their naughty spaniel. Indeed, he was one of the few people they would entrust with the care of their beloved pet.

'Yes, and I'll ask Mrs Smith if she can care for Rascal,' Kitty agreed.

Matt rose from his seat. 'Right, I expect I shall have to go down to Torquay to see the agent in person to pay deposits since the trip is at quite short notice. If I'm not back before you leave, give my love to Alice and congratulate her once again on her engagement.' He dropped a kiss on the top of Kitty's short blonde curls.

'Hmm, you didn't seem as surprised by the engagement announcement as I was.' Kitty gave him a keen glance.

'Really?' Matt grinned at her and made good his escape. He had been sworn to secrecy a long time ago by Robert Potter about a number of matters. It was better he left for Torquay now before his wife tried to wheedle more information from him.

* * *

Kitty's eyes narrowed as she watched her husband depart inside the house to make their unexpected travel arrangements. She knew that Robert Potter, her friend Alice's new fiancé, often confided in Matt. When Alice and Robert had fallen out some eighteen months or so ago Alice's lips had been sealed on what had prompted the parting.

She knew that Matt had known much more about it but had given his word to Robert not to say anything. Although it had killed Kitty with her innate curiosity, she hadn't pressed her friend for information. She knew Alice and Robert had started to see one another again, but until the engagement had been announced she hadn't liked to ask much about how things were going. Matt had obviously known a lot more about the matter.

Kitty usually met Alice once a week for a regular date to attend the local cinema, followed by a fish and chip supper. They also usually talked on the telephone a couple of times a week, but Alice had been very busy of late with her shop. Kitty too had been away, so it had been a while since their last meeting, giving them lots to talk about.

Alice had telephoned her with news of the engagement before it had gone into the local newspaper and Kitty and Matt had sent a card and had a china tea service delivered as an engagement gift. Kitty was looking forward now though to hearing all of the details and seeing Alice's ring for the first time.

Kitty heard Matt's cheery whistle, followed by the front door closing and the dull roar of his Sunbeam motorcycle engine starting. She guessed he must have had to go to the travel agency in person as he had suspected. Still, he had sounded very cheerful, so he clearly didn't mind taking a short holiday to France. She just hoped it would be more relaxing than their last trip there.

Matt hadn't returned home by the time she had eaten lunch, walked Bertie and tidied the sitting room. She left him a note telling him their housekeeper had prepared him a cold supper in the pantry and set off to Paignton to meet Alice.

She parked her little red car at the kerb outside the front of her friend's shop and waited. Alice had to close up and give her young assistant her instructions for the next day before she could escape to join Kitty for their evening out.

Presently, Alice emerged and locked her shop door, testing the handle to ensure it was secure before coming to join Kitty.

'I'm sorry I'm a bit late. It's been a busy day today, lots of people wanting their new summer dresses altered,' Alice exclaimed breathlessly as she seated herself in the passenger seat.

'I don't mind. I'm thrilled business is so good and you are so busy.' Kitty grinned at her friend. 'Well, don't keep me in suspense, let me see your ring.'

Alice's cheeks blushed as red as her auburn hair as she drew off her glove to reveal a neat gold band set with three diamonds.

'Oh, how lovely,' Kitty exclaimed as she admired the stones as they twinkled in the late afternoon sunlight.

'Thank you. I think he made a good choice.' Alice smiled at her friend. 'Thank you too for the lovely tea set. It arrived yesterday.'

'It was our pleasure. I remembered it wasn't something you had already in your bottom drawer,' Kitty said as she turned the key in the car ignition.

'No, you were right. It's so pretty. I love those new modern designs with the geometric shapes.' Alice tucked a stray strand of hair back under her straw hat and they set off to travel the short distance to the picture house near the station in the pretty seaside town.

Kitty parked just off the seafront, and they walked together arm in arm to the imposing red-brick cinema with its cream-coloured stone detailing.

'I am not the only one with news anyway I suspect. How is your grandmother? I went to visit her a couple of days ago and she still seemed very low.' Alice looked concerned.

'I know. I have been very worried, but her spirits seem to have improved today.' Kitty told her friend about the letter from Eliza and the plans for a short trip to Paris.

'Oh, you lucky duck. A Paris couture show! I should love to go and see what's new and coming out. It would give me so many ideas for my own dress designs. You will have to take lots of notes for me,' Alice said as they drew near to the entrance of the cinema.

'If we do get to go to a show I will, I promise. What are we watching tonight by the way?' Kitty asked as she prepared to take out her purse ready to buy her ticket.

'*The Prince and the Pauper*. It's got Errol Flynn.' Alice took on a dreamy expression as they headed for the box office.

Kitty grinned. She knew her friend loved movies and their stars and read all of the latest magazine articles about their lives. The dashing Errol Flynn was one of Alice's new favourites. Before long they were happily ensconced in their favourite seats and enjoying the film and the accompanying newsreel.

'He married her then, that Mrs Simpson,' Alice said a couple of hours later as they exited the cinema ready to go and get their supper. The Pathé News reel had shown a short clip of the wedding in the South of France. 'She always looks very smart and has some lovely jewellery though.'

'It would seem so. It was a nice suit and hat.' Kitty knew her friend, much like herself, had been saddened by the former king's abdication and decision to marry the American divorcee. The decision might have been romantic but it had also been quite shocking for the nation.

The air had cooled somewhat while they had been inside the picture house and the sun had begun to sink over the sea. Kitty shivered as they walked back towards the promenade and their favourite fish restaurant.

They decided to eat their supper inside at one of the tables in the small restaurant section of their usual fish and chip shop as the breeze had started to come in. Alice was unwilling to risk her new hat with the marauding seagulls who appeared to be patrolling the front for unwary holidaymakers bearing fish suppers wrapped in newspaper.

Once they were at their table and had liberally applied vinegar and salt to their meal, Kitty broached the subject at the front of her mind.

'Come on then, tell me everything about your engagement.

Matt has been like an oyster, and I know he knows much more about it all than me.' She snuck a glance at her friend. 'I am your best friend, after all.' Kitty speared a plump, golden chip with her fork.

She tried not to sound reproachful, but she had been puzzled that Alice hadn't confided in her about what had gone on.

Alice blushed. 'I didn't want you to think I was being silly when I stopped walking out with Robert. Everything was so muddled in my head, and you had to go away to France on that job for the government. Your cousin Lucy helped me a lot to get things right in my mind though and I didn't want to say anything until, well, until I knew for certain myself what I wanted to do.'

CHAPTER THREE

'I'd never think you silly.' Kitty couldn't help but feel hurt that her best friend hadn't felt able to confide in her. She knew Alice had really been upset when she had fallen out with Robert. Kitty had done her best to support her, despite not knowing the reason behind the split.

Alice stared down at her supper and prodded at the crispy, golden batter on her fish. 'You know that I was in love with Robert and, well, we'd talked about marriage.' She raised her gaze to meet Kitty's.

'Yes, I knew you had your bottom drawer all started and you always seemed so well suited together,' Kitty said.

'The problems really began at the Christmas and came to a head after Valentine's Day. I was hardly seeing him and it all felt a bit, well, forced. It was as if seeing me was just another job he had to tick off his list. It was like it were just expected we should get married as we'd been walking out for so long.' Alice frowned as she tried to explain.

'I remember you being unhappy. He forgot Valentine's Day, didn't he? Until the last minute?' Kitty had remarked on it to

Matt when Alice had shown her the limp bunch of flowers and belated box of chocolates that she had received.

'Yes, and he didn't make much effort at Christmas. It wasn't like we'd had words or a big row or something though,' Alice said, her face earnest. 'Then there was this quiz in one of my magazines. You know how they do them for fun. Well, this one was "Does your boyfriend take you for granted?"'

'Ah.' Kitty could see where this was heading. 'And you were being taken for granted?'

'Yes. It was as if Robert just thought I would fall in with whatever he suggested or wait around twiddling my thumbs while he built up his business. Then I was to be the little wife at home. I could see my life rolling out in front of me with no one asking me what I wanted.' Alice stabbed at her fish now with her knife.

'What brought it to a head?' Kitty wondered what Matt's part had been in all of this.

'I found something out by accident.' Alice's cheeks turned pink. 'I found as Robert was working on a cottage. It was to be a surprise apparently. Our first home. First home! I hadn't even said as I would marry him. No discussion about it, nothing. I hadn't even seen it. In fact, I still haven't. He just assumed that I would go along with everything as he decided. It was the last straw. I told him I wasn't going to go out with him no more. I thought as we wanted different things in life, and we should part ways.'

'This was just before we went to Enderley Hall and then Matt and I got sent to France and you stayed on there with Lucy?' Kitty had taken Alice with her to her aunt and uncle's home near Exeter at the time, hoping to give her friend a change of scenery.

'That's right.' Alice looked at Kitty. 'Talking to your cousin helped as she didn't know us as well and so she weren't likely to be biased. Not that you would have been, but I was so unhappy and confused. That was when I decided to set up my business. I wanted to prove that I was a person who could do things. I had ideas and ambitions of my own.'

Kitty dropped her fork down on her plate and reached across the table to squeeze her friend's hand affectionately. 'Of course.'

'I wanted Robert to see me as a person and to realise that if we were to be together then things had to change. He needed to actually talk to me. He's not good at talking but he's working on it. If he couldn't have done that, then we would have to stay apart.' Alice's lower lip quivered slightly.

Kitty's heart ached for her friend. She knew how difficult it must have been for Alice to take those decisions.

'Why didn't you tell me? And where does Matt fit into all of this?' Kitty asked as she resumed eating her supper.

'I felt stupid, and it made me too upset to talk about it. Mother kept prying and all, trying to get to what were going on. Then Robert, well, he didn't come after me or anything to try and get me back.'

'I know Matt was still going out with Robert and his father for their weekly billiard games and a pint at the Ship,' Kitty said.

'Robert had told Matt his plans. He knew about the cottage and that Robert had this ring for me. I think as Matt might have been to see the place. It has outbuildings and some land for Robert to keep his vehicles there. I don't know how he come to have enough to buy it. There's probably a reason why it was so cheap at the auction, apart from needing a lot of work. Robert was going to propose on my birthday he says, but I broke it off,' Alice said.

'Then he risked his life to swim out and save you that night when you were in the river.' Kitty had been horrified when Alice and Robert had been caught up in a case she and Matt had been working on at the time at Stoke Gabriel. Alice had almost lost her life and only Robert and Matt's bravery had saved her.

Alice blushed and nodded. 'That was when we started to see one another again. There was a lot of things we had to say and work out.'

Kitty smiled. 'I'm so very glad you did. Do you have an idea for when you'd like to get married? And will you live in this cottage Robert has for you both?'

The colour in Alice's cheeks deepened to a dark red. 'No date yet and I'll have to think about the cottage. There's a lot to be done to it apparently. He's not taken me to see it yet, he still says he wants to surprise me, and I'll take against it if I see it in the state it's in now. He has promised though as if I don't like it as he'll sell it and we can look together for a home.'

'Well, I am delighted for both of you.' Kitty raised her water glass and clinked it against Alice's. 'Cheers to you both.'

They finished their supper and Kitty dropped Alice back at her home above her shop. She promised once again to take copious notes of the Parisian fashion for her friend while she was away.

When she arrived home, Matt was in the sitting room. A pile of travel brochures and guidebooks were on the table beside him and Bertie was snoring happily on the hearth rug.

Kitty kissed her husband and took a seat on the black leather and chrome modern-style sofa. 'Did you manage to make the travel arrangements?' she asked, eyeing the booklets.

'Indeed, we are all set. We are to leave the day after tomorrow so just enough time to pack. I called in to the Dolphin to see your grandmother and we telephoned Madame DeTourner together. She is very excited we are to visit.'

'How thrilling!' Kitty couldn't help feeling a buzz of pleasure now at this sudden unexpected trip. It seemed her husband had been very speedy. She hoped the holiday would be everything her grandmother was hoping for.

'Your grandmother certainly appears to be in much better spirits. Like a new woman in fact,' Matt remarked with a grin. 'I have arranged for us to stay in Paris for a week. That should be enough time to attend the private fashion show, meet Julian's friend and see some of the sights.'

'Thank you, darling.' Kitty smiled back at him. 'I know that Grams will appreciate it so much. I must admit I'm curious to meet Eliza and Julian again. It's been such a long time since I last saw them. I vaguely recall Julian being an annoying child trying to tug my pigtails when I was younger. The photograph Grams showed me was of a very handsome young man.'

'Should I be concerned?' Matt's smile widened and the dimple flashed in his cheek.

Kitty swatted at him playfully with one of the pamphlets. 'Don't be so silly. It will be nice though to take a break. It's been a very busy year so far and it's coming up to our most hectic time of year.'

Summer in Torbay always provided them with a lot of work. The hotels, gardens and elegant surroundings attracted a wealthy clientele. This unfortunately also often meant an influx of petty thieves and conmen.

'How was your evening with Alice?' Matt asked. 'Did she tell you all about her engagement?'

Kitty told him everything Alice had said.

'I wish I could have said something to you before, but I promised Robert. He planned to propose thinking the cottage would be a wonderful wedding gift. It does need work but he'll be able to use it as a base for his business.' Matt's expression sobered.

'I'm glad you kept your word, even if it killed my curiosity being kept in the dark,' Kitty said. 'I'm so thrilled they are back together now though. They always seemed so well suited.'

. . .

The next day was swallowed up in a whirlwind of packing and sorting. Early on the morning of their departure they were collected by private car and driven to an airfield near London for the airplane journey across the channel to Paris. Kitty was touched by how careful Matt had been about the arrangements so that her grandmother could travel in ease and comfort.

Her grandmother certainly seemed to be much more like her old self as they boarded the plane. They seemed to have been barely in the air before they were setting down on French soil and heading for the waiting delights of Paris. The elegant buildings, pale-stone bridges and the Seine sparkling in the sunshine all appeared enticing from the taxi. Matt had booked a suite at the Ritz Hotel on the Place Vendôme in the city centre.

When Kitty's eyes had widened at this unexpected luxury her husband had merely smiled and told her that she and her grandmother deserved it.

'I've heard that Coco Chanel the fashion designer has a suite here too,' her grandmother whispered as the uniformed porter collected their luggage from the taxi, and they were escorted inside by the liveried doorman.

Kitty admired the open reception with its beautiful marble and the elegance of her surroundings. Her sharp hotelier's eyes noting all the small details which marked the Ritz out as a truly luxurious hotel. The carpets and ornate glass and gold light fittings, plants and air of quiet wealth. She glanced at her grandmother and was privately amused to see she was doing much the same thing as they booked in.

The suite proved to be just as delightful as everything else they had experienced so far. It was surprisingly spacious with private bathrooms, two bedrooms and a lounge area. Kitty insisted her grandmother rest on the rose-silk canopied bed in her room while she unpacked their luggage with Matt's assistance.

Matt had arranged for Madame DeTourner and Julian to

join them downstairs later for afternoon tea. Kitty was pleased to see that Grams appeared refreshed and rested by the time they were due to meet her godmother. It had been some time since she had last seen them as Eliza had been unable to attend hers and Matt's wedding due to illness.

They had scarcely had time to take their places in the elegant salon when Eliza bustled towards them, accompanied by Julian. Matt rose to greet her and to shake hands with Julian who was easily as tall as Matt and attired very elegantly in a well-tailored suit. They all exchanged kisses and greetings before sitting down once more around the pristine white table.

'I cannot begin to tell you how thrilled I am to see you all here.' Eliza beamed around at them all. Pearl earrings matched the single row around her plump neck and her dress was an elegant silk crêpe in palest lilac. 'I have such plans for your stay.'

'It's been far too long since we last met,' Grams agreed as she studied the leather-bound tea menu. 'Julian has grown up into such a handsome young man. I rather think you were in short trousers the last time I saw you.'

Kitty bit back a smile as a hint of colour crept into Julian's cheeks at this remark.

'Now, Julian and I have arranged for us to attend a private showing tomorrow afternoon at the House of Dido. It's a small but exclusive fashion house. They are having a little premiere of their upcoming winter collection. It is just for their most valued customers, but we have managed to get you an invitation,' Eliza told them excitedly. 'The owner of the house, Marie Dido, is a dear personal friend. Julian too has a connection there.'

They paused in their conversation for a moment to give their order for tea to the waiter.

'How kind of you. I know it must seem a tad silly, but it's been a dream of mine for years to see inside a French couture business and to attend a show. I know that since then you have been to several shows. We used to dream of it years ago, back when we were younger. Do you remember, Eliza? You used to design your own dresses then too.' Kitty's grandmother smiled fondly at her friend.

'Yes, I did. In that sketchbook that I took everywhere. It seems so long ago now. We had such plans. Then poor darling Elowed went missing, and we were both so busy.' Eliza looked distressed for a moment.

Kitty swallowed the lump in her throat that had surfaced at the mention of her late mother. It had been such a long, difficult time spent searching only to finally learn her fate. Awful though the discovery of her mother's body had been, they had finally been able to hold a funeral and Kitty now had a place to go to pay her respects.

'This recent illness of mine has been very upsetting for Kitty, so I'm glad she and Matthew are here to share this little holiday with me. Even if it does mean indulging a foolish old lady in achieving a girlhood dream.' Her grandmother's eyes were watery as she spoke.

Eliza patted Kitty's grandmother's arm. 'Not silly at all, my dear. I find as I've grown older the things of my youth have become much more important.'

Tea arrived, delivered by what seemed to Kitty to be a veritable squadron of waiters. An elegant gilt and china stand laden with delicate finger sandwiches and all manner of dainty patisserie delights was placed before them.

After many murmurings of '*merci*,' the waiting staff poured their tea and left them to enjoy their repast.

'*Maman* tells me that you are no longer managing the hotel, Kitty. She said that you and your husband are private detectives?' Julian looked at Kitty and Matt as he added sugar to his tea.

'That's right. The Dolphin has a very competent manager, and I just oversee things there once a month. Matt and I are in business together. We have our own agency.' Kitty smiled at Matt as she selected several of the dainty sandwiches.

'That must be most fascinating. You must have had very interesting cases,' Julian said.

'Indeed, we get quite a variety of commissions, ranging from petty theft and lost dogs to murder,' Matt agreed affably, before biting into an egg and cress sandwich.

'Dear me, that sounds most unpleasant.' Eliza looked alarmed. 'You surely don't have to be involved with, well, any of the murder cases, Kitty?'

Kitty's grandmother choked on the tiny strawberry tartlet she was eating and Kitty had to pat her back.

'My dear Eliza, I swear murders follow Kitty around. We can never seem to be able to go anywhere without her or Matthew stumbling over a corpse.'

'My goodness!' Eliza pressed her hand to her ample bosom in alarm.

'It must be most interesting.' Julian appeared unmoved by his mother's squeamishness. 'Perhaps when *Maman* is not listening, you and Matthew can tell me about some of your cases.'

'Of course. You work in the city?' Kitty turned the tables on Julian as she smiled at Eliza's expression at her son's suggestion.

'Yes, I manage some investment accounts and, of course, all of my mother's financial matters. My father had a lot of interests in various companies, and I have to represent *Maman* at the board meetings. You know, that kind of thing,' Julian said.

'You are not married yet, Julian?' her grandmother enquired with an arch smile.

Again, there was a flash of colour on Julian's cheekbones. 'No, alas, not quite yet, although with luck, perhaps soon.'

Kitty noticed his mother stiffen at this comment and she wondered if she did not approve of the young lady in question.

Her grandmother had mentioned that Eliza's invitation had hinted at some objection to Julian's lady friend.

'Most intriguing. I do hope we shall meet her during our stay?' Her grandmother appeared not to have noticed her friend's discomfort.

'You shall meet her tomorrow. Simone is the leading model for the House of Dido.'

'Then we shall look forward to it,' Grams assured him.

CHAPTER FOUR

Matt rose early the following morning. He had not slept well despite the cozy dinner he and Kitty had enjoyed at a romantic restaurant near the Eiffel Tower. Mrs Treadwell had declared herself still full up from tea and tired from the journey, so had remained in the suite. Kitty's grandmother had, however, been insistent that he and Kitty go out and enjoy themselves.

He went out of the bedroom into the salon. He sat on the velvet-covered sofa and watched the sky turn a soft pearlescent pink as the sun rose and the city started to come to life. The pantiles on the roofs glowed and the outlines of the city sights were silhouetted in the distance. Eliza and Julian had arranged to meet them after lunch at the House of Dido in time for the fashion show. The intention was then to go out together for dinner later, so they could get to know Simone, Julian's girlfriend, better.

Matt called down to reception for a pot of tea. Then let the waiter in a few minutes later, signalling the man to be quiet so that Kitty and her grandmother were not disturbed. Left to himself he would have preferred not to attend the fashion show. Couture ladies fashion was not something that interested him.

He suspected that Kitty was only interested so she could take notes for Alice. While Kitty's grandmother was still weak from her recent illness though, he felt that he should accompany them.

At least they would see this girlfriend of Julian's. He had noticed that Eliza DeTourner did not look very happy when her name was mentioned. Perhaps it was because the girl was working as a model at House of Dido. He knew that not everyone of Eliza's generation considered modelling a suitable occupation for a young lady. Madame DeTourner certainly appeared very traditional in her outlook and protective of her son. Hearing about Kitty's work had definitely shocked her.

Kitty appeared in the salon just as he was finishing his second cup of tea. She was already dressed for the day in a cherry-print cotton summer dress.

'I wondered where you had gone,' she said as she came to sit beside him on the sofa. 'I don't suppose there is any tea left in that pot?' She peered hopefully at his tray.

'Sorry, darling. It's pretty much all gone. Why don't you send down for some more while I dress,' he suggested, dropping a kiss on her cheek.

'Very well. I thought we would want an early breakfast if we are to visit the Eiffel Tower before the crowds arrive and it becomes too hot and too busy,' Kitty said as he rose to go and prepare for the day. 'I saw in the paper on the airplane that there is a trade fair on at the moment and the sights may be very crowded.'

'Good idea. Your grandmother said she would meet us here at lunchtime, so she is well rested for the afternoon,' Matt called back in a low tone.

Kitty's grandmother had announced her plans the previous evening and Matt suspected she was not yet as strong as she had thought. Personally, he considered it prudent that the older woman paced herself. He knew from experience that Paris could be a very lovely but very tiring city.

When he returned to Kitty she had finished her tea and had ordered breakfast in bed for her grandmother.

'Shall we go downstairs for our breakfast?' Kitty asked, slipping her arm through his. 'I'm quite starving. It must be the change of air.'

Matt laughed and shook his head in despair. Kitty was always hungry. He often wondered where a woman so petite managed to put so much food. They went down to the elegant dining room and ate their fill of croissants and strawberry jam before setting out into the streets of Paris to behave like tourists for the morning.

* * *

Kitty enjoyed seeing the sights of Paris from the top of the Eiffel Tower. It was even larger in real life than in the pictures she had seen. The views of the city were astounding, and she was fascinated by the restaurant within the tower. She had visited Paris a couple of times before but had never had the opportunity to take in the sights as a tourist.

After a pleasant stroll along the bank of the Seine admiring the various small stalls and trinkets that were for sale, they met her grandmother back at the hotel. They decided on a light lunch at a pavement café nearby where they could watch the world go by as they dined. Kitty was pleased to see her grandmother's cheeks were pink and she had some of her old spark back in her eyes.

'Are you excited for this afternoon, Grams?' Kitty asked as they sipped their tiny coffees after lunch in the warmth of the Parisian sunshine.

'Darling, I cannot begin to tell you how excited I am. I feel as giddy as a schoolgirl. Eliza is too, too kind to have arranged this. Oh, and you too, Matthew, my dear. I so appreciate all your hard work to make this such a splendid holiday.' Her grandmother smiled fondly at Matt.

Kitty knew that ordinarily her husband wouldn't care to attend a fashion show, so she appreciated his support.

'Not at all, it's our pleasure. We should set off soon if we are to meet Eliza and Julian at the House of Dido,' Matt said as he waved the waiter over to settle their bill before flagging down a taxi.

'And we shall meet this mysterious Simone, who seems to have won Julian's heart,' Grams said with a smile.

Kitty enjoyed watching the sights of Paris through the taxi window on their short drive to the House of Dido, which was situated in a street of tall, elegant terraced buildings. Eliza and Julian were waiting for them outside the entrance. Her godmother had a tiny black poodle tucked under her arm.

'*Bonjour*,' Eliza greeted them affectionately with kisses on their cheeks. She put her little dog down to sniff interestedly at their ankles. 'Don't mind Violette, she is such a darling.' Eliza smiled affectionately at her pet.

Julian pressed the brass doorbell beneath the discreet black and gold plaque beside the front door.

A young maid, immaculate in a black dress with white cap and apron, opened the door. She instantly appeared to recognise both Eliza and Julian and permitted their party to enter into the lobby of the fashion house.

The lobby was an elegant square space. The floor had black-and-white tiles in a chequerboard fashion. On the walls were various large, framed photographs of famous people all dressed presumably in clothes from the House of Dido. A staircase with a black wrought-iron balustrade curved up to the next floor.

A tall, thin man in his late forties was descending the staircase towards them. The faint pinstripe on his trousers seeming to extenuate his height and physique. A scarlet carnation was in his buttonhole, and he greeted Eliza and Julian with a flurry of kisses and rapid-fire French.

Violette regarded him with a lack of interest that argued they had met many times before.

'Yves, may I introduce my dear friend, Mrs Treadwell, and her granddaughter, Kitty, and her husband, Captain Bryant. I told you they were visiting from England. My dears, this is Monsieur Yves Mangan. The marvellously talented head designer for House of Dido,' Eliza presented them to the Frenchman.

'*Enchanté, mesdames, monsieur.*' He kissed Kitty and her grandmother's hands and bowed his head to Matt in greeting, taking them somewhat by surprise.

'*Eh bien*, we have the most delightful small showing for you today. Please do ascend and take some champagne.' Monsieur Mangan stood aside so they could go up the stairs to the next floor.

At the top of the stairs was a broad light-filled landing. A white painted door stood open with a podium outside where a tall, slender woman of a similar age to Eliza was marking names from a list. A uniformed maid stood close by bearing a silver tray of champagne coupes. The faint strains of chamber music wafted out onto the landing and the air seemed to be faintly perfumed with roses and vanilla.

The woman was beautifully clad in a dress of iridescent shot-green silk with her blonde hair arranged artfully on top of her head. Intricate pleats highlighted the narrowness of her waist. Kitty thought that Alice would have adored seeing the woman's dress. She made a mental note so she could tell her everything when she returned home.

'Eliza, *chérie, et* Julian.' Once more Eliza and Julian were greeted warmly. Eliza repeated the introduction she had made to Monsieur Mangan and Kitty learned that this was Marie Dido, proprietor of the House of Dido.

'You are all very welcome. Please go in and take a drink and a seat. The models are preparing and we shall begin shortly,' Marie instructed.

They each took a glass from the maid's tray and entered the spacious sunny room. Rows of gilt chairs with red velvet padded seats had been placed on either side of a strip of crimson carpet which led back to a low stage draped with matching red velvet curtains. Green fronded plants in stone urns had been positioned on either side of the runway.

A cellist and a violinist were playing at the rear of the room and many of the seats were already occupied by ladies of various ages and a smattering of smartly clad gentlemen, who appeared to be accompanying them.

'Ah, Sir Humphrey Engels is here, I must introduce you all.' Eliza sighted an upright man of about Matt's age who rose to greet them as they approached. Kitty thought she saw a scowl cross Julian's face when they met.

Once more introductions were performed and they quickly took their seats as the curtains on the stage parted and Monsieur Mangan began the announcements.

Kitty gathered that this show was an exclusive preview of some limited edition designs which House of Dido was only making for favoured clients for the winter season. Eliza explained that the focus of the show was on evening and cocktail wear.

Kitty's grandmother sighed happily and relaxed in her seat as she sipped her champagne. A procession of three very pretty young women started their walk along the carpet between the rows of chairs. Kitty tried to make mental notes of the types of fabrics and the trims. She knew Alice would be eager for every detail.

She wondered which one of the girls was Julian's girlfriend. They all appeared very attractive, and she noticed the Parisian ladies were making approving sounds and nods as the various designs were paraded through the salon. One young woman did seem to be the lead model, a stunningly pretty brunette with a certain air about her person that marked her out from the rest.

Eventually the show closed, and all the models joined Marie Dido and Monsieur Mangan on the stage to take the plaudits of the audience. Kitty noticed Julian was smiling warmly at the young woman she had noticed on the catwalk. It seemed that now more champagne was to be supplied, and Marie and Yves were busy taking orders while the models went to change.

'Well, what did you think?' Eliza turned to Kitty's grandmother as Julian excused himself to go and wait near the backstage door for Simone.

'It was simply marvellous. Everything I could ever have imagined.' Grams sighed happily. 'A dream come true. Thank you so much for the invitation, my dear.'

Sir Humphrey had also wandered off and Kitty wondered why he had been at the fashion show. It was clear that he attended often from the way Eliza had greeted him. Perhaps he was shopping for his wife or daughter as a special gift.

'Where has Julian gone?' Eliza tutted after a few minutes when they had finished their drinks and most of the audience had begun to dissipate. 'I suppose he is waiting for that girl.'

'You don't approve of this Simone?' Grams asked.

'Simone is, well, not my first choice for Julian. She is ambitious and greedy. I have also learned something else about her which worries me.' Eliza moved her silk-clad shoulders in a tiny shrug. 'Still, what can one say? He is of an age to make up his own mind.'

Kitty looked around and saw the other two girls who had been modelling talking to Marie Dido. 'The other models are over there. Oh, and there is Julian too.'

Eliza looked, her frown deepening when she saw Sir Humphrey had joined the group. 'The girl with the dark hair is

Simone's sister, Nathalie. The auburn-haired girl is an American, Patricia Maddox. They all share an apartment.'

'We should leave soon if we are to go for tea. It would be nice to stroll around the shops for a while before returning to the hotel,' Kitty said as she checked the time on her watch. The show had run for longer than she had anticipated. 'Perhaps we could meet Julian's friend some other time if she is busy with her work.'

Eliza stood and collected her handbag ready to depart. Violette emerged, yawning from where she had been snoozing under her mistress's chair during the show. Kitty noticed that Julian appeared to be arguing with Yves Mangan, waving his hands in Gallic fashion and gesticulating towards the backstage area.

'Julian, darling, is something wrong?' Eliza moved swiftly over to her son.

'Simone has not yet come out. Nathalie and Patricia are already changed. Simone is usually very swift, and she knows we are waiting for her.' Julian glowered at Monsieur Mangan.

Nathalie and the other girl joined the conversation.

'She should be out very soon. No doubt she is taking extra care of her appearance to make a good impression,' Nathalie suggested.

'Sure, we called to her just before we came out front and she said she'd only be a minute,' Patricia said.

'Would you like me to go and see where she is?' Nathalie asked.

'*Merci.*' Julian glowered at Monsieur Mangan. 'It would seem I am not permitted backstage.'

'No, silly.' Patricia looked shocked at the suggestion. 'You know that is not allowed.'

Nathalie slipped away and disappeared through a nondescript door at the side of the stage, half hidden by the curtain. A few minutes later a series of piercing screams rang out. Matt joined Julian and Monsieur Mangan as they rushed through the door at the side of the stage.

Kitty and Sir Humphrey were not far behind them. In the backstage area next to the rail of clothes which had so recently graced the salon, Simone's body lay lifeless on the floor in a pool of dark-red blood. Nathalie was crouched beside her sister, a sharp and bloodied pair of tailoring scissors in her hands.

She looked up at them all with wide, shocked eyes. 'I have just found her. These scissors... she is dead.' The girl stared aghast at the scissors in her hand and her body started to shake.

'We must telephone for an ambulance, the police,' Sir Humphrey said and rushed back out again. Kitty could only suppose that was what he had gone to do.

'Simone!' Julian moved as if going to touch the dead girl.

'Nathalie, place the scissors beside your sister. We must all touch nothing until the police come,' Matt instructed. His tone was firm and authoritative.

Julian straightened and translated into French for the stricken girl, before placing his arm around her shoulder to guide her away after she had placed the scissors on the floor.

'This is terrible! Who could have done such a thing. *Pauvre* Simone. She is our star model and much in demand everywhere.' Monsieur Mangan appeared equally distraught.

'We can do nothing for her now. Go and tell Madame Dido what has happened if she has not heard already from the others,' Matt instructed him.

The man nodded briefly and scurried off, leaving Kitty and Matt with the body of the dead model.

'It looks as if the scissors were the weapon.' Kitty shuddered at the wound in the girl's abdomen.

'Well, any chance of fingerprints have probably gone since Nathalie picked them up.' Matt looked around the tiled floor in case there might be any clue to who could have killed the girl.

Kitty gazed around the room. There were a couple of

leatherette-topped stools, a countertop with a sink and a mirror. It seemed well lit, with hair pins and other cosmetic items near the sink. On the far side of the room she could see there was a toilet and a curtained cubicle area which she guessed was probably used for clients fittings.

'Simone must have been in the toilet or behind the curtain when the other girls came out or they would have seen her getting dressed,' Kitty said.

'Indeed, they said she called to them so that implies she was out of sight and there are few options for that in here,' Matt agreed.

Kitty shuddered. The girl had changed into a pale-lemon dress, and she was wearing a dainty hat of white and lemon with a scrap of netting. A few more minutes and she would have been out in the salon with the other girls.

'Who on earth could have done such a thing?' Kitty asked.

Matt placed his arm around her. 'We had better join the others before the police arrive.' His expression was grim.

Kitty took one last glance before permitting her husband to lead her away. It was such a dreadful end to a wonderful afternoon.

CHAPTER FIVE

They went back into the salon where a chaotic scene awaited them. Nathalie, the dead girl's sister, was sobbing loudly and hysterically. Patricia, her fellow model, attempted to calm and console her. Julian was white-faced and clearly distraught as he paced back and forth. Madame Dido had produced a bottle of cognac from somewhere and was pressing glasses on everyone.

Sir Humphrey was also pacing up and down the strip of red carpet having apparently called the police. Kitty immediately looked at her grandmother to see if she was all right. She was seated with Eliza who had Violette on her lap. Although she could see her grandmother was shaken she didn't seem unduly perturbed. Unlike Eliza who was sipping cognac and dabbing delicately at her nose with a wisp of a lace-edged handkerchief.

Monsieur Mangan alternated between issuing streams of angry-sounding French at Madame Dido and muttering unhappily under his breath. Fortunately, it seemed that the other attendees of the show had all departed. There had only been a couple of people left when they had found Simone's body, and they too must now have gone.

'Julian, darling.' Eliza reached out her hand to her son, but he shook her away and stalked over to the window to stare moodily out at the street below.

Kitty wished she knew what Monsieur Mangan was saying to Marie Dido. Her schoolgirl French was struggling to pick up the context. She thought, however, that he was saying something about the designs and theft.

Marie appeared to be attempting to silence him. She also kept glancing anxiously at Sir Humphrey and Kitty wondered if perhaps he had some kind of financial interest in House of Dido. Or a romantic interest, perhaps, in Madame Dido. It would certainly account for his presence at the fashion show if that were the case.

The maid who had let them in on their arrival now appeared in the doorway. She was accompanied by two uniformed gendarmes and a tall man in his late forties dressed in a smart grey suit.

Marie Dido went immediately to greet him, accompanied by Sir Humphrey. The policeman cast an assessing glance around the room before heading for the door at the side of the stage. One of the gendarmes went with him. The other took up a post at the doorway to prevent anyone from following. It seemed clear that they were all to stay put for the time being.

After a few minutes the inspector reappeared at the same time as a man, who was clearly the doctor, arrived and was shown into the salon. There was a brief huddle between the doctor and the policeman, before the doctor too went through the door backstage.

'*Bonjour, mesdames et monsieurs*. My apologies for keeping you all here. I can tell this has been most distressing occurrence for everyone. I am Inspector LeJeune and I shall be investigating this most dreadful murder. I would ask that you remain here for a little while as I need to speak with all of you to help me determine what may have happened to the *pauvre* Mademoiselle Belliste.' The inspector looked around as he spoke.

His words triggered a fresh bout of noisy sobs from Nathalie at the mention of her sister's name.

'Madame Dido, do you perhaps have an office I can use?' the inspector asked, looking at Marie.

'*Oui*, monsieur.' She led the inspector from the room and returned a second later. She crouched down at Nathalie's side. 'Nathalie, he wishes to speak with you first,' she said in a sympathetic tone.

The girl nodded and rose from her chair. She wobbled as she stood and steadied herself with a hand on the back of one of the other gilt chairs, before making her way from the room.

Kitty wished she and Matt could have attended the interviews. She would dearly like to know what everyone was going to say when they were questioned. Julian came to sit beside Patricia once Nathalie had left the room. He leaned forward and buried his face in his hands, while the young model placed a sympathetic hand on his shoulder.

Sir Humphrey came to sit beside Eliza and Kitty's grandmother.

'This is such a dreadful way for us to make your acquaintance, Sir Humphrey. Did you know this girl, Simone, at all?' Kitty's grandmother asked.

'Yes, oh yes, very well. She was a very talented young woman. This is a tragedy, an absolute tragedy,' Sir Humphrey remarked in a sorrowful tone. 'I can't believe it.'

Eliza peeked quickly over at Julian as Violette yawned and settled on her mistress's lap, clearly bored by whatever was going on.

'It does seem so incredible. I mean, who could possibly have wished to harm the girl?' Grams mused.

Matt glanced at Kitty, and she could see the twinkle in his eye. It seemed clear who Kitty had inherited her investigative nature from.

'I have no idea. Simone was well liked.' Sir Humphrey shook his head.

'Her sister was found holding the murder weapon,' Matt said. 'Did they get on well?'

Sir Humphrey looked surprised. 'I believe so. Simone adored Nathalie. She would do anything for her. She even got her the job working for House of Dido, I believe.'

'I suppose someone will have to tell the girl's parents what has happened,' Grams said.

'Alas, they are orphans. Their parents died a few years ago when Simone was eighteen, Julian told me. It was some sort of motor accident in the snow,' Eliza said.

The police doctor re-emerged from the side door, a sober expression on his face. He hurried from the room and Kitty presumed he must have gone to tell the inspector of his findings so that they could move the dead girl's body.

Inspector LeJeune entered the room and asked Patricia to come with him. Kitty guessed that since the Belliste sisters shared an apartment with the American model, he wanted to get her opinion on relationships between the girls. She was also one of the last people to speak to Simone. It would be advisable too, she suspected, that if Patricia was seen next then she could accompany her flatmate home. That was if the police had not arrested Nathalie already.

It had certainly appeared suspicious to find the girl bent over her sister's body with her hands covered in blood. Then there was the matter of her holding what seemed to be the murder weapon. Those tailoring scissors certainly looked very sharp and pointed.

A shiver danced along Kitty's spine. The murder had taken place in such a short space of time. The girls had barely been off stage for ten or fifteen minutes before Patricia and Nathalie had come out into the salon. Then it had probably been only another ten minutes or so before Nathalie had gone backstage again to find Simone.

If Nathalie had not stabbed her sister, then who else could have done it and why? The other attendees had all gone by the time the models had come back out into the salon. The only remaining clients had been giving their orders to Madame Dido. Kitty saw that Madame Dido and Monsieur Mangan were now huddled together over their order book, and she wondered if they were worried the orders from today would be cancelled once word got out about Simone's murder.

Inspector LeJeune came back and this time he asked Julian to accompany him. Kitty saw a distressed expression flash across her godmother's face. Marie Dido crossed back over to them bearing the bottle of cognac.

'*Ma chère amie*, more brandy? I am sure Julian will not be with the inspector for long. The poor boy must be most upset, indeed as are we all,' Marie soothed as she poured more alcohol into the crystal tumbler that Eliza was still nursing.

'Yes, I'm certain he will be out soon. It's such a terrible end to such a wonderful day. We were so looking forward to meeting Miss Belliste,' Grams said.

'I don't know who could have wished to harm the girl. Yves is convinced someone was trying to steal our designs or sabotage our event and Simone must have disturbed them. He is keen to get backstage to check the garments and the pattern books for any sign of theft or tampering.' Marie glanced at her colleague who was still looking unhappily at the order books.

Kitty hadn't thought of this as a possible motive for the girl's murder. But if it were the case, then how had someone managed to get in, steal something, kill Simone and get out without anyone noticing them? The time frame had been so short, and it seemed to her that the girl's murderer must be someone close at hand.

'Simone was well liked then, madame?' Kitty asked.

'*Mais oui!* She was at the top of her game and had such talent. She, Nathalie and Patricia were as thick as thieves. Simone had even begun to turn her hand to designing. Yves showed me a few of her sketches. They were a little crude but not without promise. She wished to change direction in her career. It is so sad,' Marie said.

'Poor Julian,' Grams said with a sigh. 'He must be heartbroken.' She reached out and patted Eliza's hand affectionately.

Violette opened her eyes and glared at Grams.

The inspector reappeared and beckoned to Madame Dido. She set the bottle of cognac down and went out of the room.

'What's happening? Where is Julian? Why has he not come back?' Eliza fretted.

'They may have asked him to wait in another room until we have all seen the inspector. Sometimes they will do that so that people's memories of events are their own. Also, they don't always want people to know what the questions may be until they are seen,' Matt explained.

'Matt's right. I'm sure Julian is fine. He may also have escorted the girls back to their apartment. They were dreadfully upset. Do they live near here?' Kitty asked.

'No, they live in a different arrondissement. It is too expensive for them to reside this close to the city centre,' Eliza said, before taking another gulp of her cognac.

Monsieur Mangan was the next person to be summoned, leaving just the English contingent in the salon. More people arrived and the covered remains of Simone Belliste were taken away.

Eliza shuddered and Sir Humphrey appeared distressed as the sad party departed downstairs and out of the building.

'Do you attend many of the fashion shows here, Sir Humphrey?' Kitty asked once the door had closed, and the gendarme was back in his post.

'I have been to quite a few, yes. Marie invited me, she was a friend of Gilda, my late wife. That's why the business has an English name instead of a French one. I am a shareholder in House of Dido, so I try to support Marie,' Sir Humphrey said.

'I hope this tragedy doesn't affect poor Marie's business,' Eliza said.

'It's hard to say what will happen. Although, it's not something one would wish to get into the press,' Sir Humphrey said.

Before Kitty could ask him anything more he was called in to see Inspector LeJeune.

'We are clearly most unimportant.' Kitty smiled at Eliza, hoping to prevent her godmother from worrying.

She was concerned now about her grandmother who was starting to look tired and uncomfortable. She hoped the police would speed things along since Grams could probably do with returning to the hotel to rest.

'Madame DeTourner, *s'il vous plaît*,' Inspector LeJeune called for Eliza.

Her godmother set her little poodle down and they left the room with the policeman.

'Oh dear, poor Eliza,' her grandmother said. 'I do hope she will be all right. She must be very worried about Julian. It makes it harder that she wasn't fond of the girl.' Her grandmother shook her head.

'Are you all right, Grams? We'll go right back to the hotel when the inspector lets us go and you can rest,' Kitty said.

'I must confess I am feeling rather weary now. Nothing that a good strong pot of tea and a little lie down won't make better.' Her grandmother smiled affectionately at her. 'Only you, darling, could bring me away to Paris as a treat and stumble straight into a murder.'

'It's a gift I would rather not possess,' Kitty said.

'I can imagine.' Her grandmother's smile widened. 'Your dear mother, however, had a very similar talent for finding trouble.'

The door of the salon opened, and Inspector LeJeune came to join them. 'My apologies for keeping you all so long. I think I may as well see you all here together since I understand that you did not know the young lady who was killed?'

The inspector spoke good English with a faint French accent. He took a seat and surveyed them all with sharp grey eyes. He produced a small black leather-bound notebook and flicked it open.

'No, we were going to meet her after the show. My godmother, Madame DeTourner, told us that her son, Julian, was seeing Simone, and he wanted to introduce us,' Kitty explained.

'I see. Madame DeTourner explained that you have recently arrived from England and are here for a short holiday.' The inspector paused for them to confirm that this was correct.

'Eliza knew it had been my dream since I was young to attend a couture show. She is friends with Madame Dido so arranged this afternoon as a treat,' Grams explained.

'Did you know any of the other people attending this show today?' Inspector LeJeune asked.

'No, we didn't know anyone at all,' Kitty said.

'You did not know of any arguments or disagreements or witness anything that may have given you pause for thought?' the inspector persisted.

'Nothing at all. The first we knew of something being wrong was when Julian became concerned that Simone had not come out of the backstage area. We were all to go to tea together. He was very keen for us to meet her. Then Nathalie offered to go and look for her sister, and, well, you know what she discovered.' Grams lifted her hands in a helpless gesture.

'Of course, Madame Treadwell. Most distressing for the young lady. I understand that you, Captain Bryant, and Mrs Bryant also went back there with Sir Humphrey and Julian DeTourner?' Inspector LeJeune looked at Matt.

'That's correct. We discovered Nathalie bent over Simone's body. She was holding a pair of tailoring scissors, and her hands were covered in blood. She appeared very shocked and distraught. She said she had found her sister dead and had picked up the scissors without thinking.' Matt's tone was calm and factual.

Kitty recognised it as the way he often gave evidence in court cases.

'*Merci.* Did you think that Mademoiselle Nathalie may have killed her sister, or did you believe her, that she had acted on instinct and picked up the scissors when she found Mademoiselle Simone?' Inspector LeJeune asked.

Matt looked at Kitty. 'Either scenario is possible. Nathalie certainly seemed to be very shocked and there has to be a reason why Simone had not come out just after the other girls. Both girls said she answered them when they said they were going out to the salon.'

'Hmm, *eh bien.*' Inspector Lejeune scribbled some notes in his book. 'Mademoiselle Patricia said they called to Simone as they left the room, and she said she would follow them shortly. Is this also your understanding of what happened?'

'Yes, that's exactly what they told us,' Kitty confirmed.

'But none of you heard this conversation?' Inspector LeJeune asked.

'No, the musicians had finished and were leaving and people were saying goodbye after placing their orders with Madame Dido and Monsieur Mangan, so the room was quite noisy.' Kitty's brow wrinkled as she tried to recall if she had heard something before the girls had appeared.

'I see, *merci,* Madame Bryant. Madame DeTourner mentioned that you and Captain Bryant are private investigators in England?' Inspector LeJeune looked enquiringly at them.

Matt took a card from his silver card case and passed it across to the inspector.

'*Merci*, you permit that I retain this?' the policeman asked and at Matt's nod of assent he tucked the card in the back of his notebook. 'Did you see anyone enter the backstage in the time between the end of the parade and the time Mademoiselle Simone was discovered?'

Kitty looked at Matt. She hadn't been looking in that direction once the show had finished. In fact, she hadn't even realised the door was there until Nathalie had gone to find her sister.

'I'm sorry, Inspector, I'm afraid I didn't,' Kitty said.

Matt and her grandmother shook their heads too. 'No, I'm afraid we didn't see anyone either,' Matt said.

'Very well. Madame DeTourner said you would be in Paris for a few more days. May I have the name of your hotel in case there is further need for me to speak with you?' Inspector LeJeune asked.

Matt gave the name of the hotel, and the inspector made a note before closing his book and returning it to his pocket.

'*Merci beaucoup* for your patience. I believe your friends said they would be waiting for you downstairs.' The inspector stood and they were dismissed.

Kitty wondered if this was the last they would hear of the case as they made their way out of the salon.

CHAPTER SIX

Matt followed Kitty and her grandmother down the elegant marble staircase into the hall. Eliza DeTourner was standing waiting for them with Marie Dido at her side. Violette gave a short volley of barks as they approached. There was no sign of Julian and Matt assumed that he must have decided to escort the two models back to their apartment.

'Julian seems to have gone, and he has left no message,' Eliza's lament cut into his thoughts.

'I expect he will arrive home later once the shock of what has happened has worn off. He must be most dreadfully upset,' Kitty's grandmother attempted to soothe her friend.

'Yves has gone with one of the gendarmes to the workshop to identify which bench the scissors came from.' Marie looked troubled as she looked down the hall to a discreet door marked *privé* at the rear. 'I do not know how they came to be up there. They are not the kind of scissors we would usually have upstairs.'

'That is troubling,' Matt said. 'Is the door to the workroom usually kept locked?'

'When there is no one in there, then yes. The problem is

that the lock has been broken this last week and the man to mend it has not yet come to make the repair,' Marie explained.

'I suppose though that usually your staff are all in there working?' Kitty asked.

'Of course, *mais maintenant* the room is empty since today was a show day and the staff had all put in so many extra hours they had been permitted the afternoon off. The girls left at lunchtime.' The frown on Marie's brow deepened.

Kitty's grandmother swayed slightly, and Kitty steadied her. 'Let us go and get a taxi. Perhaps a pot of tea, Grams. You look tired.'

Matt immediately went to the door.

'There is a taxi rank just three houses down the street,' Eliza said.

He went out, found the rank and got a car to come to the fashion house. Kitty assisted her grandmother and Eliza into the back, before getting in herself. Violette sat obediently on Eliza's lap. Matt took a seat beside the driver after they had said goodbye to Marie Dido.

They headed for the Ritz and persuaded Eliza to join them for tea before she returned to her own apartment. The streets of the city were busier than ever as the afternoon was almost gone, and people had begun to leave work to return home. The patisserie on the corner had almost sold out of its mouthwatering confections and the flower stall was emptying their buckets of water.

Matt offered his arms to the two older ladies once they exited the taxi, and he escorted them inside the hotel. Once they were installed in a quiet corner of the residents' lounge and a pot of tea ordered, Eliza settled her dog on the floor beside her seat.

A tray of tea was quickly delivered and a dish of water for Violette. Eliza drew off her light-cotton gloves and set them on top of her handbag. 'Oh, I am in need of this tea. Kitty, *ma chérie*, can you pour?'

Kitty duly obliged and passed out the china teacups for them all to add their own milk and sugar.

'Is it usual for the workshop to be empty on the day of a show?' Kitty asked Eliza.

Her godmother frowned. 'I think so. There is so much preparation work and House of Dido has only a small staff compared to many of the larger houses. The girls go in early to prepare the racks and I think Marie then permits them to leave. I know Marie outsources some things like complicated embroidery to specialists.'

'And the models today, Simone, Nathalie and Patricia, do they only work for House of Dido or do they work for other people?' Matt asked.

Eliza selected one of the small, plain biscuits from amongst the petit fours that had accompanied the tea and snapped it in half. She gave a piece to Violette who ate it daintily while Eliza considered his question.

'The girls work for various houses. The more popular they are the more work they get. Marie was worried that she soon would not be able to book Simone because so many places wanted her, and she had asked Marie for more money. Simone also wanted to do less modelling and more designing. We were talking about it while I waited for you to finish with the inspector,' Eliza said.

'What about Patricia and Nathalie?' Kitty asked.

'Oh well, Simone usually gets Nathalie some bookings, but she is not as good as Simone. She lacks a certain finesse when she moves and I think Julian said she is not always reliable. Patricia has a distinctive look, so she often gets more work for sportswear and outdoor clothing.' Eliza gave her poodle the other half of the biscuit.

'Did that cause a problem between the sisters?' Kitty asked. 'With Simone being more successful?'

'I'm not sure, I don't think so. Julian said that Simone wished to get away from modelling. She thought she was becoming too old. Too old! I ask you. The girl was only twenty-two. She hoped to become a designer. At least that was what she said.' Eliza gave a small derisive sniff.

'You didn't think that was possible?' Kitty's grandmother asked.

'I don't know. Marie said that Yves didn't think much of her designs and if you ask me the girl was merely hunting for a rich husband.' Eliza picked up her teacup.

'That was why you were concerned that things were becoming serious between her and Julian?' Kitty's grandmother looked at her friend.

'Among other things. She was playing Julian for a fool and he did inherit a great deal of money when his father died. I saw her and Sir Humphrey together one day. They were at lunch in a secluded corner, heads together. Bah.' Eliza pursed her lips.

'Did you tell Julian?' Kitty asked.

'He would not have listened if I had said something. He knew that I was not keen on Simone anyway and he would have thought I was just trying to poison him against her. I have tried to warn him of her low morals,' Eliza said. She drained her teacup and placed it back on the saucer.

Matt looked at Kitty. He knew she was taking in all of this information.

'My dear Gwen, I must get off now. I'm anxious to see if Julian has arrived home. Shall we meet tomorrow for lunch? I hope we can put this terrible event behind us so you can enjoy the rest of your holiday,' Eliza said as she gathered her things together.

'That sounds delightful. Please don't worry, my dear, I'm sure Julian will be home soon,' Kitty's grandmother agreed. The older ladies arranged a time to meet, and Eliza said she would book a restaurant.

Matt escorted Eliza out of the hotel and waited with her while the doorman called a taxi for her and Violette.

'Thank you, Matthew. You are taking very good care of Kitty and Gwen. I cannot believe what has happened today.' Eliza kissed his cheeks, and he waved her off in the car.

* * *

'Are you feeling a little better now, Grams?' Kitty asked once Matt had walked off with Eliza to get her a taxi. She thought her grandmother had a little more colour now she had drunk her tea, but she looked tired.

'I am, darling. The show this afternoon was so lovely, it was a terrible shame it ended the way it did. Poor Eliza, she worries so much about Julian,' Grams said with a sigh.

'Perhaps if you rest in your room, we can go for dinner in the hotel this evening?' Kitty suggested.

'You and Matthew must not curtail your pleasure in this holiday by worrying about me. No, my dear, you and Mathew go out. I shall dine in the suite. I have some correspondence to do. You know Millicent will expect a letter and now it seems I have much to tell her.' Her grandmother's eyes twinkled mischievously at the mention of Millicent Craven.

She knew that Mrs Craven and Kitty were often at loggerheads. After their recent case on Dartmoor things had become even more complicated.

'I suppose she will,' Kitty agreed, smiling back at her grandmother.

Matt returned to join them and after finishing their tea they headed to their suite. Grams retired to her room to rest, while Kitty flung herself down on the sofa and patted the cushion next to her in an enticing manner.

She eased off her shoes and grinned at her husband as he came to join her.

'Another murder then?' She looked at Matt.

'It would seem so.' Matt draped his arm along the back of the sofa across her shoulders. 'Now I suppose you are going to tell me all the reasons you think we should be assisting Inspector LeJeune.'

Kitty's smile widened. 'Whether he wants our help or not, you mean?'

'It certainly seems a strange case. The window for killing Simone was quite small and realistically there are not many suspects,' Matt said.

'The musicians had packed their instruments and were at the far end of the room so they can be ruled out. The maid wasn't in the room so we can eliminate the staff,' Kitty said.

Matt smiled. 'I think your grandmother and Eliza can also be ruled out. I didn't see them stir from their seats. I'm sure we would have heard Violette if Eliza had gone anywhere without her.'

'It would be hard to stab someone whilst holding a dog, even though Eliza clearly disliked Simone.' Kitty smiled before her expression sobered. 'I know we are making light of this, but it was truly awful. Simone was so young and vibrant when she was showing off those lovely clothes.'

'She was and yet someone hated her enough to murder her.' Matt frowned. 'No one heard a scream or a fight so whoever killed her must have been someone she knew who she permitted to get close enough to her to stab her.'

Kitty shuddered. 'Those tailoring scissors were a wicked weapon. The blade was at least six inches long and they were razor-sharp.'

'The position she was lying in on the floor didn't indicate she had been trying to run away. I didn't notice anything unusual or out of place in the room. Did you?' Matt asked.

She shook her head. 'Nothing at all. So, who are our suspects?'

'Nathalie is an obvious one. She was Simone's sister, and she was found crouched over the body holding the scissors with blood on her hands,' Matt said.

'What do you think? She said she found her sister dead and automatically picked up the scissors.' Kitty could see how Nathalie could have done that. Equally, she could see how the girl could have murdered her sister in that moment before they had all entered the backstage area.

'She did seem to be very shocked at finding her sister dead. Motive though? I suppose, if as Eliza says, Nathalie got most of her work through Simone and Simone planned to give up modelling...'

'She may not have liked that. She may also have been jealous of her sister being more successful.' Kitty picked up on Matt's unfinished thought.

'What about the other girl, Patricia, the American model? She shares an apartment with the Belliste sisters and probably knows them both very well. She could have harboured some kind of resentment against Simone for some reason,' Matt suggested.

'True, but she left the room at the same time as Nathalie, and she said she heard Simone call to say she would be out in a moment. She didn't go backstage again after Nathalie found her sister dead,' Kitty said.

'But she could have gone back in before Nathalie found Simone,' Matt pointed out. 'We don't know that she didn't.'

'Hmm, but I think the motive would have to be stronger than some imagined professional jealousy at Simone's success. From what Eliza told us Patricia is doing pretty well herself anyway.' Kitty couldn't see that the American model had much reason to wish her flatmate dead.

'What about Marie Dido?' Matt asked.

'Simone was her most successful model and she was thinking of leaving. She had already raised her fees, making it harder for Marie to keep her. I know Alice has told me before that many of the couture houses align themselves with certain models to be the face of the house. She could have argued with Simone and stabbed her in a flash of temper,' Kitty tried the theory out for size.

'She would have had a slim chance I suppose while she was taking the orders for the new line and saying goodbye to some of the clients. She was moving around a lot, as was Monsieur Mangan.'

'He didn't seem very fond of Simone. I don't know what it was but something about the way he talked about her, I don't know, I just had the feeling he disliked her.' Kitty looked at Matt. 'What did you think?'

Matt frowned. 'He was very dismissive of her designs, wasn't he? Marie said Yves didn't rate them. He certainly had the opportunity to go backstage and kill Simone.'

Kitty ran her hand through her blonde curls. 'All of these people would know where the scissors were kept and that the workshop would be empty too.'

'I wonder if it was bad luck or planned that the door lock had been broken.' Matt's gaze met Kitty's, and her heart thumped. Taking the scissors upstairs and damaging a lock spoke of premeditated murder. Not someone arguing and seizing a weapon to hand and blindly striking out.

'Dislike isn't usually enough to wish to stab someone. Perhaps Simone's designs were good after all. He is House of Dido's main creative designer. He may have seen Simone as a threat.'

'That brings us to Julian.' Matt's arm around her shoulders tightened in a comforting hug. She knew he disliked having to place her godmother's son on the suspect list but she also knew he had no choice.

'I'm afraid it does. Julian was Simone's boyfriend. He told us he saw a future with her. Maybe she didn't feel the same way. He had the opportunity to go backstage. He certainly resented being stopped from going to find Simone. He was gone for a few minutes. Wasn't he waiting for her? I wonder if he saw anyone else hanging around the stage door?'

'He may have known what Nathalie would discover. He disappeared very quickly after he had seen the inspector.' Matt's tone was sympathetic.

'It could have been grief or concern for Nathalie, but, yes, he wasn't worried about Eliza, was he? Then there is Sir Humphrey. Eliza thought that Simone was seeing him as well as Julian. He could have been resentful or jealous of her, perhaps making things more serious with Julian,' Kitty suggested.

'Both men would have a motive for killing her in a fit of jealousy,' Matt said.

'Taking those scissors from the workshop speaks of a planned attack though.'

'It does but we don't know that for certain. Someone may have taken them up for an innocent reason and the murderer spotted them lying there and used them.' Matt gave her a hug. 'Anyway, this speculation is all very well, but we are on holiday, and this is Inspector LeJeune's case.'

Kitty placed a hand on his knee. 'I know, you're right, but to have someone killed literally right under our noses. That is not something I can easily put to one side.'

Matt chuckled. 'I didn't think you would.'

Kitty jumped up and went to peep in at her grandmother to ensure she was resting peacefully. She wondered if the inspector would arrest Nathalie Belliste and if the model really did murder her sister.

CHAPTER SEVEN

They spent the following morning shopping at the Galeries Lafayette. Kitty had heard a lot about the magnificent steel and glass coupole roof and was keen to see it for herself. Her grandmother was equally enthusiastic.

Kitty suspected much of her enthusiasm was intended to divert Kitty and Matt from further discussion of Simone Belliste's murder. The huge domed roof, however, was something of a landmark in the city. The department store was a showcase for fashion, cosmetics, shoes, jewellery and fine fragrance. Kitty thought Alice would have loved it. Perhaps she should suggest Paris to her friend as a honeymoon destination.

Matt was soon laden down with parcels and packages as Kitty and her grandmother happily shopped amongst the boutiques. By the time they returned to the Ritz to deposit the shopping in their suite, Kitty was more than ready to meet Eliza for lunch.

Eliza, accompanied once more by Violette, was seated on one of the leather-covered chairs in the spacious lobby when they went downstairs.

'*Bonjour!*' She jumped up when she saw them approach

and kissed their cheeks fondly in greeting, while Violette permitted herself somewhat grudgingly to be petted.

Kitty thought her godmother looked exhausted despite the artful use of cosmetics to try and disguise the dark smudges under her eyes.

'I take it Julian is not joining us today. Did he return home all right after yesterday?' Kitty's grandmother asked as they waited for the doorman to summon them a cab from the rank.

'It was very late when I heard his key in the door. He did not come in to say goodnight like he usually does, and he had gone out again when I rose this morning.' Eliza looked distressed. 'I wish he would confide in me and allow me to comfort him.'

'Let's go to lunch and we can discuss it then. I'm certain everything will settle down once the shock of what happened at the fashion show has worn off,' Grams soothed as the taxi pulled to a halt.

The doorman opened the car doors for them and Matt gave the man a discreet tip. Eliza gave the driver the address and they were soon moving through the busy sunlit streets. Kitty admired the view as they crossed one of the bridges over the Seine and headed up the hill into the Montmartre area of the city. The area was known for the steep picturesque cobbled streets, views of the city and thriving artistic scene. It also housed a number of elegant restaurants and pavement cafés and bistros.

The taxi pulled to a stop outside one of these canopies. The entrance of the restaurant was flanked by two bay trees in pots. Gold lettering on the dark-green canopy over the door and plate-glass window bore the legend, '*Les Saveurs*'.

They followed Eliza and Violette inside the restaurant where she was greeted warmly and shown to what appeared to be her regular table. Violette settled herself beneath Eliza's chair and watched the other diners with a disdainful air.

Burgundy leather-bound menus were produced, a carafe of water placed on the table and wine decided upon.

'I take it you dine here often? I remember we always loved this part of the city,' Grams remarked after they had given their food orders with many recommendations from Eliza about what she thought they might enjoy.

A cloud passed over Eliza's face. 'We did indeed. I used to come here with my husband. I've had many delightful times here. It's somewhere I shall miss when I return to England.'

'Have you decided where you will live when you come back? I hope the brochures I sent you arrived?' Grams asked.

Eliza shrugged. 'They have, thank you. I thought I might rent a place to begin with. Perhaps on the Riviera near you, one or two properties seemed very promising.'

'That would be most delightful. I'm more than happy to view them for you. Millicent will be pleased to see you as will the rest of the girls. Julian will remain in Paris, I assume. You said he will take a smaller apartment?'

The waiter returned with their wine and the conversation paused while it was tasted and approved.

'That's right. His work is here, of course, and he has many friends. He has lived here his whole life, but our existing apartment is much too large for one person alone. Also, he wished to live somewhere livelier I think. Now, of course, he may change his mind,' Eliza said.

'How does he feel about you returning to Devon after all these years in France?' Matt asked.

Eliza gave a wry smile. 'In some ways I think he would prefer me to remain here but in other ways I think perhaps I cramp his style, as the Americans say.'

The first course was placed before them. Kitty sniffed the delicious aroma appreciatively. They had all opted for a classic French onion soup on Eliza's recommendation. She had advised them to save room for the main course and the desserts, which she said the restaurant was renowned for.

The soup tasted as good as the aroma suggested, and the fresh crusty chunks of baguette loaded with creamy yellow butter made the perfect accompaniment.

'Do you think Julian will change his mind then about staying on in Paris after yesterday? He seemed to have serious intentions towards Simone Belliste, and he has clearly taken her death badly,' Grams said to Eliza as she set her spoon down in the now empty delicate white china soup dish.

'His work is here, and he has friends so I don't know that he would wish to leave. I really don't know though. I must admit I hadn't realised until recently that his infatuation for the girl had gone quite so far. Or perhaps I hoped it had not. Julian is not the kind of son who shares his emotions with his mother.' Eliza smiled wryly.

'Had Julian known Simone long?' Grams asked.

'About six months or so I think. They met when I attended a fitting for some new clothes. I lost a lot of weight after my husband died. You know, not eating, so I desperately needed to buy some new things. Julian accompanied me on one of those trips to House of Dido and he met Simone and her sister then,' Eliza explained.

There was another short pause while the empty soup dishes were collected and removed by the waiter.

'Did you know Simone well?' Kitty asked. She was curious to discover the extent of her godmother's relationship with the dead girl. It was clear that seeing Simone with Sir Humphrey had influenced her feelings towards her. She wondered though if Eliza had always disapproved of Mademoiselle Belliste's relationship with her beloved son.

Kitty savoured the aroma of the duck confit with roast potatoes and green beans as the waiter set her plate before her. Matt had chosen steak with pepper sauce, whilst Eliza and her grandmother had selected a fish dish.

Eliza picked up her cutlery and waved away the waiter as he offered to refill her wine glass.

'I knew her before Julian since she modelled for Marie. However, when she began seeing Julian I came into contact with her and Nathalie more often. She was always very polite and pleasant but had a somewhat cool manner about her.' Eliza cut a piece of her fish.

'And then you saw her with Sir Humphrey?' Grams said.

'Well, it placed me in such a dilemma. Not just over Julian but also Marie.' Eliza looked distressed.

'Why Marie?' Kitty asked.

'Well, because Sir Humphrey has a small stake in House of Dido and Marie had hoped he would invest more. She also had hopes of, well, marrying him. He is a widow, he inherited the shares in the business from his wife. He and Marie had been out for several dinners, and she is much more his age than Simone.' Eliza gave a tiny shrug of her shoulders and began to eat her fish.

'Goodness me, I can see that did place you in a quandary. Did you ever say anything to her?' Kitty asked. If Eliza had told Marie Dido about Simone and Sir Humphrey, then it might well give the owner of the fashion house a motive to remove the model.

Eliza picked up her wine glass and took a sip before replying. 'I did. I felt dreadful but I thought it better that she should know. That was about two weeks ago now. I wished Julian could see what was going on.' Eliza sighed and resumed her meal. 'It is so difficult as a mother seeing your child become involved with someone unsuitable.'

'Did you know Nathalie well too? You said you often saw her with her sister?' Grams asked.

'Nathalie was often with Simone. I think it frustrated Julian at times that they were often together. I rather think Nathalie has a crush on Julian. She was always hanging around. It used to make me wonder why Simone didn't discourage her,' Eliza said.

'You said the sisters shared an apartment with Patricia?' Matt appeared to be enjoying his steak. Kitty noticed it was almost gone. She had no doubt though that her husband had been paying close attention to what Eliza had been telling them.

'Patricia is a dear girl. Her father is an industrialist from Detroit, I believe. Her mother was half French and Patty came here initially to meet her *grandmère*. The old lady has since passed away and Patty decided to stay in Paris. Her great-aunt still lives here and is quite frail. Patty owns the apartment, but she was lonely living alone so rents a room to the other two girls.' Eliza finished her meal and set her cutlery down neatly on her plate.

'Monsieur Mangan didn't seem fond of Simone,' Kitty observed as she finished her own meal.

'Yves rarely has anything good to say about anyone.' Eliza chuckled. 'I rather think he was threatened by Simone wanting to become a designer. He told Marie the girl's designs were poor, but I must admit I rather liked them. They were admittedly not for Marie's usual clientele. Normally, Gwen, Marie caters for ladies of a more mature age such as ourselves. These designs were for younger women in cheaper fabrics as a more off-the-peg type range.'

'Do you know if Simone had shown her designs to any other houses?' Matt asked.

'Julian said she had plans to show them elsewhere if Marie was not interested. I don't know how far that had progressed.' Eliza picked her wine up once more.

The waiter returned for their plates and they all stopped talking to consider the dessert menu. Kitty chose *baba au rhum*,

Matt selected the *tarte tartin* and her grandmother and Eliza the cherry *clafoutis*.

It crossed Kitty's mind as she eagerly anticipated her dessert that Simone may have been killed for her designs. Either to prevent her from selling them or for someone else to steal them. Was that what Monsieur Mangan had been referring to? Where were those designs now? Had Simone kept them at her apartment or had she taken them to the House of Dido?

The *baba au rhum* was delicious and Kitty focused on her food and the coffee which followed, while Eliza and her grandmother changed the conversation onto sights they could go to see in Paris during their stay.

Eliza had to leave immediately after lunch as she had an appointment at her hairdressers. She and Violette said farewell and departed in a taxi. This left Kitty's party free to wander around the charming streets of Montmartre enjoying the views and the tiny boutiques.

This passed a very pleasant hour or so away and allowed time to digest their meal. When Kitty noticed her grandmother beginning to look fatigued she nudged Matt, and he found a taxi to return them to the hotel.

Grams excused herself to go up to the suite to rest while Kitty and Matt decided to go into the lounge to order a cool drink. The afternoon sun had been quite strong, and they were both thirsty.

They took seats at a table where they could observe the comings and goings in the lounge and the lobby of the hotel.

'I am so warm.' Kitty fanned her face with her hand. 'I can understand why everyone leaves Paris in August for the coast or the mountains. It's hot enough now.'

'It is rather warm,' Matt agreed as he flagged down a passing waiter and ordered two lemonades. 'At least it is somewhat cooler in here with the draught from the doors.'

Once they had their drinks Kitty looked at her husband.

'Go on, darling, I know you are simply bursting to talk about what Eliza told us at lunch.' Matt grinned at her and raised his glass to take a sip.

'It certainly shed a light on a lot of things, didn't it?' Kitty said. 'It gave virtually everyone a motive, with the possible exception of Patricia. I can't help feeling Eliza knows something more about Simone that she hasn't told us.'

'Yes, I got the same impression. I wonder how much of this background information Inspector LeJeune is aware of.' Matt looked at her.

'If this were Devon we would go to Chief Inspector Greville or even Inspector Lewis and tell them,' Kitty agreed.

'But we are in France where we don't know anyone and are not fluent in the language,' Matt reminded her.

Kitty sipped her lemonade, enjoying the cold sharpness of the drink. Matt's French was much better than hers but even so the Parisians spoke very quickly and were often impatient with tourists' attempts at their language.

'What do you suggest we do?' Kitty asked.

'I'm not certain.' Matt frowned. 'If we were to encounter Inspector LeJeune again then obviously we could tell him what we've learned today. However, I'm conscious that this information also gives Julian more of a motive too and it may distress your godmother.'

'If we were to tell the police the information that she has given us you mean?' Kitty could see how that might cause an upset between Eliza and her grandmother.

'Inspector LeJeune may already know much of this anyway. Eliza had told Madame Dido about Simone seeing Sir Humphrey and the police already know of Simone wishing to leave modelling to become a designer. I'm sure that Monsieur Mangan would have given them his view on that,' Matt said.

'I was thinking about the designs. I wondered where they

were. Do you think Simone had them with her at House of Dido that afternoon or do you think they are at her apartment?'

Matt scratched his chin thoughtfully. 'Do you think the designs might have been a reason why Simone was killed?'

Kitty traced a forefinger up her glass to remove some of the condensation that had formed there. 'I think it's possible. I don't know. That's assuming, of course, that someone other than Nathalie killed Simone.'

'The girl could well have been telling the truth. It's hard to say. I wonder if Inspector LeJeune will find anyone else's fingerprints on those scissors,' Matt said before taking another sip of his drink.

'That's a good point,' Kitty said. 'Luckily you told Nathalie to place them on the floor beside Simone before anyone else might have been tempted to handle them.'

Matt suddenly straightened in his seat.

'What is it?' Kitty asked.

'I rather think that's Patricia over there. She's just said goodbye to someone.' Matt raised his hand in greeting as Kitty followed his gaze to where the model was standing, looking somewhat uncertain beside the reception desk.

The girl suddenly appeared to recognise them and came over to their table. Matt stood to greet her.

'*Bonjour*, you were with Madame DeTourner yesterday afternoon at the show? You are friends with Julian?' Patricia said.

'That's right, won't you sit down and have a drink with us.' Kitty smiled up at the girl as she extended the invitation. 'That was such a dreadful shock yesterday, wasn't it?'

Patricia sat daintily on the edge of one of the smart black-leather and chrome modern-style armchairs as Matt got the attention of a passing waiter. She ordered a lemonade and settled back in her seat.

'It was simply ghastly. Poor Nathalie has been absolutely

distraught. I was very grateful to Julian yesterday for accompanying us back to the apartment. It must have been so difficult for him too. He was totally in love with Simone,' Patricia said. 'I must confess I was glad I had a visit planned for today with my father so that I could get out of the apartment for a while.'

The waiter placed Patricia's drink on the table and departed.

'Is your father visiting Paris?' Kitty asked.

'He flies to London in a couple of hours. I was just saying goodbye to him. He wanted to stay when he heard what had happened at the show. I told him though that there was no point in him worrying.' Patricia took a long sip of her drink.

'Do you know of anyone who would have wanted to harm Simone?' Kitty asked.

The model shook her head, her auburn curls bouncing against her cheek. 'No, not at all. Simone wasn't the kind of girl to make enemies. She was clever and ambitious. If she didn't like someone she wouldn't argue or fall out with them the way some girls do. She would just very politely drop them gradually from her circle.'

'Eliza, Madame DeTourner, was saying that Nathalie relied on her sister for much of her work,' Kitty said.

'That's true. She was a little upset with Simone over her plans to wind down her modelling work. Nathalie gets some jobs, of course. She's a very pretty girl, but she doesn't have Simone's flair and poise. Simone had that star quality, you know.' Patricia gave a shy smile. 'I'm more in demand for sportswear and other lines. I know my limitations and, of course, I'm fortunate in that I inherited money from my mother so I can pick and choose my work.'

'Eliza said Simone had aspirations to move into designing?' Matt said.

Patricia gave a sad smile. 'Yes, she had some wonderful designs. She had shown them to Yves Mangan and he had said he would let Marie Dido see them for her opinion. I don't think he was happy about doing it, mind you. Simone had to press her case.'

'Simone didn't just want to show Madame Dido directly?' Kitty couldn't see why the model had decided to show Monsieur Mangan first. She must have known what his attitude towards her designs would be like.

'I think she and Madame Dido had fallen out over something. Marie was definitely acting kind of cool with her,' Patricia said. 'Maybe she thought too that there might be some merit in Monsieur Mangan's opinion. He is a very experienced designer.'

Kitty's brows lifted slightly. It seemed there were plenty of people who might have had a motive to harm Simone Belliste.

CHAPTER EIGHT

Matt was interested in what Patricia was telling them about the relationships between the people working at House of Dido.

'I take it you saw Simone's designs? What did you think of them? Were they good?' Matt asked.

Colour crept into Patricia's cheeks. 'Sure, I thought they were marvellous. We talked a fair bit about them when she was drawing them and sourcing fabric samples. They were young and fresh. Monsieur Mangan's designs are good and all, but they are a bit well, old-fashioned, staid. I know Madame Dido had spoken to him about it. She thought the house was losing business to the newer more forward-looking places. You know with Coco Chanel making a bit of a splash, things need to change, modernise.' Patricia looked at Matt. 'You know what I mean?'

'I'm obviously not that au fait with ladies' couture but, yes, I do understand.' Matt smiled at the girl to put her at her ease.

'When Madame Dido wasn't interested in her designs how did Simone take that? Did she plan to show them elsewhere?' Kitty asked.

Patricia took another sip of lemonade before replying. 'She

had interviews lined up I think at a couple of places where she had modelled. Rivals to House of Dido. Marie was hemming and hawing so Simone thought she wouldn't go for it. She also said something about finding a backer and setting up on her own.' Patricia shrugged. 'I don't know how serious she was about doing that. Simone could be a bit secretive sometimes. She would take these little trips and not say where she had been.'

'Did Marie Dido know about Simone's plans?' Kitty asked.

Patricia's eyes widened. 'Oh my goodness, yes. They had quite the argument just before the show started. I don't think Marie could afford Simone's terms and I think Simone felt they were messing her around. Monsieur Mangan certainly wasn't happy. Simone took back her portfolio from Marie and told her if she wasn't interested then she knew others that were.'

Matt's gaze met Kitty's. He could see his wife was turning all this new information over in her mind.

'So, she had her designs with her at the show?' Matt said.

'Yes, a few of them. Most were back at the apartment, but she had given a few to Yves to show Marie and those were the ones she took back. He brought them up to her. They were in a big brown envelope backstage.' Patricia frowned. 'Now I come to think of it, I didn't see those afterwards. Nathalie didn't bring them back so far as I know. Gee, I guess they must still be there at the salon.'

'I expect Nathalie will have them returned to her once the shock of everything has settled down,' Kitty said.

Patricia, however, was still frowning. 'You know, I don't know. Maybe that's why Simone was late coming out. I don't recall seeing that envelope at the end of the show. It was on the countertop by the mirrors. Do you think it had been moved, and she was searching for it?'

'I don't know. I suppose you could ask Nathalie. Maybe she

had it ready for her sister after all and Simone hadn't realised?' Kitty suggested.

Matt's brow creased as he tried to recall the handbags the girls had been carrying when they had emerged from the backstage area. He seemed to recall Patricia had been holding a small cream bag. His frown deepened. Nathalie had thrust her bag at Patricia before going to look for Simone. It had been a large circular straw design. It could easily have held an envelope of design sketches.

When they had found Simone, her handbag had been on the floor near her body. That had been a dainty dark-blue leather affair that had matched her shoes. It certainly wouldn't have been large enough to contain drawings. He doubted that Simone would have folded her precious designs.

'I guess. Nathalie is so upset though. That police inspector called to see her again this morning. I think he thinks that she killed Simone. You know, with her being found holding the scissors and all.' Patricia looked unhappy. 'Even my father asked if I was totally sure she was innocent. He wants me to stay with my great-aunt for a spell.'

'I suppose it's only natural for him to be concerned for you,' Kitty said.

'I guess. Julian said something about you both being private investigators back in England. Do you really think Nathalie could have killed Simone?' Patricia gave Kitty and Matt a worried look.

'I think there are a number of people who may have killed her but I'm sure Inspector LeJeune will get to the bottom of things very quickly. Are you worried about Nathalie staying with you until her name is cleared?' Kitty asked.

'No, of course not. I mean, I guess everything is all right. It was just when Pops started asking questions it made me feel kinda funny about it.' Patricia didn't sound confident in her assertion.

Matt guessed the girl was just beginning to realise the implications if Nathalie was responsible for Simone's death.

'It's only natural that you should feel uncomfortable,' Kitty said. 'You could always do as your father suggests and stay with your great-aunt for a couple of nights just until everything settles. That is, if you didn't want to stay at your apartment right now. I think it might ease your father's concerns.'

Patricia looked a little uncertain at first but then nodded her head slowly. 'Yeah, I think you might be right. Mrs Bryant, could I ask a favour of you and Captain Bryant?'

'Certainly.' Matt leaned forward in his chair and set his empty glass down on the table.

'Would you come back to the apartment with me. Just while I come up with an excuse about why I'm going to stay with my great-aunt and pack a bag? I just feel a bit nervous now about going back in case she doesn't take it well or something. I'd feel better having someone there.' Patricia gave them a pleading look.

'Of course,' Kitty agreed. 'We'd be happy to help.'

Patricia's apartment was only a short taxi ride away through the busy streets to a different arrondissement. This one was more residential with three- and four-storey buildings lining the streets. The apartment block was old and had broad ledges between each storey ornamented with ornate stone work.

Matt paid for the taxi as Patricia fished the keys to her apartment out of her handbag.

'My apartment is on the second floor so there are a few stairs,' she explained as she led them inside the building. A dark narrow hall gave way to a steep flight of stairs which curved upwards with a metal and wooden bannister.

Kitty was slightly breathless when they arrived at Patricia's landing.

'Nathalie!' Patricia called out as she unlocked the door of the apartment to alert her friend to their arrival.

The apartment had a tiny hallway with a door leading to the sitting room and kitchenette. A further three doors led to Patricia's bedroom, the bathroom and a larger bedroom which the Belliste sisters had shared.

Nathalie was in the sitting room. She was lying on the sofa covered with a lightweight blanket. An eye shade of dark-green silk was on the table beside her along with an empty glass and a small plate covered in crumbs.

'We have company. Are you feeling any better?' Patricia asked as she whisked the glass and the plate into the sink in the kitchenette.

Nathalie opened her eyes and looked startled to see Kitty and Matt standing in the compact room.

'My head is still aching after this morning,' she complained as she sat herself up and moved her blanket so that Kitty could sit down.

'What time did Inspector LeJeune finally go?' Patricia asked.

Matt took a seat on one of the pair of armchairs.

'*Je ne sais pas*, perhaps eleven. Just after you went to meet your father,' Nathalie said.

'*Et* Julian?' Patricia looked at her flatmate.

'He also left then. He said he had to go to work. I thought that might have been him returning.' Nathalie sounded a little sulky.

'I ran into Captain and Mrs Bryant at the Ritz when I was saying goodbye to Pops. You remember Julian told us they were private investigators in England?' Patricia continued to bustle about as she spoke, tidying various things away and straightening them up.

'*Mais oui*.' Nathalie had a wary expression in her dark-brown eyes.

'I don't know if they might be able to help you at all to clear your name with the inspector,' Patricia said as she paused for a moment to look at her friend. 'You seemed so worried this morning.'

'*Merci*, that is very kind of you,' Nathalie said. '*C'est vrai*, I am frightened the inspector doesn't believe me when I told him that I found my sister dead. I wish I had not picked up the scissors. I don't know why I did so. It was the shock I think.'

'You don't know of anyone who wanted to harm Simone. Anyone she had quarrelled with or who may have threatened her?' Matt asked.

'*Non*, Captain, there was no one. At least no one who would kill her. She argued with Marie Dido and also Monsieur Mangan. Even, I think, she had sharp words with Sir Humphrey but nothing serious.' Nathalie sounded sincere.

'And you were on good terms with Simone?' Kitty asked the question this time.

Nathalie plucked a lace-edged handkerchief from under her pillow and dabbed at her eyes. 'We quarrelled sometimes, of course. She was my sister, but it was nothing. I loved her.'

'Was your quarrel to do with Simone wishing to become a designer and to move away from modelling?' Matt looked at the girl.

A tear leaked down the girl's pale cheek. 'I told her to forget about it for a while. She was doing well, we both were. She was the face of the House of Dido and was commanding good fees from other houses. Why would she walk away from that to set up as a designer?'

'What did Simone say to this argument?' Kitty asked.

Nathalie sniffed and blew her nose. 'She was cold. She said it was not a matter for discussion. She had someone who would back her if she couldn't find a fashion house to take her seriously.'

'Did she take it badly when Monsieur Mangan was not

keen on her designs. Eliza said he had shown some to Madame Dido,' Kitty persisted.

'She said they were foolish and short-sighted. Marie was messing her around, keeping her waiting for a decision. She said she would take her designs back.' Nathalie wiped her eyes once more.

'She had some of them with her yesterday. Monsieur Mangan gave them to her before the show, remember? Do you know where the designs are? Did you bring them back here?' Patricia asked as she glanced about the room.

'I don't know. I remember she said Yves had a few sketches and some fabric swatches. I'm not certain if Simone had them back from him. I was changing so I didn't take much notice.' Nathalie's brow puckered.

'They were in a brown envelope near the mirrors in the changing room,' Patricia prompted.

'Perhaps, I don't know. Simone's design folio is in our room,' Nathalie said.

Patricia went out of the room, returning a moment later with a large black portfolio. She presented it to Kitty.

'These are Simone's designs.'

Kitty opened the folder to reveal sketches that had clearly been drawn by a talented hand. A few clever pencil strokes annotated in French with a hint of colour here and there. Pinned to some pages were tiny pieces of fabrics, silks and cottons.

The folder was divided into seasons and each season appeared to show day wear and evening wear. There was even a small section of bridal designs.

'I am not very knowledgeable when it comes to fashion. I wish my friend Alice were here. She is the most talented seamstress and does some designing herself. These though, they seem to be really good to me,' Kitty said.

Simone appeared to have planned her collections meticulously and there were even pages of notes about what seemed to be costings and suppliers for the fabrics she had chosen. One section was empty. The design pages were missing with only Simone's careful notes and the costings pages present. Kitty assumed these must have been the designs which the model had shown Monsieur Mangan.

'Simone was frightfully clever,' Patricia said.

'The designs from this section are missing. Are these the ones she may have had with her at the fashion show?' Kitty showed the folder to Nathalie and Patricia.

The two girls studied the folder carefully. Nathalie flicked back through the pages. '*Oui,* I think you are correct.'

'There are definitely designs missing,' Patricia agreed. 'I think they must have been in that envelope.'

'*C'est possible,*' Nathalie agreed. 'My sister would only show them a small sample of her plans. She didn't want her ideas stolen or copied.'

'Did she believe Madame Dido or Monsieur Mangan would copy her ideas or claim them for themselves?' Matt asked.

The girls exchanged glances.

'The fashion world is very competitive, Captain Bryant, and ruthless. Every house wants the next hot thing. The design that someone in the public eye will be seen wearing and then other women will clamour to wear it too,' Patricia said.

'Madame Wallis Simpson is a case in point. If she could capture the heart of a prince, then maybe if you wore such similar clothes then you also might do the same thing,' Nathalie explained. 'The House of Chanel, that is very avant-garde at this moment. Her name is on the lips of all the rich women of Paris. Stealing or copying designs is always possible.'

'And your sister's designs might be valuable?' Matt looked at Nathalie.

'*Oui, c'est possible,*' she agreed with a shrug. 'Do you think that Simone was killed for her designs?' The girl's eyes widened at the thought.

'It's possible there was some kind of connection. I expect Inspector LeJeune will need to be told about this. Especially as it seems some of Simone's designs have gone missing,' Kitty said. She felt more strongly than ever that she and Matt should go and see the inspector or telephone him to tell him what they had discovered.

'It is very strange that the envelope with her designs is missing. I could have sworn it was on the side right by the mirror when we finished the show and were packing up,' Patricia said.

'We will telephone Inspector LeJeune when we return to the hotel and pass the information on. In the meantime, Mademoiselle Nathalie, I think you should ensure your sister's designs are kept safely,' Matt suggested as Kitty closed the folder and passed it back to the model.

Nathalie took the folder from Kitty, a worried look on her face. 'I wish I knew who would have wanted to kill Simone. It's so strange.'

'Madame Dido said the scissors you found were usually kept downstairs in the workshops. She said the lock had broken on the door there last week, but she had no idea why the scissors would have been upstairs or who could have carried them up there,' Kitty said.

'*Oui, c'est vrai.* The door is usually locked when there is no one in the workshops. The designs are very sensitive, and I suppose there is always the risk of theft as some of the materials are *très* expensive,' Nathalie said.

'I didn't see any scissors while we were showing the clothes. Mind you, it's so hectic as you hop from one frock to another and tidy your hair and so on, there's no time to look,' Patricia said with a wry smile.

'That is exactly so. For big shows there is a wardrobe mistress, but Madame Dido was assisting us while Monsieur

Mangan was out front announcing the dresses in the collection.'
Nathalie nodded in agreement.

'It was awful busy after the end of the show, and we were clearing away. Madame Dido had to go out front to talk to clients. We did most of all the hanging everything back up and putting the shoes away ourselves once we were dressed.' Patricia frowned.

'What did Simone do?' Kitty asked.

'She hung up her last dress and put on her own clothes. She was tidying her hair and reapplying her lipstick while we were changing too. She was excited to meet you and your grandmother. Then she disappeared off to the toilet while we saw everything was clean. We went to come out and called to her to say we were going out front.' Patrica glanced at Nathalie who had begun to cry once more.

'You didn't see her?' Kitty asked.

Nathalie shook her head and dabbed at her eyes with her handkerchief. '*Non*, Madame Bryant. We just heard her call. I said to Patricia that she must be coming after us.'

'We knew that Julian had told her that he wanted to introduce her to you and your grandmother. Like I said, she was excited to meet you all. I guess we thought she would be right out,' Patricia said.

'The two of you came out together?' Matt asked.

'Yes, I was first, and Nathalie was right behind me,' Patricia confirmed.

Kitty suppressed a sigh. It seemed that the killer must have entered the backstage between the girls leaving and Nathalie discovering Simone's body barely five minutes or so later. A very narrow time frame indeed.

CHAPTER NINE

Patricia had just made her excuse to Nathalie about why she was going to be away from the apartment for the night when there was a ring on the doorbell. She hurried to answer the door.

'Julian, please come in. Captain and Madame Bryant are here.' Patricia's voice carried from the front door to the sitting room.

Nathalie immediately sat up straighter and produced a tiny compact mirror from her bag to quickly check her appearance before Julian entered the room.

'Kitty, Matt, I didn't expect to find you both here.' Julian stretched out his hand to shake hands with Matt before kissing Kitty on her cheeks.

Kitty thought Julian looked unwell. His eyes had dark circles under them and his cheeks seemed to have sunk overnight.

'We ran into Patricia at the Ritz and she invited us to come over,' Kitty explained as Julian greeted Nathalie.

'Are you assisting Inspector LeJeune?' Julian asked. 'He was here this morning talking to Nathalie and Patty.' He nodded his head toward the American girl who was collecting up the last of her things to put in her overnight bag.

'I have told them already of my ordeal. Oh, Julian, I said to them how *très terrible* it was, so many questions. He is thinking it was I who killed Simone. I would never have harmed my sister, never. I should have never picked up those scissors.' Nathalie took hold of Julian's arm and turned her face to look imploringly at him.

'I can understand that it looked bad for you, Nathalie, but he hasn't arrested you so he must not be convinced of your guilt.' Julian looked uncomfortable. 'He has to ask awkward questions if he is to find who did this. I thought I'd call in here on my way home to see if you or Patricia had heard anything else from the police.' He turned to Kitty. 'I take it you haven't heard anything?'

'No, we've been out for most of the day. We met your mother for lunch, and she hadn't spoken to the inspector since yesterday,' Kitty said.

Julian paced restlessly up and down the room. 'It's like a nightmare. I keep going over and over what happened in my mind. Matt, Kitty, will you be investigating Simone's death?' he asked.

Kitty exchanged a glance with her husband. 'That would be tricky. Inspector LeJeune is in charge of the investigation. We are in a foreign country and there is no reason to believe the inspector won't do a good job and catch the person responsible for Simone's death.'

Julian appeared to consider what she'd said. 'I don't know, Kitty. I wish I could be as confident. I don't want whoever did this to escape justice.'

'It is so awful to feel that I am under suspicion and could be arrested for something I haven't done,' Nathalie said. 'I agree with Julian. Whoever killed my sister must be caught.'

'We intend to speak to the inspector about a couple of

things when we return to the hotel. We really cannot promise that there is much more that we can do. It really is down to the police to solve Simone's murder,' Matt said.

Patricia gave a discreet cough. 'I think Captain Bryant kinda has a point. They are here on holiday, and to spend time with your mother.'

'If while we are here we discover anything more that might help Inspector LeJeune, then we'll naturally talk to him,' Kitty promised.

Julian looked slightly mollified by this, but she could tell he was not entirely happy.

'I must get going, my great-aunt is expecting me thanks to Dad's promise that I'd look in on her. I'll telephone tomorrow, Nathalie, you have my great-aunt's number if you need me for anything. I hope they catch Simone's killer soon.' Patricia slipped out of the room and a few minutes later they heard the front door close.

'I wish I was not here alone tonight.' Nathalie looked at Julian. 'Suppose whoever killed my sister comes here for me. They might want the rest of Simone's designs.' She looked at the folder lying on the table.

'Do you think that was why she was killed? For her designs?' Julian looked at Matt.

'Some of Simone's designs are missing. It may be connected to her death. It might be a mere coincidence. That's why we need to speak to Inspector LeJeune,' Kitty explained.

Julian dropped onto a chair and placed his head in his hands. 'I know she was hoping to find a backer for her designs. She had mentioned them to Sir Humphrey and she thought he might help her. Madame Dido was interested in them too, but she didn't want to upset Monsieur Mangan since he had been with House of Dido for so long. Simone was frustrated that Marie couldn't seem to decide what to do. She had said she had given them long enough to make up their minds.'

'Is this what Simone told you?' Kitty asked.

Julian raised his head to look at her. 'Yes, she said that Sir Humphrey had shares in House of Dido, He could probably persuade Marie to consider making and showing some of her designs. She said Yves Mangan was jealous of her and was old-fashioned. Simone was ambitious, she wanted her own label.'

'Hmm, it seems there was a lot happening for Simone,' Kitty said.

It sounded to her as if the motives for several people to kill Simone had become a lot stronger. It also sounded as if Julian was aware of Simone seeing Sir Humphrey. Had Eliza misinterpreted what she had seen in the restaurant?

'I think we should go back to the hotel. We need to try and telephone Inspector LeJeune,' Matt said, rising from his seat.

'Of course. Julian will stay for a little while, no doubt, and your *grandmère* will wish you back,' Nathalie said.

'Yes, you're right, time is moving on and Grams will start to wonder where we are.' Kitty followed her husband's lead and collected her bag ready to go.

She was starting to feel uncomfortable in the small apartment with Julian and Nathalie. She was glad that Patricia had heeded their advice to stay elsewhere with her great-aunt.

If Nathalie was Simone's murderer it was better that Patricia was out of the apartment. If Patricia was the murderer then they were protecting Nathalie. Not that she could quite work out a good motive for Patricia to kill Simone.

They said goodbye to Julian and Nathalie and made their way back out of the building. Kitty tucked her hand in the crook of Matt's arm as they strolled along the street towards one of the main boulevards in the hope of spotting a taxi.

'My head is spinning with everything we've learned this afternoon,' Kitty said as they turned the corner to emerge onto the much busier broad avenue that led towards the city centre.

'I feel the same way. I do think we now need to telephone

the inspector. We seem to have uncovered information, especially about the missing designs, that he may not be aware of,' Matt said.

He raised his hand to flag down a taxi.

When they arrived back at the Ritz they decided to take tea downstairs before going up to their suite. Kitty felt as if she needed to sit quietly and digest all they had learned before they tried to talk to Inspector LeJeune.

Matt appeared to feel the same way. He ordered their tea, and they seated themselves in a quiet area of the lounge. Neither of them spoke for a moment, content just to sit and wait for their refreshments to arrive before debating what they had learned.

'Shall I pour?' Kitty asked with a smile after the tea tray had been placed on the low table before them and the waiter had departed.

'Please.' Matt leaned forward in his seat as Kitty raised the lid of the pot and stirred the tea leaves.

She replaced the lid on the pot and carefully poured the tea through the metal tea strainer into the china cups. Matt added his own milk and some sugar.

'It seems we have a lot to share with the inspector,' Kitty said once she was settled back in her chair and had taken her first sip of tea.

'Yes, this business about the missing designs is concerning,' Matt said. He set down his cup and saucer and began to look in the pockets of his jacket for the inspector's card. The police had given one to all of the people they had interviewed at the show.

'Do you think the designs were why Simone was killed?' Kitty asked.

'I don't know. It certainly sounded as if there was a lot more going on behind the scenes at House of Dido than we first thought.' Matt placed the card he had been searching for down on the table.

'*Pardon*, Captain Bryant, you have a most urgent telephone call at the desk.' One of the hotel receptionists had approached their table and stood waiting for Matt to reply.

Matt rose from his seat looking puzzled. 'Of course, do you know who is calling?'

'A Chief Inspector Greville,' the man replied.

Matt hurried away with the receptionist to take the call at the desk, leaving Kitty to wonder what could be so urgent that Chief Inspector Greville needed to talk to Matt about. She waited anxiously on the edge of her seat until Matt returned a few minutes later.

'Well? What did the chief inspector want? Nothing has happened to the house, has it? Or the hotel?' Kitty knew if something bad had happened then she would have heard from more people than just the chief inspector. Even so, the unexpected nature of the call had raised her anxiety levels.

Matt resumed his seat, he appeared perplexed. 'No, nothing at all like that. No, this is to do with Redvers Palmerston.'

'Oh? I take it that a pretty big development has taken place. Have they caught him?' she asked as she picked up her cup and took another draught of tea.

'Not exactly. It's all something of a puzzle. There has been a big fire in Plymouth near the docks. A lodging house has burnt down. Unfortunately, there were several casualties including one fatality. A man they are struggling to identify.' Matt looked at Kitty.

'I presume they have reason to believe the unknown man may be Redvers?' Kitty asked.

Matt nodded. 'Whoever this man is he was wearing Redvers's signet ring. The one that was stolen a few months ago from Redvers's son. The man was badly burned so they cannot use the injury Redvers suffered years ago to his ear as a means of identification.' Matt's expression was grave, and Kitty could only take that to mean that the man must have suffered dreadful injuries.

Redvers had lost part of one ear during the Great War and the old injury had been very useful in identifying him previously.

'That's terrible.' Kitty was not sympathetic to Redvers's crimes, but she hated to think that anyone could have perished in such a terrifying way.

'The chief inspector is anxious to confirm if the body is that of Redvers. They cannot keep him for long in the mortuary so wish to hold the inquest swiftly,' Matt continued.

Kitty had a feeling she knew what was coming. 'How does he plan to do that?'

The corners of Matt's mouth quirked upwards in a humourless smile. 'He has requested that I fly back to Devon to look at the corpse. He doesn't wish to ask any of the ladies who have been recently connected to Redvers. He feels it would be too distressing.'

Kitty privately felt the impact of looking at Redvers's possible corpse might not be good for Matt either. She knew though that her husband would feel compelled to oblige the chief inspector. She just hoped that it wouldn't trigger the horrific nightmares and memories that plagued her husband from his time in the Great War. A time when he and Redvers had been brother officers as impossibly young men.

'What shall you do?' she asked.

'I can fly out this evening and possibly be back here by tomorrow evening or if not the morning after that, depending on airplanes. It would mean you and your grandmother managing alone for the day here,' Matt said.

'What about Inspector LeJeune? Shall I telephone him? I presume you need to arrange tickets to fly back to England,' Kitty said. She hoped the inspector's English was as good as she had thought when they had first met. Her French was likely to prove inadequate if the conversation became complicated.

'Chief Inspector Greville is booking my flight. He says that one is leaving in two hours, and he has reserved a seat. He does send his apologies for interrupting our holiday,' Matt admitted.

'I see. Then we had better head upstairs and contact Inspector LeJeune before you leave and I can pack you a small travel bag. It's a good thing I brought the carpet bag as well as the case,' Kitty said. She drained her tea, and they headed up to their suite to break the news to Grams.

Her grandmother, like Kitty, was shocked by the news of Redvers's potential fate. However, she quickly reassured Matt that she and Kitty would be perfectly all right in Paris together until he returned.

'We have Eliza and Julian should we need assistance with anything.' Grams smiled at him, her eyes sparkling with mischief. 'Don't worry at all about us. I promise too that I shall keep Kitty from doing anything reckless in your absence.'

Matt smiled back at her. 'Well, if you can do that then my mind will be perfectly at ease.'

Grams laughed girlishly.

They left her to continue her perusal of a novel Eliza had loaned her and returned to the sitting room of their suite. Matt took a seat and studied the number on Inspector LeJeune's card before dialling.

'*Bonjour*, Inspector, this is Captain Matt Bryant. We met at House of Dido.'

Kitty tried her best to listen in to the call, but the conversation was mostly in French. Although she could follow some of what was being said, the rest proved too quick for her.

'*Merci, bien sûr.*' Matt finally hung up the receiver.

'What did he say? Was he all right about us contacting him with information?' Kitty asked.

'Yes, he was very grateful. He is continuing his investigations and will follow up on what we've just told him,' Matt said. 'I've explained that I have to return home on a case for a day or so but that you will be here if he needs to check anything.'

Kitty placed his shaving things in his bag. 'I wonder what he'll discover about those missing designs. It all sounded very complicated.'

Matt passed the inspector's business card across to her and she tucked it safely inside her handbag.

'I don't know but I hope he'll share it with us at some point.'

Kitty caught sight of the time on her watch. 'Oh, Matt, we had better hurry and get the last things packed, or you'll miss your flight.'

She accompanied her husband down to the lobby and waved him off in the taxi to the airport with a farewell kiss. With Matt gone, it was now down to her to continue with a little discreet sleuthing in his absence.

* * *

Matt took the evening flight, followed by the early morning train from London to Plymouth the next day after a night spent in London. He had telephoned Kitty on his arrival in London and hoped she would be all right whilst he was away.

Chief Inspector Greville met him at the station in Plymouth, ready to take him straight to the morgue.

'I really do appreciate you returning so promptly, Captain Bryant. I hated disturbing you and Mrs Bryant on your holiday, but this matter really cannot wait,' the chief inspector explained as they climbed into the black police car.

'No, I do understand. I gather that the body is in a pretty bad way since you said it would be unwise to ask any of the ladies to view him.' Matt glanced across at the chief inspector who was now steering the car into the city traffic.

The chief inspector's moustache twitched. 'I'm afraid so.

The fire was very intense. Luckily everyone else managed to get out relatively unscathed. The lady who owned the lodgings sustained some burns to her hands and arms from where she tried to extinguish the blaze.'

'Do you know what caused the fire?' Matt asked.

Chief Inspector Greville glanced at him. 'The fire service believe it was started deliberately. They found the remains of some rags that smelled of petrol and an empty can in the back alley behind the lodgings.'

Matt's brows rose. 'I see, sir. That puts a very serious complexion on the matter.'

He hoped that Redvers had not been responsible for the fire, even if it turned out that he had indeed perished in the flames. A woman had been injured and her home and livelihood destroyed. Other innocent people could have been seriously injured or killed. Surely his former comrade had not sunk so low.

CHAPTER TEN

The following morning, Kitty and her grandmother enjoyed a leisurely breakfast while they waited for Eliza to come and join them. Kitty had received a telephone call late in the evening from Matt to say he had arrived safely in London. She guessed that by now he would be on his way to Plymouth, if he wasn't there already. She hoped that at least this might be an end to the sorry saga of Redvers's crimes, even if it had gone horrifically wrong for him to die in such a dreadful way.

Grams had telephoned Eliza after supper to let her friend know that Matt had been temporarily recalled to England. Eliza had been shocked and sympathetic, promising to escort them to lots of lovely places to make up for his absence.

'*Bonjour, bonjour,* I hope you have left room for our luncheon later.' Eliza bustled into the dining room just as they were finishing their pastries and coffee. She greeted them as usual with kisses.

'Good morning, Eliza. You seem brighter this morning,' Grams observed as her friend perched herself on a vacant chair at their table.

'*Oui*, Julian was at home last night and he seemed a little happier. I can only hope that the inspector catches whoever killed Simone swiftly. Then Julian can put this all behind him,' Eliza explained. She certainly looked as if she had recovered somewhat from the upset at the fashion show.

'Let us hope so, poor boy,' Grams agreed. 'Now, where are we going today?'

Eliza had planned that they should visit the Louvre Museum to look at some of the pictures in the gallery. Then she had booked them a lunch on board one of the boats that travelled up and down the Seine.

'It is a little tourist-like, but you are on holiday, and I shall be returning to England soon myself. It may be our last chance to do something like this,' Eliza explained as she patted Gram's hand.

'It sounds delightful,' Kitty agreed. 'I'll just run and get my hat. Grams, is there anything you wish me to fetch?' She rose from her chair ready to head to their suite.

'My parasol please, my dear. The heat was quite fierce yesterday and I know we shall be inside for a while but better safe than sorry,' Grams said.

When Kitty returned the two ladies were seated in the lobby near the door.

'*Splendide.*' Eliza beamed as Kitty handed the delicate old-fashioned lace parasol to her grandmother. A moment later they were heading for the Louvre in a taxi, admiring the sights of Paris as they travelled.

The Louvre was busy with other holidaymakers all keen to get a dose of culture whilst in the French capital. The paintings were duly admired and discussed as they wandered amongst the crowds through the many rooms. Kitty privately thought many of the pictures were rather muddy and decided she must not have a good eye for art.

The sun was warm as they strolled out of the museum and made their way back towards the Seine. Kitty was relieved to be back outside. They had paused for refreshments and for Grams to rest partway round the tour, but Kitty thought her grandmother was starting to flag again with the heat.

'Ah, here we are,' Eliza said as they arrived at a rather jaunty blue and white boat tied up at a quay on the river. A discreet dark-blue sign with gold lettering announced, 'Dîners-croisières privés'.

Eliza produced tickets from her handbag and a smartly attired gentleman assisted them down the steep steps and showed them to their table on board the boat. It was clear the company was quite exclusive since there were only a few tables and everything was laid out impeccably.

The tablecloths were of fine pale-blue linen with matching napkins and the crystal glasses shone in the sunlight pouring in through the large windows.

'This is a rather new enterprise but it has been extremely popular and the food is said to be remarkably good,' Eliza confided when they had been seated and supplied with an aperitif.

'It certainly looks wonderful,' Kitty agreed, pleased to see her grandmother seemed more comfortable now she was seated at the table.

Once the remaining guests had arrived and were seated, the boat cast off from the quay and began a leisurely progression along the river. Kitty was fascinated by the sights of Paris as they floated past the other vessels. The view of the bridges and buildings from the water was delightful and she wished Matt was there to enjoy it with her.

Having lived beside a river for most of her life she was used to all kinds of crafts, from yachts to commercial boats and leisure vessels. The Seine seemed to offer the same varied traffic but in greater numbers. This offered an extra source of pleasure to the trip.

The first course to be served was shellfish and Kitty enjoyed passing L'Île de la Cité while dining. Eliza was delighted at their enjoyment and appeared to be taking as much pleasure in the outing as Kitty and her grandmother.

Pont Neuf and Notre-Dame Cathedral were pointed out to them by Eliza even though they could hardly fail to miss the magnificent cathedral. The perspective from the river added to its grandeur as they sipped a delicious cold Chablis with their noisettes of lamb.

Some of their fellow diners took the opportunity to take photographs with their Box Brownies as they floated by the various beauty spots. The Eiffel Tower appeared even more impressive in size from the river. Grams seemed to be as taken with the excursion as Kitty, marvelling aloud at the height of the tower.

The boat turned as the dessert course of lemon syllabub was served.

'This really has been quite wonderful, Eliza. Thank you so much, my dear.' Grams smiled happily at her friend.

'I felt so dreadful about what happened at the fashion show. I really wanted you to have a lovely time while you were here. You were so good to me when my husband died,' Eliza said.

'Nonsense, my dear, you and I have been friends for so many years and what else are friends for?' Grams said stoutly.

'We had such fun in Paris when we were young.' Eliza finished her dessert and placed her spoon on her plate with a small sigh.

'We did indeed. It's so nice to share some of that with Kitty.' Her grandmother smiled at her.

'Marie Dido telephoned me last night after I had spoken to you. She's still terribly distressed about what happened, poor thing. Simone's murder was in the paper. She thinks there will be more today since Simone was well known and, of course, they always make a meal of such things. She thinks she may lose her business,' Eliza confided, lowering her voice so as not to be overheard by the surrounding diners.

'Oh dear, that's very concerning for her,' Kitty said.

'She has had a few orders cancelled and lots of ghoulish enquiries about Simone's death from the press and from people asking the most peculiar questions. She has had to send her staff home as they were being harassed on their way into work.' Eliza gave a disapproving tut at this turn of events.

'That does sound bad,' Kitty's grandmother said as she placed her cutlery down on her empty plate.

'She is very worried that Sir Humphrey may even withdraw his support for the business,' Eliza confided.

'Does he own part of it? I thought that was what he said?' Kitty was still a little unclear about exactly how large Sir Humphrey's stake in House of Dido was and how he had come to invest in it.

'Sir Humphrey's late wife, Gilda, was an old friend of Marie's. When Marie started the business Gilda loaned her the money and in return Marie gave Gilda a third of the business. When Gilda died, Sir Humphrey inherited Gilda's shares. Since then he has invested some more money, I believe. Or, at least, Marie was hoping he would invest more. Although she had hinted, before Simone was killed, that he was unsure if he wanted to continue with his investment. Marie was a little worried, but I think she thought that perhaps he was interested in her romantically. If he was, then she might be able to persuade him to continue.' Eliza gave them a meaningful look.

'But if he did decide to sell his shares, what then?' Kitty asked, placing her napkin down on the table.

Eliza's brow creased as she pondered the question. 'I don't know. I doubt Marie has the money to buy him out so I suppose another couture house might merge with House of Dido, or the business could fold.'

'It sounds most precarious if you ask me,' Grams said.

Kitty could see that her grandmother disapproved of House of Dido's business arrangements.

'Yes, I suppose so. Marie is terribly down about it all. I wondered, Kitty, my dear, I know this is a terrible imposition, but perhaps you might meet her for tea this afternoon? I think your experiences of dealing with these kinds of unpleasant situations may help her.' Eliza looked at Kitty with a pleading expression.

Kitty was taken somewhat by surprise by the unexpected request. 'Of course, if you think it would help, but I don't know how useful my experiences might be really. I mean this is France and things may be different here.'

Her grandmother sipped her wine but stayed silent on the matter.

'I know, but it would mean so much if you could,' Eliza said. 'You did have that case on the Riviera at Nice, so you have a little knowledge of how long these things are likely to take and what happens in an investigation. Poor Marie is struggling and Monsieur Mangan is not making things any easier for her,' Eliza said.

'Is Monsieur Mangan afraid of losing his job?' Kitty asked.

If the House of Dido were to fold even an experienced designer might find it difficult to get taken on elsewhere in a similar position. She would have thought that most couture houses already had people in place who led their design teams. While she wasn't sure if her experiences would be helpful, she wasn't going to turn away an opportunity to do more sleuthing.

Eliza followed Kitty's lead and dabbed the corners of her mouth delicately with her napkin before dropping it on the table. 'Marie was not explicit, but she said he had been asking her all kinds of difficult questions, and I think she is just not in a good place at this time. Please do say you will see her, Kitty, just for an hour?'

Kitty looked at her grandmother. She could tell that she was as curious as Kitty to try and find out more information.

'I see no harm in helping the poor woman. She was very kind to allow us to see the fashion show and it was hardly her fault that things turned out as they have,' Grams said.

'Very well, shall we say four o'clock at the Ritz?' Kitty agreed as the waiter cleared their plates and returned to serve coffee in dainty china cups.

She was curious about the set-up of House of Dido, and she wondered if Marie might be able to shed more light on Simone's murder.

'*Merci beaucoup*, Kitty. I shall go to fetch Marie once we are docked. We can meet you at the hotel.' Eliza's eyes brightened and Kitty hoped she wasn't making a mistake by agreeing to see Marie.

* * *

The morgue was situated in a small red-brick building sited discreetly at the rear of the hospital in Plymouth. It looked to Matt as if it was of a more recent construction than the large Victorian main building. He suspected it had been added during the Great War when the death rate had risen, and the original building had proved insufficient.

Chief Inspector Greville pulled the police car to a halt just outside the building and glanced across at Matt.

'This won't be pretty I'm afraid, Captain Bryant,' he warned before they got out of the car.

Matt nodded in acknowledgement. He didn't expect it would be. He had been mentally bracing himself for this moment over every mile of the rail journey from London to Plymouth.

Chief Inspector Greville knocked on the green-painted door of the morgue. A small thin man in his late fifties answered and let them inside once the chief inspector had shown his credentials.

Matt followed the chief inspector. A strong smell of disinfectant greeted them as they walked the short distance through the limewashed-walled corridor and through another door into the main room. The room felt icy after being in the sun outside.

A body lay covered with a green hospital drape on the central slab and Matt guessed that the mortuary assistant had placed Redvers there ready for them to identify him.

'Firstly, here are the effects removed from the man when he was recovered from the fire.' Chief Inspector Greville signalled to the mortician who stepped forward with a wooden tray containing several items.

The man placed the tray on a small metal desk at the side of the room. Matt was glad to turn his attention to examining the items and delaying the inevitable unveiling of the body. The contents of the tray were minimal and had clearly been exposed to extreme heat. A cheap wallet, badly burned, a few coins, one cufflink, broken, and the stone that it had once held missing. Then there was the signet ring.

Matt swallowed and sucked in a breath. 'May I?'

He looked at the chief inspector for permission to remove it from the tray so he could examine it. This was the item that had led the police to believe the body on the mortuary slab was Redvers.

'Go ahead,' Chief Inspector Greville gave his consent.

Matt picked up the remains of the ring. The fire had clearly been hot enough to cause it to lose its shape, but the family crest and garnet inset was still clearly visible. He placed it back carefully in the tray.

'Is that the ring Redvers Palmerston gave you in 1916? The one you gave to his widow, and which was subsequently stolen recently from his son?' Chief Inspector Greville's question was very formal.

Matt knew that this was so he could record the facts should they need to present them to the coroner in court.

'Yes, sir. It is.'

'Thank you, Captain Bryant. If you feel ready, shall we see the corpse?' The chief inspector again signalled to the mortuary attendant who had remained silent throughout the proceedings.

Matt turned around to face the slab and moved closer to the chief inspector. He was dimly aware that mingled in with the strong scent of the disinfectant there was another smell. A charred, acrid scent that cloyed at the back of the throat.

The attendant carefully lifted the area of the cloth covering the dead man's head and immediately the burnt smell grew stronger. Matt controlled his emotions and leaned forward to examine what remained of the man's face.

He could see immediately why the ears could not be used for identification. It was very hard to tell if the sorry remains were those of Redvers or not. Matt tried to focus on aspects of his former brother officer's face that were unlikely to have altered.

'I'm sorry, sir. I cannot say for certain that this is Redvers Palmerston. The man here, judging by his size under the covers, looks shorter by at least three inches. I cannot tell from his face, but I can see no points of resemblance that I can rely on. I don't believe that this is our man,' Matt said as the technician, at another signal from the policeman, covered the face back up.

'Thank you, Captain Bryant.' The chief inspector looked disappointed.

Matt waited as the chief inspector thanked the mortician before they walked out of the building back into the warm, summer sunshine.

'I'm sorry we seem to have spoiled your holiday with a wild

goose chase,' Chief Inspector Greville said as Matt breathed in the clean air of the hospital car park.

'No matter, Chief Inspector. That is definitely Redvers's ring. I don't know who that poor soul is or how he got hold of it, but we do know their paths have crossed and recently,' Matt said.

CHAPTER ELEVEN

Once they had disembarked, Eliza dashed away in a flurry of au revoirs and kisses to collect Marie, while Kitty and her grandmother returned to the hotel.

'Darling, would you mind terribly if I retired to rest while you meet Madame Dido and Eliza? I am feeling rather fatigued. We seem to have done a great deal of walking this morning and that lovely luncheon has made me quite sleepy.' Grams smiled apologetically as they entered the lobby of the Ritz.

'Oh, of course you must go and rest. I love Eliza dearly, but she can be quite exhausting.' Kitty smiled back at her grandmother, and they exchanged understanding glances. 'I'll come up to join you after Marie and Eliza have gone. I'm hoping Matt might telephone me later to let me know what has happened in Plymouth and when he is able to rejoin us.'

'Thank you, darling. I hope Matthew has been successful and is able to return soon. We only have a few more days before we go home and there is still so much to see,' Grams agreed.

Kitty walked with her grandmother to the impressive brass and metal elevator and saw her safely inside before returning to sit in the lobby. It didn't seem worth going up to the suite and she enjoyed sitting watching the world go by from one of the Ritz's comfortable chairs.

She didn't have to wait long before Eliza and Marie Dido strolled in through the doors of the hotel. Violette accompanied them on her leash, trotting at her mistress's heels with a pink satin bow in her fluffy black topknot.

'Madame Bryant, I cannot tell you how grateful I am that you have agreed to see me.' Marie Dido sank down onto a chair opposite Kitty's, while Eliza organised herself and her little dog in a seat beside her friend.

Kitty could see the older woman no longer seemed the confident proprietor of a successful couture house. Despite her elegant, fitted pale-pink summer two-piece and charming hat, she looked pale and afraid.

'Not at all, madame. You were so kind to allow Eliza to bring us to the show and for it to end so terribly was awful. It must have been even more distressing for you since you knew Simone so well,' Kitty said.

The waiter delivered their tea to the table in front of them and departed. Eliza took it upon herself to serve the drinks and to offer the delicious bite-sized patisserie confections around. Violette received her fair share of the treats.

'The newspaper people have been outside the salon all day. They have harassed my staff, my neighbours, even the woman who does the cleaning. They have tried taking photographs and demanded to be let inside. In the end I had to ask the inspector to send a gendarme. It is all too much.' Marie's hand trembled as she picked up her teaspoon to add sugar to her tea.

'It is true. I had to go around to the back door of the salon and even there a man was concealed amongst the dustbins.' Eliza smoothed the silk fabric of her skirt and Kitty suspected that her godmother was secretly a little excited by the drama.

'I have never been in the middle of such a scandal. It is

awful.' Marie stirred her tea, the sound of the spoon clinking against the china made Violette stare.

'Murder is always shocking, and I expect the way Simone was killed, and the glamour of a couture house has obviously drawn the attention of the journalists,' Kitty said.

'I have tried to speak to Sir Humphrey to ask his advice, but he has not been at his apartment today.' Marie looked at Eliza.

'Eliza said Sir Humphrey is your business partner in House of Dido?' Kitty said.

Marie nodded. 'He inherited his late wife's shares. She was a great friend and supporter when I first set up the business. Sir Humphrey has always supported me too.'

'Eliza said you were worried about the future of House of Dido?' Kitty continued her probing as gently as she could. She knew Marie was distressed but she was curious about the things they had learned so far about the couture house.

Marie's face crumpled and she hastily drew a fine-linen monogrammed handkerchief from her patent leather bag. 'This business could be the end of House of Dido.' She dabbed at her eyes. 'My order books, they were already slim. That is partly why we did the extra show, to get more new orders. Yves is a very good designer, but he is seen as a little old-fashioned now and customers are hungry for new ideas. Everyone is talking about the clothes of Madame Wallis Simpson and her jewels. I was looking for more investment and perhaps a new designer to work alongside Yves.'

Kitty's brows rose. 'Did Monsieur Mangan know this?'

'He did. He is very unhappy about it. Simone was aware of my plans. I presume Sir Humphrey must have told her. I'd hoped he would increase his investment.' Marie sniffed and blew her nose, before composing herself with another sip of her tea.

'You said Monsieur Mangan had shown you some of Simone's designs. You weren't impressed?' Kitty asked.

'The designs were very different to our usual style. Cheaper fabrics and more of a ready-to-wear collection. Yves disapproved, of course. I needed more time to consider. They were not immediately commercial you understand. Also, Simone was asking quite a lot in return from me,' Marie said.

Eliza took the last of the pastries from the stand and gave it to Violette. 'What a terrible position to be in, Marie. You obviously would not wish to upset Monsieur Mangan but it sounds as if Simone's designs may have been the new direction you wanted.'

'This is true but if I had taken Simone on as a designer I knew Yves would probably make life *très difficile* for everyone.' Marie set down her cup and saucer. 'Sir Humphrey also was keen that I consider Simone. I felt under so much pressure.'

'Simone's designs, the ones you saw, were they in a large brown envelope?' Kitty asked.

Marie looked puzzled. '*Oui*, they were a sample. I think she had a full folio, *mais naturellement* she would not share the whole thing unless I was serious about perhaps producing her designs. She wanted to have her own label within House of Dido. I think this may have enraged Yves more than anything. He was very angry about it.'

Kitty wondered if his anger may have led him to murder his would-be rival.

'Oh dear. Did you see the envelope with the designs the day of the show?' Kitty asked.

Marie frowned. 'I don't know. Oh, wait, *oui*, Yves had them and gave them to Simone before the girls started their walk. Simone had been asking for their return, and they were in his office downstairs. She was insistent on having them back. She was most unpleasant about it but with the show there was no time for further discussion.'

'You didn't see the envelope again after the show?' Kitty was conscious of Eliza gazing curiously at her.

Marie shook her head. 'I didn't notice it. Why? Is this important?'

Kitty shrugged. 'I don't know. Nathalie mentioned the designs seemed to have gone missing.'

'Maybe the police have taken them?' Eliza suggested. 'You know, as evidence or a clue to the murderer?'

'Perhaps.' Kitty kept her response noncommittal. She was fairly sure the police didn't have them, or Matt would have discovered that during his telephone call to the inspector.

'What do you think I should do, Madame Bryant? About all this business with the press and the murder?' Marie asked. 'Eliza said you have a great deal of experience in these matters.'

'Don't talk to the journalists and advise your staff to do the same. Direct any enquiries to the police and Inspector LeJeune. The less you say the better. The interest will die down in a day or so and hopefully the police will have made an arrest by then,' Kitty advised.

'Has it affected your orders, Marie? You were worried people would cancel,' Eliza asked her friend.

'A few but I suspect most people cannot even get through on the telephone. I had to disconnect it because it kept ringing with the newspaper people,' Marie said.

'You knew Simone well, madame, was there anyone who may have held a grudge against her or who wished to harm her?' Kitty asked.

Violette stirred restlessly on her mistress's chair and Kitty suspected her godmother would announce their departure soon.

'I don't know. She could be secretive at times. Yves was unhappy with her, but I cannot think my head designer would go so far as to murder the girl. She and her sister, they would sometimes quarrel. It worries me that Nathalie was found holding those scissors.' Marie shuddered. 'She looked so shocked, I cannot think though she would harm Simone. She loved her. As for Patricia, she and Simone never had a cross word to my knowledge. It is a complete mystery. If not for the nature of her death it almost seems like a bizarre accident or perhaps she harmed herself,' Marie suggested.

'An interesting idea.' Kitty didn't believe for one moment that Simone would have stabbed herself with the tailoring scissors. She certainly couldn't have plunged them into her abdomen accidentally.

Marie sighed. '*Merci beaucoup* for seeing me, Madame Bryant. I appreciate your help. I feel a little calmer after speaking with you and your advice seems very good.'

'My pleasure. I'm glad to have helped you,' Kitty said as Marie and Eliza gathered up their bags. Eliza scooped up Violette from her chair and murmured endearments in her poodle's ears.

'Let us hope whoever did this terrible thing is caught soon,' Marie said.

Eliza murmured her agreement. Kitty hoped the inspector would catch the murderer soon as she watched the two women depart with Eliza still carrying her dog.

* * *

Chief Inspector Greville drove Matt back to the train station so he could try to get an evening flight back to Paris from London.

'You'll be cutting it fine, I'm afraid,' the policeman said as he sped along the Plymouth streets to the railway station.

'That's all right. I'm glad I came. I'd love to know how our mystery man came to have Redvers Palmerston's ring though,' Matt said thoughtfully.

'He could have stolen it, found it, got it in payment of a debt if your man had fallen on hard times.' Chief Inspector Greville glanced at him.

'The landlady had no idea who the dead man is?' Matt asked. 'Usually they keep a register?'

'Charles Palmers she reckons was the name he gave her. Palmers and Palmerston are pretty similar so add in the discovery of that ring...' Chief Inspector Greville pulled the police car to a halt outside the station.

'Quite so. A most extraordinary coincidence, don't you think?' Matt reached over and collected the carpet bag containing his things from the rear seat of the car.

'I'll get my men making enquiries to see if we can pin down the identity of the dead man. If we can't find who he was, then he'll have to go down as a John Doe.' Chief Inspector Greville looked most dissatisfied.

'I had best be off. Please let me know if anything else happens. We're due back from Paris in a few days' time. Kitty and I can pick up the threads again then,' Matt said.

'Safe travels.' The chief inspector raised his hand in a farewell gesture as Matt hopped out of the car to go in search of the ticket office.

Matt hurried away and discovered his train was due in the next ten minutes. He purchased his ticket and went to the platform to wait. He hadn't discussed the murder in Paris with the chief inspector since there had been no time. It was a great pity as he would have been interested in the policeman's thoughts on Simone's murder.

The train was punctual, and he should have just enough time when he reached London to place a long-distance telephone call to the Ritz to inform Kitty that he was on his way back.

* * *

Kitty had just seen Eliza and Marie out and was about to head upstairs to her suite when a movement near the potted palms caught her attention. A familiar figure in a well-cut grey suit was clearly attempting to conceal themselves behind the large stone pots and waving green fronds.

'Monsieur Mangan!' Kitty stood and called over to the designer.

'Madame Bryant, *quelle surprise*, I didn't know this was where you were staying.' He emerged from behind the ferns looking a little flushed and sheepish at having been seen.

'Why on earth were you trying to hide behind the foliage? Were you spying on Madame Dido?' Kitty asked sternly.

The designer sank down on the chair so recently vacated by his employer and placed his head in his hands. 'Forgive me, Madame Bryant, I was concerned. This affair of Simone's murder, you understand.'

Kitty fixed him with a steely glance. 'I'm afraid I don't understand. Did you follow Marie and Eliza here this afternoon?'

Yves sighed. '*Oui*. I was at House of Dido when I saw Madame DeTourner come to the back door and Marie slip out. It was clear they were not wishing to be noticed. I managed to get a taxi and followed them here. I wanted to know what was going on.'

'What do you think is happening? Why are you so concerned, Monsieur Mangan? Do you have something to hide?' Kitty asked.

The designer groaned, his body rocking slightly to and fro in his seat. 'I do not expect you to fully understand my difficulties, Madame Bryant. It is a business issue. My job is under threat. House of Dido is beginning to struggle. Our clientele they are demanding, always looking to be not just fashionable but for the best materials. Marie, the route she is considering for the business is, in my view, short-sighted. This *prêt-à-porter* fashion is just a nonsense. Then Simone is killed, am I suspected because she wished to take my job? Is Marie wishing to be rid of me?'

'Let me see if I have understood you correctly, Monsieur

Mangan. You followed Madame Dido because you thought she was plotting to terminate your employment and that she suspected you of killing Simone Belliste?' Kitty stared at him.

'I know, it is not perhaps rational to you, madame, but couture is my life. I have worked hard to secure my position.' Yves raised his head from his hands to meet her gaze.

'Did you harm Simone? You said you were threatened by her wishing to become a designer. I know you were critical of her work and tried to discourage Marie from employing the girl,' Kitty said.

'*Oui*, I admit I was concerned. As I said I do not think House of Dido should be producing a ready-to-wear collection. Our focus should be on our clients who wish for beautiful, exclusive, one-off classical garments that speak of luxury and style. Simone wanted her own label, it was ridiculous. A mere slip of a girl such as her, pah! *C'est impossible.* That does not mean I intended to harm the girl. If only I had not...' His voice tailed off.

'If you had not what?' Kitty was certain now that she was onto something. She sensed Yves Mangan was about to admit to something significant.

'It was I who took the scissors from the workshop upstairs to the changing rooms,' Yves confessed.

'You? For what reason? To kill Simone?' Kitty was thoroughly alarmed now and glanced around the lobby to check that there were people around should Yves attack her.

'*Non, non*, that was not my purpose. Marie had asked me to return Simone's designs to her. She had been making a huge fuss about them. I picked them up and went to go upstairs when I saw the scissors lying on a bench.' He paused and scrubbed at his face with his hands before continuing. 'I am not proud of my thoughts or my actions, Madame Bryant. Jealousy took over me. I did not have time to act then but I thought I will return these designs, but I shall cut them into little pieces first.'

Kitty blinked. 'You took the scissors intending to destroy Simone's work before giving it back to her?'

'There was not time before the show commenced so I left the envelope near the mirror in the changing rooms and the scissors were near the clothes rail. I hid them under the shoes.' Yves looked uncomfortable.

It was no wonder, Kitty thought, considering what he had just told her. 'You are saying the murderer must have found the scissors you hid and used them to kill Simone?'

Yves nodded miserably. '*Mais oui*, madame, what else can have happened? I did not murder the girl. It was her designs I intended to destroy not Simone herself.'

'Why should I believe you?' Kitty asked. 'Did you think Marie knew you had taken the scissors? Is that why you followed her to try and hear what she was going to tell me?'

'I heard that you and your husband are private investigators. I thought perhaps Marie had seen me with the scissors and thought I was Simone's murderer. I wanted to discover what was going on.' He gazed at her imploringly. 'You must believe me, Madame Bryant, I acted foolishly in thinking to destroy Simone's work, but I did not kill her.'

'Simone's designs are missing. That envelope you said you left near the mirror in the changing room has vanished.' Kitty watched him closely to see his reaction to this news.

'*Je ne comprends pas.* The designs were there. I intended to try and retrieve them once the show had ended. Then when Nathalie screamed, and we rushed to her aid I never even thought of them. I was so shocked at the sight of Nathalie holding those scissors, Simone lying there and the blood.' He stopped and swallowed, the Adam's apple bobbing in his throat.

'You need to tell all of this to Inspector LeJeune,' Kitty said firmly. 'The longer you leave it the worse it will be. The police may well have found your fingerprints on those scissors.'

The high colour in Monsieur Mangan's face receded as swiftly as it had risen.

'Madame Bryant...' He stopped. '*D'accord*, I understand, yes, you are right. Unpleasant though this will be. I must speak.'

'If not, then you know that I will tell the inspector myself. I suggest you go right away.' Kitty rose from her seat. She wanted to get away to the quiet safety of her room. His revelations had left her feeling quite shaken.

'*Très bien, au revoir*, Madame Bryant.' Yves Mangan tipped his hat to her and walked briskly away through the hotel lobby.

CHAPTER TWELVE

Kitty checked in on her grandmother when she returned to the suite and was relieved to see that she was asleep in her room. The adventures of the last few days had clearly exhausted her. Kitty slipped off her shoes and padded into her own room. The broad expanse of the bed looked inviting, so she settled herself down and tucked the pillows comfortably under her head.

The sound of the telephone ringing in the lounge area of their suite was the next thing she knew. She slid off the bed feeling slightly confused from being woken so suddenly and hurried to answer the call. The hotel receptionist connected her and she heard Matt's voice in her ear.

'I'm just about to board my flight. I'll be back soon.' He sounded crackly and very far away.

'Wonderful, I have so much to tell you. Take care. I love you.'

She heard him chuckle softly. 'I love you too, darling. See you later.'

The line went dead, and she replaced the receiver on the stand.

'Who was that, Kitty? Was that Matthew?' Her grandmother appeared at the door of her room.

'Yes, he'll be with us later this evening. He was waiting to board his flight.' Kitty attempted to smooth her short blonde curls with her hands. She still felt disorientated from the sudden awakening.

'Are you all right, Kitty, dear? You seem a little out of sorts?' Her grandmother eyed her keenly. 'Was everything all right when you saw Eliza and Madame Dido?'

'Yes, we had an interesting talk.' Kitty sank down on the sofa. 'It was what happened afterwards that has made me feel quite confused.'

'Oh?' Grams asked as she came to join her. She took a seat at the other end of the sofa to Kitty. 'What happened?'

'I found Monsieur Mangan lurking amongst the flowerpots in the lobby. He had followed Eliza and Marie and was trying to eavesdrop on the conversation,' Kitty explained.

Her grandmother looked shocked. 'How dreadful! What on earth did he think he was doing?'

'It seems he was the person responsible for the scissors being in the changing room.' Kitty told her what Yves had said.

Her grandmother's eyes were wide by the time Kitty had finished. 'Oh, my dear! This is awful. You must tell Inspector LeJeune at once, don't you think? I know he has denied it, but he could easily have killed that poor girl. He could have attacked you.'

'He promised to go straight to the police. There were lots of people in the lobby at the time, so I was quite safe,' she hastened to reassure her grandmother, who was looking appalled at what Kitty had just told her.

'Do you think he has gone to the police? I mean, he could be making good his escape. We don't know how trustworthy he may be, not after what he disclosed to you.' Grams sounded unconvinced.

'I don't think he lied to me. You do have a point, however. Matt has left the inspector's card here next to the telephone. I suppose there would be no harm in checking if he has gone to meet Inspector LeJeune.'

Her grandmother was right. Matt always told her she was too trusting. She would never forgive herself if he had killed Simone and she had permitted him to escape. Kitty checked the number on the card and placed a call to the police station. She gave her name to the man who answered and asked for the inspector in careful French.

'*Un instant*, madame.'

Kitty waited while the gendarme put her call through.

'*Bonjour*, Madame Bryant. I believe I have to thank you for sending Monsieur Mangan to see me.' Inspector LeJeune's cultured tones reached her, and she breathed a silent sigh of relief.

'Yes, Inspector. That was really why I was calling, to make certain that he had kept his word. He told you about the scissors, I presume?' Kitty asked.

'*Oui*, madame. His admission and our discoveries about the House of Dido's financial structure have added a new complexity to our investigations,' the inspector said.

'I presume you are aware of Sir Humphrey's involvement and his shares in Madame Dido's company then?' Kitty asked. She glanced at her grandmother who was listening attentively to the conversation.

'That is correct. For now, we have allowed Monsieur Mangan to go but we are grateful for your assistance in Mademoiselle Belliste's murder. I would ask, however, Madame Bryant, that since the newspapers are very interested in this case that you refrain from communicating with any journalists,' Inspector LeJeune warned.

'No, of course. I understand completely. Thank you.' Kitty wished the policeman a pleasant evening and ended the call.

'Monsieur Mangan has made a clean breast of it after all, then?' her grandmother said as she settled a cushion in the small of her back.

'Yes, thank goodness. I must say I don't envy the inspector his task. It seems that any number of people had a reason to wish Simone dead. It makes it even more awful that we seem to know them all too,' Kitty said. 'I shall be glad to see Matt later to tell him everything. Perhaps he will see it all more clearly than I do at the moment.'

Her grandmother reached out and gave her hand a comforting pat. 'I think you should stop trying to do Inspector LeJeune's job for him and just enjoy our time in Paris. We cannot go around suspecting everyone we meet. It may be that there is someone else we are unaware of who has a motive for killing the girl.'

Kitty smiled. 'I'm sorry, Grams. You're right, this is all really none of my business. Now, Matt won't be returning until late so shall we dine out tonight? Eliza recommended that charming-looking restaurant just along the street. We wouldn't even require a taxi.'

'That sounds most delightful. Call down to the desk, my dear, and get them to make a reservation for us. I shall go and dress. A nice night out will be just the ticket,' her grandmother instructed.

Kitty booked the reservation and went to change for the evening. Her grandmother was right that an enjoyable evening dining out would be lovely. However, she couldn't stop thinking about Simone's murder. She would be glad when Matt was back in Paris so she could get his thoughts on the latest developments.

The restaurant was just a little way along the treelined street, and it was a pleasant stroll in the warm evening air. *Le Petit Chien* was a glamorous venue. The green-canopied doorway was flanked on either side by manicured bay trees in pots. Small black cane tables with bentwood chairs stood out front for clients wishing to dine al fresco.

Kitty gave their name to the maître d' and they were escorted to a charming table set with starched white linen, silver cutlery and crystal glassware sparkling in the light from the venetian glass chandeliers above their heads.

'This all seems very pleasant,' Grams remarked after they had ordered their wine and were happily engaged in studying the menu. 'This brings back so many happy memories for me of when Eliza and I were younger, and we would dine out together on the Champs-Élysées.'

Kitty gazed round at the busy restaurant that was filling up fast with well-heeled diners. There was a hum of chatter and the faint, delicious scent of steak in the air.

'It is very nice, here,' Kitty agreed. Perhaps her grandmother was right. She should stop thinking about Simone Belliste's death and let Inspector LeJeune do his job.

For the next hour or so she focused on enjoying the beautifully presented meal that was served to them by the attentive waiters. She listened to her grandmother's reminiscences and savoured the fine, crisp bottle of white wine they had ordered to accompany their fish.

'What time will Matthew return? Did he give you an estimate?' Grams asked as the waiter removed their dessert plates.

Kitty consulted her tiny gold wristwatch. 'I would have thought he would be at the hotel for around eleven. That is, of course, providing all went as planned with the departure,' she said.

'Splendid, we have plenty of time then to enjoy our coffee,' her grandmother said, beaming at her as the waiter returned bearing their drinks.

Kitty added cream to her cup from the delicate silver jug and savoured the fresh scent of the coffee. The restaurant was full now and the waiters darted about between the tables. The noise levels too had risen, and the place was alive with chatter, laughter and cigarette smoke.

'Kitty, darling, is that Sir Humphrey over there?' Grams broke into Kitty's train of thought. 'I can't quite see who he is with.' She inclined her head towards a table on the far side of the restaurant, partly obscured by the waiter's station.

Kitty was forced to discreetly twist her head to try and see the table. 'Oh, yes, I rather think it is. He has a lady with him, and it isn't Marie.' She turned her head back again in case Sir Humphrey looked up and saw her.

'Yes, you're right. I wonder who she is. He certainly seems to move swiftly, doesn't he?' her grandmother remarked. 'Quite the ladies' man it would seem.'

They finished their coffees and called the waiter to pay the bill. Kitty took the opportunity when they rose to collect their wraps to take a better look at Sir Humphrey's companion.

The lady certainly wasn't anyone she recognised. She was elegantly dressed in dark-grey crêpe de chine with embroidered flowers in shot-silver silk thread. Her shoes were both expensive looking and distinctive. Her dark hair was immaculately styled, and she appeared to be paying close attention to Sir Humphrey's conversation.

There was something about the way the woman was listening and her poise that made Kitty think that this wasn't a romantic dinner after all, but was perhaps more of a business meeting. As if to confirm this idea the woman produced a tiny notebook and a silver propelling pencil.

Kitty dawdled collecting her handbag while she snooped discreetly near the waiter's station. The woman made several notes in her book before returning to her meal. She toyed with the idea of going over to say hello to Sir Humphrey but decided against it. Instead, she followed her grandmother out of the restaurant. Once back on the pavement she tucked her hand through her grandmother's arm to support her, and they walked back slowly to their hotel.

It was a little after ten when they arrived in the lobby and they went straight up to their suite. Her grandmother retired to bed while Kitty changed into her night attire and waited up for Matt to return.

She didn't have to wait for too long before the door to the suite opened and Matt entered. He looked tired, Kitty thought as he greeted her with a warm embrace.

'Phew, it's nice to be back for a couple of days.' He took off his hat and dropped his bag down beside the chair.

'Let me get you a drink? Have you eaten? Shall I send for something?' Kitty asked as her husband sank down on the end of the sofa.

'A drink would be rather marvellous. They served us supper on the plane so I'm not hungry,' he said.

The suite had a small bar with a couple of bottles and a soda syphon. Kitty mixed her husband a brandy and soda and brought it over to him.

'How did you get on in Plymouth? Was it Redvers Palmerston who was in the fire?' she asked after he had taken his first reviving sip.

He told her everything that had happened.

'Oh dear, that sounds awful. So, it was another poor soul who died? And he had Redvers's ring? That's quite extraordinary.' Kitty was horrified by Matt's news.

'At least Chief Inspector Greville is still on the hunt for Redvers. He remains hopeful that he'll turn up again soon like the proverbial bad penny. He said he would try to identify the man who died but I don't know if he'll have much luck. We think the name on the boarding house register is false,' Matt said before taking another sip of brandy. 'Now, what have you been up to while I've been gone?'

Kitty told Matt everything that had happened. How Yves

had been the one to take the scissors to the salon from the workroom and all the other things she had found out. Her husband listened carefully, a grave expression on his face.

'Hmm, I'm glad Inspector LeJeune is aware of all of this. Let's hope he discovers who killed Simone soon. It's an unpleasant business.'

They were woken the next morning by the telephone ringing in their suite. Matt got out of bed and went to answer. Kitty tugged on her robe and followed behind him, wondering who could be calling so early.

'Hello.' Matt had barely spoken before Kitty overheard a torrent of hysterical English mixed with French coming from the other end of the line.

Matt quickly passed the receiver to Kitty. 'It's Eliza.'

'Eliza, it's Kitty. What's wrong? What's happened?' Kitty sank down on a nearby velvet-covered armchair and waited for Eliza to take a breath and compose herself.

'*Chérie*, it's terrible. This morning Marie has telephoned me. Nathalie has been attacked in her apartment. She is at the hospital now. Some masked man has broken in and she has been injured. Thank goodness she was not killed.' Eliza rushed her words out. 'Now the police have been here looking for Julian. He stayed at a friend's house last night, so he did not come home. Oh, Kitty, I think they believe he is responsible.' Eliza broke into a sob.

'Please don't worry. I'm sure they just want to ask him some questions to eliminate him from the investigation, that's all. Do you want Matt and I to come over to you? Grams is still asleep.' Kitty glanced at her grandmother's closed bedroom door.

'If you would be so kind. I am frightened and don't want to be alone. You and Matthew know so much more about this kind of thing. My poor Julian.' Eliza broke into a fresh bout of sobbing.

Kitty reassured her as best she could before replacing the receiver back on the stand. Matt had already gone to shave and dress. Kitty scribbled a note for her grandmother explaining their absence and hurried to get ready to leave.

She hoped Eliza was all right and that Julian would soon be exonerated. If not, then things were about to become very difficult indeed.

CHAPTER THIRTEEN

Matt organised a taxi while Kitty dressed. He saw she had left a note for her grandmother before they hurried downstairs. He was curious to see where Eliza lived. Kitty had said her godmother resided a little out of the city centre in a slightly more rural upmarket arrondissement.

The taxi took them away from the city centre and the shops. They were soon in an area where there were more trees and parkland in between the immaculate apartment blocks and stylish crescents of elegant, terraced mansions.

They stopped outside one of the apartment blocks opposite what seemed to be a small woodland. Matt paid the driver, and they made their way inside the building through the revolving glass and brass door. A concierge was on duty at the desk and Matt gave Eliza's name.

The concierge directed them to the elevator, and they went up to the top floor where Eliza occupied the penthouse apartment. Kitty's godmother was waiting for them at the door, and he assumed the concierge must have called up to say they were on their way.

Violette was at Eliza's side and the little poodle yapped a welcome as Kitty kissed her godmother's pale cheeks.

'Oh, Kitty, Matthew, come in, I am so upset. I didn't know what to do, who to call.' Eliza wrung her hands together, the diamonds on her rings flashing in the morning sunlight.

They followed her inside the spacious apartment and Matt could see the place was in disarray with large packing cases. There were spaces on the wall where pictures had obviously been hanging and all of the ornaments which he guessed would have been present had been packed. The faint aroma of fresh paint lingered in the air.

'You said on the telephone the police had been here to see Julian?' Matt asked.

'*Oui, c'est vrai*, they came just after Marie had called. I was so confused. They asked me where he was and I gave them his friend's address.' Eliza looked helplessly at them. 'Why would they think Julian might be involved?'

'Marie said Nathalie was attacked at her apartment?' Kitty asked.

'Yes, she is in the hospital. Marie had a telephone call from the hospital about Nathalie. She was due to see her today at the fashion house to discuss future work. The nurse at the hospital, I think she made the call. She told Marie that Nathalie was injured and had called for the police and an ambulance. It was all very confusing. Marie was upset and I don't know how much the nurse knew of what had happened, except Nathalie said a masked man broke in.'

'Did you telephone Julian to let him know the police were on their way to his friend's house to see him?' Kitty asked.

Eliza sank down on one of the armchairs beside a packing case. 'No, I only have the address of Julian's friend, not his telephone number. I've misplaced the directory with all of the packing.' She waved her hand helplessly in the direction of the cases.

'I'm sure Julian will telephone you soon to reassure you that he's all right,' Kitty said.

'I hope so. What on earth is happening? Why would someone break in to Nathalie's apartment?' Eliza pressed her trembling hands together on her lap.

'Let me go and make you some tea,' Kitty offered. 'We'll stay here with you for a while until you hear from Julian.' She glanced at Matt, and he nodded his agreement.

* * *

While Kitty went off to the kitchen in search of tea things, Matt seated himself near Eliza.

'Do you know when Julian last saw Nathalie? I know he escorted her and Patricia home after Simone's death and called again the following day to check on her,' Matt said.

Eliza shrugged. 'My son doesn't tell me his every move. But I don't think he has called at the apartment since then. I know he telephoned her, or she called him. Patricia has not been staying there so Nathalie I think was feeling lonely. It was a blessing that Patricia wasn't home. She too could have been injured. Do you think this man who attacked Nathalie could have been the same person who killed Simone?' Eliza asked as Violette jumped up beside her and placed her head on her mistress's knee.

Matt frowned. 'I don't know. Obviously Inspector LeJeune is party to much more information about the case than either me or Kitty. I think though that it's a possibility. I wonder what this burglar was looking for? Or if he stole anything?'

The whole thing was quite curious. Had the Belliste sisters been mixed up in something that they knew nothing about? Was this why they had been targeted?

Kitty returned with a tray of tea. Matt moved a small pile of papers from the table in front of them so she could set the tray down.

'I hope Nathalie will be all right. I admit I am not very fond of either Simone or Nathalie, but I would not wish them to come to any harm,' Eliza said as Kitty poured her a cup of tea.

'Eliza, forgive me, but I get the impression that there was something else about Simone that you disliked. Something you mentioned you had discovered?' Kitty asked.

Eliza sighed, a pink tinge colouring her cheeks. 'When Julian seemed to be becoming more serious about the girl I took it upon myself to make some enquiries about her. They were from Nantes originally. Orphans, as I think I told you. Well, I discovered that Simone has a child, a daughter born when she was sixteen. She left the child in the care of the nuns at the convent back in Nantes. She sends money for her upkeep. Heaven knows who the father might be. Obviously I was shocked and concerned.'

'Did Julian know this?' Kitty asked.

Eliza nodded. 'I spoke to him. I had to. He was so angry with me. He said it was none of my business and I was not to say anything to anyone. Simone had told him all about the child already.'

Matt wondered who else knew about Simone's daughter. Obviously, Nathalie must know. Did the child have anything to do with Simone's death? A vengeful ex-lover perhaps?

Violette lifted her head and stared meaningfully at the small plate of biscuits on the tray. Matt's stomach rumbled, reminding him it had been a long time since he had eaten supper on the plane and neither he nor Kitty had eaten breakfast.

Kitty raised an eyebrow and offered him the biscuits, before taking one and giving it to the patient poodle.

'When we were at Nathalie's apartment with Patricia, there

didn't appear to be anything of much value there. Nothing that would cry out to a burglar,' Kitty mused as she stirred her own cup of tea. This revelation about Simone having a child had shocked her but she wasn't certain if it had anything to do with their case.

'No, the girls are not rich. Patricia is the one who has money. She owns the apartment, and her father provides her with a generous allowance. The Belliste sisters were just ordinary working girls.' Eliza helped herself to a second biscuit and gave half to Violette.

There was a loud knock at the door and Eliza pressed her hand to her bosom in alarm as Violette began to bark.

'I'll go,' Matt offered and went to the door. He was surprised the concierge had not telephoned to let them know someone was coming.

He opened the door to discover Inspector LeJeune accompanied by a uniformed gendarme on the other side.

'Inspector, please come in. Madame DeTourner called us over to keep her company. She was distressed from your earlier visit when you were looking for her son.' Matt stood aside to allow the policemen to enter.

'*Bonjour*, Captain Bryant, Madame Bryant.' The inspector raised his hat to Kitty as Eliza tried to quiet Violette.

'How may I assist you, Inspector? You have news? Is Julian all right?' Eliza turned frightened eyes towards the policeman.

'Monsieur DeTourner is currently assisting us with our investigation at the police station, madame. I have here the necessary papers to search parts of your apartment.' The inspector reached inside the breast pocket of his jacket and produced a bundle of documents which appeared to bear an official seal.

'You are welcome to search where you please, Inspector. There is nothing untoward in my home, I assure you,' Eliza said stiffly.

'*Merci*, madame, your cooperation in this matter is much appreciated.' Inspector Lejeune nodded to his gendarme who set off down the hall to the bedrooms.

'May we ask what you are hoping to find, Inspector?' Kitty asked.

'There are items missing which belong to Mademoiselle Nathalie Belliste and her late sister, Simone. Mademoiselle Nathalie was uncertain if anything more may have been taken this morning when she was assaulted at her home.' Inspector LeJeune had commenced looking inside the partly filled packing cases.

'But Julian didn't return here last night. He was at his friend's home.' Eliza looked bewildered. 'Certainly, neither I nor Julian have anything that belongs to Nathalie or Simone so far as I am aware.'

'Is this to do with Simone's missing designs?' Matt asked.

The inspector merely looked at him but declined to answer. Matt drew his own conclusions from this. Looking at Kitty he could see his wife had also reached the same conclusion.

The gendarme returned empty-handed to the sitting room and the inspector sent him to search the kitchen. The inspector continued his search, finishing the one case before then moving to the next. Eliza watched from the sofa with Violette beside her.

Kitty continued to calmly drink her tea and watch while the police concluded their search. The gendarme returned again, once more empty-handed and the inspector too had clearly discovered nothing of interest.

'*Merci* for your patience, madame,' the inspector said, stepping away from the last of the packing cases.

'Will you be releasing my son?' Eliza asked.

'He has not been charged with anything yet, madame. He is merely assisting us,' Inspector LeJeune said.

'Is Nathalie Belliste all right? Was she seriously injured? I take it she will recover from her injuries quickly?' Kitty asked.

'*Oui*, Madame Bryant, I believe so. She was more shocked than gravely harmed but the whole thing was most unpleasant. It was fortunate that the perpetrator ran away without harming her more seriously,' Inspector LeJeune said.

'Did something disturb this man? Or was it that Nathalie managed to fight him off? Was that why he ran away?' Kitty persisted.

'We are unsure if one of the neighbours may have startled him or if it was Mademoiselle Belliste screaming that drove him from her apartment,' the inspector said as he prepared to leave.

'Did the neighbours see him? Perhaps recognise him at all?' Kitty asked.

Matt could only admire his wife's skill and determination to prise information from the inspector.

'*Non*, madame, no one saw him leave the building that we have discovered as yet. He was masked and a discarded knitted mask was found outside the building. He must have dropped it as he made his getaway,' Inspector LeJeune said.

He made his farewells to them all and departed with the gendarme.

'I wonder if he is going to visit Monsieur Mangan and Sir Humphrey next,' Kitty mused after he had gone.

'You think he is also going to search their homes too?' Eliza stared at her.

'Well, it would seem logical, don't you think?' Kitty said. 'They must be suspects too.'

'I suppose now you mention it, then yes.' Eliza frowned. 'Do you think Julian will be back soon? That the police will let him go?' she asked.

'If they have no reason to suspect him, then, of course,' Kitty said in a reassuring tone.

'Perhaps though, it may be worth speaking to your lawyer.

Just so he is aware of what is happening. Then, if he is needed it may make things smoother. Hopefully he won't be required but I think it's a sensible precaution to protect Julian's reputation.' Matt phrased his advice as gently as he could to try not to alarm Eliza.

'Yes, that's a good idea,' Kitty spoke up to support him. She patted her godmother's hand. 'Taking legal advice is always helpful in these circumstances. It will make you feel less alone.'

Eliza glanced at them both before giving a decisive nod. 'Yes, you're both right. It would be good, and I can ask him to go to the police station to support Julian.'

With Eliza clearly in a much calmer frame of mind they said their goodbyes and left her and Violette to contact her lawyer.

* * *

Kitty slipped her arm through Matt's as they strolled along the street enjoying the morning air. 'What shall we do now? I must admit I'm starving.'

'Shall we find a café for breakfast and then we had better go and tell your grandmother what's happened?' Matt suggested.

They walked on in the summer sunshine along several more streets before entering a more commercial part of the city. Matt spotted a small pavement café with tables and chairs surrounded by pots of red geraniums.

A few minutes later, a cafetière of fresh coffee was placed in front of them along with a basket of fresh-baked croissants and generous glass dishes of butter and strawberry jam.

'Do you think Inspector LeJeune will let Julian go? I can't see why he has gone after him in the first place,' Kitty said as she spread jam lavishly on her croissant.

'Except for his relationship with Simone,' Matt reminded her as he brushed crumbs of flaky pastry from his tie. 'That business about Simone having a child was quite a shock, wasn't it?'

'It was. I wonder who else might know about that or if it's important to the case? I suppose though this speculation about Sir Humphrey's relationship with Simone makes him of interest too. Perhaps even more so given his commercial connection with House of Dido. I'd love to discover who that woman was who Grams and I saw him with last night. It definitely was a business meeting of some sort.' Kitty licked a small crumb from the corner of her mouth.

'That may be true, but he could have many business interests. She may even have been giving him legal advice. Much as we have just advised Eliza to do,' Matt said as he picked up his coffee cup.

Kitty was forced to admit he was right. It just seemed so odd. Why have a business meeting on an evening in a high-class restaurant? Surely he could conduct his business during the day at the person's office or place of work. No, there was something else afoot there, she was sure of it.

They finished their breakfast before continuing along the street. The café owner had assured Matt that they would find taxis at a rank there who could take them back to their hotel.

Kitty had quite enjoyed her breakfast in the sunshine and if it were not for the investigation she would have been relishing her unexpected Parisian holiday. Grams was in the hotel lobby when they returned having taken her breakfast in the dining room.

To Kitty's surprise she was not alone. Patricia Maddox was sitting with her.

'Patty, this is a surprise,' Kitty greeted the girl warmly as Patty rose to kiss her cheeks.

'I came to see you and ran into your grandmother, and she said Eliza had telephoned you to go over. I assumed it must be something to do with this break-in at my apartment.' Patricia looked anxious as she retook her seat.

'We just saw Inspector LeJeune and he said Nathalie had not been badly hurt, so I think she will be out of hospital soon,' Kitty said.

'I feel just awful. On one hand I'm selfishly glad I wasn't there and then again I feel terrible that she was on her own. It must have been terrifying, especially after what happened to Simone,' Patricia said.

'My dear, you must not think that way. Who could have expected such a thing to happen? No, you were better off not being there.' Grams gave the girl's hand a reassuring squeeze. 'How is Eliza? You said in your note she was worried about Julian?' Grams looked at Kitty.

'It seems he is being interviewed at the police station. Inspector LeJeune and a gendarme arrived at Eliza's apartment while we were there and conducted a search,' Kitty explained.

Patricia looked horrified. 'Do the police suspect Julian? That's absurd. He would never break in and harm Nathalie. Why would he? That's plumb crazy.'

'They didn't find anything suspicious,' Matt assured her.

'I should think not.' Grams looked indignant. 'Julian comes from a very respectable home. I'm certain he would not go about assaulting young women in their homes.'

'What were the police hoping to find?' Patricia asked.

Kitty glanced at Matt. 'We asked the inspector that, but he declined to answer. We can only assume he'll also be searching Monsieur Mangan's home and that of Sir Humphrey.'

Patricia frowned in confusion. 'Why would either of them attack Nathalie? Was something stolen, do you think?'

'I don't know. Have you been back to the apartment yet to see what's been damaged?' Kitty looked at Patricia.

The girl shook her head. 'Not yet. I'll admit I was scared to go there alone. The police have all finished there now. That's why I came here to see if you would come with me. If something has been damaged I'll need to get it fixed so the place is secure. I guess I was kinda bothered in case this person came back.'

'How did you learn of the robbery?' Kitty asked.

'Marie Dido telephoned me. She knew where I was staying and has my great-aunt's number,' Patricia explained.

Kitty thought Madame Dido had been very busy on the telephone that morning.

CHAPTER FOURTEEN

The apartment block where Patricia and the Belliste sisters lived was quiet when the taxi dropped them off. From the exterior of the building there was no sign that anything unusual had taken place there that morning. The faded pale-green shutters were all open and a tabby cat sat washing its paws placidly on a nearby step.

Kitty looked around the front of the building. The block was joined on both sides to other buildings, there were no alleys that she could see, and she wondered where the assailant's mask had been found.

'Does your apartment have a view of the back of the building at all?' she asked Patricia as they entered the small, communal hallway.

Patricia looked puzzled. 'No, our apartment has all front-facing windows. The kitchen and the bathroom have no windows at all. You have to put the light on to do anything. That can be a real nuisance at times, especially in winter.' She led the way up the flight of stairs to the apartment.

'Is there a rear door to the block?' Matt asked as they reached the landing outside Patricia's apartment.

'No. These apartments are old, and each floor originally had only one. Now there are two on each floor. One faces the front, the other the rear. Ours is front-facing.' Patricia squared her shoulders and walked towards her front door.

Kitty immediately saw there was damage to the wooden frame near the lock as if someone had tried to jimmy it open with a crowbar or screwdriver. The paint was chipped and there were gouges in the woodwork.

'Try the door first,' Matt advised, 'and see if the lock is still holding. If the door opens without the key you'll need a locksmith.'

Patricia nodded and pulled her keys from her bag. She followed Matt's advice and found the door was secure. She took the key and unlocked it to allow them to enter. The tiny hall was in disarray. A glass-shaded Tiffany lamp lay smashed on the floor and Patricia's heels crunched on the broken glass.

'Be careful, Patty,' Kitty cautioned as the girl headed for the sitting room.

Patricia pushed open the door to the sitting room and gave an audible gasp when she saw the state of the place. 'Oh my goodness, poor Nathalie! My oh my, she must have put up quite a fight.'

Kitty and Matt picked their way over the broken glass in the hall to follow her into the room. Kitty could see what the girl meant. Everything was strewn about. Papers, cushions, end tables had been overturned and a couple of small ornaments lay in pieces on the floor.

'Shall I help you straighten everything up? Matt can check the front door to make certain it is secure and see what else can be fitted so that you are safe,' Kitty suggested.

'Thank you, that's real good of you. I appreciate it so much. I guess I'm just in shock looking at all of this.' Patricia shook her head, and Kitty could see she was fighting back tears at the state of her home.

'It will be all right, my dear, I promise.' Kitty gave the girl a hug. 'Now, where will I find a broom? I'll get up the glass in the hall before it carries all through the apartment,' Kitty said briskly as she picked up some of the cushions from the floor.

Patricia gave her a slightly watery smile and blew her nose on her handkerchief before replying. 'There's a tall skinny cupboard in the kitchen. The broom is in there.'

Kitty placed her handbag on the sofa and fetched a broom and a dustpan and brush. Patricia began to collect up the scattered letters and magazines while Kitty got up the glass and broken china ornaments.

'I do hope none of these had any sentimental value,' she said to Patty as she deposited the debris in the dustbin.

'No, not to me. I think the figurines that have been broken were Simone's. They were a harlequin set she was fond of. Oh, and some glass lovebirds. She got them at one of the markets here. They weren't expensive but she liked them.' Patricia looked sad.

Matt was busy in the hallway examining the door and the lock.

'The chain affair you had on the back of the door is broken. I can only assume whoever assaulted Nathalie must have started on the door. She must have heard the noise and opened it with the chain on, and he forced his way inside,' Matt said.

Kitty could see from his expression that he seemed slightly dissatisfied by this explanation.

'But why would she open the door?' Patricia asked. 'Why not just telephone the police straight away when she heard a noise?'

'She may not have been thinking straight. You know how it can be sometimes when something unexpected occurs. Especially if she was woken up,' Kitty said.

'Either way, you need a new catch for the chain. The lock

seems perfectly good. The door frame just needs a little patching and some paint, nothing much,' Matt assured her.

'That's a relief at any rate.' Patricia seemed cheered by his appraisal.

'I wonder if Nathalie will return here today?' Kitty said. 'The inspector seemed to think the hospital would discharge her and she'll need to get some of her things even if she may be too afraid to remain here alone.'

Patricia shivered. 'I feel safer now Captain Bryant has checked all of the door fittings. I think I'll wait here until tea and see if she shows up. She can decide then what she'd like to do about staying here.'

'Will you return to where you are currently staying?' Matt asked.

Patricia nodded. 'I don't think I'm brave enough to stay here. My great-aunt would have kittens if I suggested it I think. Not until whoever attacked Nathalie and killed Simone is safely under lock and key.'

Kitty could see why the girl felt that way. In Patricia's place she too would be wary about staying in the apartment.

After making quite certain that Patricia was happy to remain there alone for a short while, Kitty and Matt made their way back downstairs and out once again onto the city streets.

'We should get back to Grams. It's not much fun for her to be loitering around the hotel while we're running around all over Paris,' Kitty said.

'Yes, she's been very patient,' Matt agreed.

Kitty's grandmother was in their suite when they returned. She appeared to be happily occupied with writing a small stash of postcards that she had acquired from a newsagents shop just down the street from the hotel.

'How was the apartment? Was there much damage? Poor Patricia was very distressed when she arrived here,' Grams said as she took off her writing spectacles.

'Everything there is secure. She's waiting to see if Nathalie returns to find out what she wants to do. I don't suppose she will wish to stay there. Patricia has already said she doesn't wish to be there overnight,' Kitty said.

'Poor girl, it must be most upsetting. I've spoken to Eliza while you were out, and she seemed much better. Her lawyer has gone to the police station to support Julian. I really can't think why the police have not sent him home.' Grams tutted as she replaced the cap on her fountain pen.

'I suppose he will be back soon,' Kitty said as she glanced at Matt.

She really hoped that her godmother's son was not involved in Simone's death or the attack on her sister. Julian had told his mother that he knew Simone had a child but what if he had been lying? That might give him a motive to attack the girl and assault the only other person who knew of the child's existence.

They decided to take a late lunch and a walk through the pleasure gardens beside the Seine. Grams was able to post her cards, and they all seemed to feel the benefit of the fresh air. By the time they had explored some of the stalls on the riverside and wandered back to the hotel it was almost teatime, so they took a seat in the lounge of the hotel.

One of the reception staff approached them. '*Pardon*, Madame Treadwell, but we have taken many messages for you, and also for Madame Bryant, from a Madame DeTourner, she wishes you to telephone her at your earliest convenience.'

'Oh dear, whatever can have happened now?' Grams looked alarmed.

'I'll go and find out. May I use the telephone at the desk?' Kitty asked.

'*Oui*, madame. We have one available for guests.' The receptionist led her to a small booth near the desk where she could use the telephone. She dialled Eliza's number and waited for her godmother to pick up.

To her surprise there was no reply. She tried again, fearing she might have misdialled, the Paris telephone system being one of the few that didn't go via an operator. There was still no answer, so she was forced to return to her husband and her grandmother without having spoken to Eliza.

'There was no reply. I tried twice.' Kitty took a seat.

'How very vexing. Wherever could she have gone?' Grams poured them all some tea from the tray that had been deposited in front of them during Kitty's absence.

'I double-checked the number. I thought since she had been trying to get us all afternoon that she would have been right beside the telephone,' Kitty said as she gratefully accepted her drink.

It had been warm walking beside the river despite some shade from the trees and she was quite thirsty.

'Perhaps the police have permitted Julian to return home,' Matt suggested.

The excited yipping of a small dog drew their attention to the main doors, and they saw Eliza heading towards them. She was accompanied by Violette and Marie Dido.

'Gwen, *chérie*, where have you been? I tried calling and I left messages,' Eliza exclaimed breathlessly as she kissed Gram's cheeks.

Kitty prudently moved the plate of biscuits out of Violette's reach.

'We were out taking the air and exploring the city. We called you just a moment ago as soon as we returned and got your messages,' Grams explained as Marie and Eliza drew up chairs to join them. 'Is something wrong? Have the police let Julian go?'

Matt discreetly summoned the waiter to bring more tea.

'My lawyer let me know that Julian was at liberty to leave the police station. It seems Inspector LeJeune has made an arrest,' Eliza announced.

This startling piece of information made Kitty slop some of her tea into her saucer. 'An arrest! Who?'

'Sir Humphrey.' Marie Dido burst into tears. '*Ce n'est pas possible.* I do not believe it.'

'Sir Humphrey? Is the arrest for Simone's murder or for the assault on Nathalie or both?' Kitty asked.

'We do not know,' Marie said with a sniff.

'The police took him into the station just as Julian and our lawyer were coming out. He was in handcuffs,' Eliza said. 'They hurried him past Julian so he couldn't ask what had happened.'

'How could Sir Humphrey have killed Simone? He had no reason to do so or to attack Nathalie. Surely it must be the same person who was responsible for both things.' Marie dabbed at her eyes as the extra tea things were delivered to their table.

Eliza promptly gave Violette one of the biscuits and the poodle crunched it up happily, dropping crumbs on Kitty's shoes.

'Perhaps they discovered something incriminating when they searched Sir Humphrey's home,' Matt suggested. 'I would have thought they would search his house and Monsieur Mangan's apartment too after leaving Eliza's apartment. There was obviously something they were expecting to find.'

'What though? I do not believe it,' Marie said.

Kitty thought the woman looked quite ill. Her cheeks seemed to have sunk, and her eyes were like dark pits against her sallow skin. She looked so different from the elegant woman who had greeted them on the day of the fashion show.

'Grams and I saw Sir Humphrey last night while we were dining at *Le Petit Chien*. It looked as if he was having a business meeting of some kind,' Kitty said.

'A business meeting?' Marie looked bewildered. 'So far as I know the only hands-on kind of business he has here in Paris is with my fashion house. For the rest of his businesses he has a broker in London for stocks and shares. Who was he with?'

'A lady, very elegant and chic. She had dark hair and seemed to be in her late forties or fifties perhaps. She was taking notes with a silver propelling pencil in a tiny notebook. She had the most marvellous shoes with dark-purple patent toe caps.' Kitty crinkled her brow as she tried to recall all the details of the woman who had been with Sir Humphrey.

Marie's lips trembled and her already pale complexion was chalk white. '*Non, non*, surely he would not do this.'

'Do you know who this lady is?' Kitty asked.

'Yvette Blanc, she has her own fashion business, Moderne Couture. We are rivals. She would like to put me out of business. Surely he would not sell his shares to her.' Marie looked stunned. '*Ce n'est pas possible.*'

'Perhaps he was meeting her for some other reason,' Grams suggested.

Marie gave a vigorous shake of her head. '*Non*, Madame Treadwell, Yvette is what you English call a snake in the grass. That meeting was not for anything good, of that I am quite certain.'

'I suppose we shall have to wait to discover if Sir Humphrey is the person who killed Simone.' Eliza looked anxiously at Marie.

'My business will be ruined. It was already bad but if he is the killer, then what? He will sell his shares to Yvette, and she will steal my work, my employees and make my share of the business worthless.' Marie's shoulders slumped and she looked completely defeated.

'There is nothing you can do for now except wait to see what happens,' Matt said.

'I just don't understand. Sir Humphrey and I, well, I thought that perhaps we might in time have a future *romantique*. Then I learn he is seeing Simone and now Yvette, of all people.' Marie looked at Eliza who squeezed her friend's hand in sympathy.

'I'm pleased that Julian is in the clear though, Eliza. That at least must be good news. I imagine Monsieur Mangan will feel the same way when he hears what has happened,' Grams said.

'Do not speak to me of Yves Mangan. He is another snake in the grass. He refuses to answer his telephone, and I have heard he has given interviews to the newspapers. I have journalists still camping outside my business. Those that are still in Paris and are not stalking Madame Wallis Simpson elsewhere in France or Austria,' Marie snapped.

'*Ma pauvre*, Marie,' Eliza said. 'It has all been so dreadful for you.'

'I'm sure you must feel quite exhausted by it all,' Kitty added in a sympathetic tone.

'It has been *très terrible*,' Marie agreed. She looked at Eliza. 'I think perhaps I should return home and rest. There seems to be nothing I can do. I will wait and see what happens to Sir Humphrey.'

'I think that is a good idea. I feel quite exhausted myself,' Eliza agreed.

With that, Eliza, Violette and Marie said their goodbyes and left, promising to telephone if they heard more news.

'Well, that was all quite extraordinary,' Grams said as she set her teacup back on its saucer. 'I suppose, however, that this means you two can desist from further sleuthing. We haven't much time left on our trip. At least we may be able to enjoy the end of it now without looking for suspects everywhere we go.'

CHAPTER FIFTEEN

With Eliza and Marie gone, they settled down to discuss their plans for the evening. Matt agreed with Kitty's grandmother that it would be nice to make the most of the time they had left in Paris. Now Sir Humphrey was under lock and key and Simone's murder seemingly solved, it was time to enjoy themselves. After a little thought Matt suggested he go and ask the concierge what might be on at any of the many theatres.

Kitty and her grandmother adored seeing operas and shows so they eagerly agreed to the idea. The Parisian nightlife was famous, and it would be a pity not to see some of it. After a conversation with the concierge and parting with a generous bundle of francs, Matt secured tickets for *Rigoletto* at the National Opera.

'Were the tickets horribly expensive?' Kitty asked as they changed later that evening into more formal clothes.

'Let's put it this way, I couldn't afford to run to a box even if one had been available. There are a lot of people in Paris for the World Fair at the moment so tickets for anything are hard to come by.' He smiled at her as she brushed her hair and pushed in a small diamanté clip.

'I'd forgotten all about the fair with the business about Simone. That was why it was so busy at the Eiffel Tower and then at the Louvre Museum.' Kitty frowned at her reflection in the dressing-table mirror. 'Do you think Inspector LeJeune has the right man?' she asked suddenly, changing the subject.

'We've no reason to think otherwise,' Matt observed. He could only think the inspector must have discovered something that definitely tied Sir Humphrey to either Simone's murder or the attack on Nathalie.

'Yes, you're right. I suppose I am so used to Inspector Lewis arresting the wrong man I forget that there are perfectly competent and sensible policemen around,' Kitty admitted with a smile.

'Forget all about the case. Let's go and take your grandmother to the opera. This trip was supposed to be a nostalgic dream escape for her,' Matt said with a chuckle as Kitty rose to collect her silver evening purse and silk stole.

'Very well, let us away to the opera,' she agreed, laughing.

The theatre was very grand and very busy. Once they were seated on the plush red-velvet seats Matt had chance to look around at the golden-gilded carved embellishments and high painted ceiling. Grams had a box of chocolates on her lap and a delighted smile on her face.

Despite Simone's murder and the chaos that had followed, he thought she looked much better than when they had arrived. Now that Julian appeared to be in the clear she seemed prepared to embrace the remainder of their stay with gusto.

Kitty too seemed more relaxed and brighter eyed. He knew she had been very worried about her grandmother, and he was pleased he had been able to arrange the break for them. It had been a busy year for Kitty too. She had been caught up in the heart of several quite terrible cases back in England before they had come away. A holiday somewhere new was definitely a good idea, despite what had happened since.

For the next few hours, they lost themselves in the pleasure of the opera, enjoying the music in such a glamorous setting. Once the show had finished they made their way back to their hotel. Grams immediately retired upstairs to their suite, declaring herself worn out from the evening.

Kitty agreed to take a light supper in the hotel bar area with Matt. The hotel was starting to quieten down now that most people had returned from their evenings out. A small group of gentlemen accompanied by ladies in dazzling summer silk gowns in shades of pale blue and rose were finishing their suppers. There was a pleasant, subdued buzz to the place and the staff had started to clear away.

'That was lovely.' Kitty smiled at him as she finished her food. She raised her glass of cognac. 'Cheers to no more talk of murder on this holiday.'

'I'll drink to that,' he agreed, and chinked his own glass against hers.

They sat and finished their drinks as the bar grew quieter, and more guests left to retire to their rooms. By the time they had finished, only a handful of fellow guests remained.

Kitty placed her empty glass on the table and stretched her back, wriggling her shoulders as she did so. 'I'm ready for bed now. It's been a tiring day.'

Matt swallowed the last of his cognac and set his glass beside hers. 'I agree, time to turn in.'

They were about to depart for their suite when a man came hurtling through the doors of the bar towards them.

'Captain Bryant! Mrs Bryant! Thank goodness I've caught you.' Sir Humphrey was dishevelled and out of breath, having clearly hurried on his journey to track them down.

Kitty gave Matt a confused and slightly horrified look as Sir Humphrey collapsed, panting, onto a nearby chair.

'Sir Humphrey, forgive us, but we had heard that Inspector LeJeune had arrested you,' Matt said.

He, like Kitty, was still standing beside their recently vacated seats.

'That's right, s'all true.' Sir Humphrey looked up at him with bleary, bloodshot eyes.

It struck Matt that the man had clearly been drinking.

Kitty sank gracefully back down onto her seat. 'I don't understand. What happened? And why are you here?'

'S'obvious, dear girl, I need help. I'm being set up, framed for Simone's murder,' Sir Humphrey said.

'Perhaps if you could start at the beginning. Why did the inspector arrest you?' Kitty spoke slowly and clearly, as if talking to a small child.

Matt bit his lip in suppressed amusement at her tactics and took his seat back beside her.

'LeJeune and a couple of gendarmes arrived at my apartment this morning with some kind of legal document. Said he wanted to search the place. I had no reason to deny him, except I thought it was dashed impertinent,' Sir Humphrey said.

'What did they discover?' Matt asked. He knew the police must have found something or they would not have made the arrest.

'That's the thing. I was out last night, a dinner meeting with a lady of my acquaintance. I returned home late and when I got in there were these papers that had been pushed through my letter box. I thought they were confirmation of an appointment I'd been trying to make with my solicitor. I tossed them onto the coffee table to look at in the morning. I was tired and the matter I'm meeting him about is quite complex. When LeJeune arrived I still hadn't opened them. His gendarme started sorting through my papers.' He paused to run his hands distractedly through his hair.

'I take it the gendarme opened the envelope?' Matt asked.

'Turns out it contained some of Simone's designs. I had absolutely no idea. I told him I hadn't opened the envelope. I had no suspicion of what was inside.' Sir Humphrey's face grew rosy with indignation.

'And that was when he asked you to accompany him to the police station?' Matt asked.

'Pah, not so much of a request as a demand. Dashed cheek! I kept telling him I had no idea what was in that blasted envelope. Then he started asking me where I had been this morning. I told him, nowhere. I had been at home eating my breakfast and reading my newspaper. My servants could vouch for me. Then he said he meant earlier in the morning before breakfast.' Sir Humphrey threw up his hands. 'I said I was in bed, asleep.'

'I see. Has he charged you with any offence as yet?' Matt asked.

'He's confiscated my passport and released me on some sort of bond thing. My solicitor has dealt with it all. I have no idea what's going on. He said someone had attacked Nathalie Belliste this morning. I said, well it jolly well wasn't me.' Sir Humphrey's face was crimson now and his voice had risen, calling the bar staff to glance in their direction.

'And you've no idea who could have delivered those designs to you or why?' Kitty asked.

'No, no idea at all. I had seen Simone's designs and thought them rather good. They certainly seemed to have commercial potential to me. I discussed them with Yves Mangan, but he seemed rather cooler on their potential. As for Marie, I'm not certain what her intentions were. She can be dreadfully indecisive. Not a good thing in business.' He looked thoughtful.

'Simone didn't leave any of her designs with you?' Kitty asked.

Sir Humphrey snorted. 'No, she guarded them like they were the crown jewels. Not that I blamed her for that. There's a lot that goes on in the fashion industry, people poaching ideas and trying to steal a march on one another.'

Matt glanced at Kitty.

'Why have you come to see us, sir?' Matt asked. He was curious about what Sir Humphrey thought they might do to help him.

'Eliza said you were private investigators. She said you had a good reputation in England for solving cases. I want someone English on my side. Someone to look into Simone's death and this attack on her sister so my name is cleared. I can't be walking around Paris with everyone thinking I'm a murderer.' Sir Humphrey's voice rose once more, and he thumped his fist on the leather arm of his chair.

'No, of course, we understand,' Kitty soothed, glancing anxiously towards the now closed bar.

'You must realise though that our powers are limited here. France has different laws and regulations. We don't have the same kinds of connections that we have available to us in Devon,' Matt said.

'We are also only here for a couple more days. We are holidaying with my grandmother, and she has been seriously ill before we left home,' Kitty said.

'Look, I need some help. I have to clear my reputation. I can pay you both well. I'm sure LeJeune is just doing his job, but I can't help but think it would be rather convenient to pin this crime on an Englishman rather than some French Johnnie.' Sir Humphrey looked at them pleadingly.

Matt could see Kitty was torn between wanting to continue sleuthing and her responsibilities toward her grandmother.

'Very well, we are only here though for another couple of days. We can't extend our stay any further as we have obligations back in Devon. If Kitty is willing, we will do what we can in that time.' Matt looked at Kitty and she gave a brief nod of acquiescence.

'Thank you, thank you both.' Sir Humphrey leapt up from his seat to grasp first Matt's hand and then Kitty's in a hearty and clammy handshake. 'Here is my card. Let me know if you find anything at all that will help to clear my name.'

He produced a card from his silver card case and pressed it on Matt before saying goodnight and heading out of the hotel.

Matt looked at the card and then at Kitty. 'So much for enjoying our holiday, old thing.'

* * *

Kitty slept badly that night. Her dreams were plagued by memories of Simone's lifeless body on the floor of the salon and Yves Mangan's confession that he had carried the scissors from the workshop. She slipped out of bed without waking Matt and wandered into the sitting room area of their suite.

She telephoned reception and ordered a pot of tea for their room. Her grandmother's door remained firmly shut and Kitty knew she was unlikely to rise until later. She tipped the young porter who delivered her tea generously and set the tray down on the low table in front of the sofa.

Outside the window the sun was rising over the rooftops of Paris casting a pink and rosy glow across the city. Kitty poured her tea and settled back cradling the cup between her hands. She watched the sky change colour from palest gold, and pastel pink to soft, clear blue.

How were they to combine trying to find evidence to clear Sir Humphrey's name and ensuring her grandmother had a lovely holiday? Come to that, was Sir Humphrey as innocent as he made himself out to be? If he hadn't murdered Simone, then they were back to square one again, suspecting everyone. Kitty sighed and sipped her tea.

It seemed to her that they needed to talk to Nathalie to see if there was anything more they could learn about who may have attacked her. She also suspected that it might be helpful to try to speak to Monsieur Mangan again to discover where he had been when Nathalie was assaulted.

Then there was also the thorny problem of Julian. She didn't want to believe that her godmother's son could possibly be guilty of such awful crimes, but perhaps he might know something more about Simone that could help them. She wanted to ask him about Simone's child.

Kitty poured herself some more tea from the pot and pondered over what they already knew. Everything seemed very jumbled and so many people seemed to benefit from Simone's demise. She frowned as she added the milk to her cup. She couldn't see why someone would attack Nathalie.

Perhaps that was when Simone's designs had been stolen or did the envelope found at Sir Humphrey's home contain the ones which had gone missing at the time of the model's murder?

The door of her grandmother's room opened.

'Good morning, darling, you're an early bird today.' Her grandmother tied the belt of her pale-green silk dressing gown more securely and came to join her on the sofa. 'Is Matthew still asleep?' she asked.

'Yes, I couldn't sleep and fancied a cup of tea. There's some in the pot and an extra cup if you'd care to join me,' Kitty said with a smile.

Her grandmother poured herself the remainder of the tea, after adding some hot water from the silver jug that had accompanied the teapot.

'We had a late-night visitor at the bar downstairs after you had gone to bed.' Kitty told her grandmother of Sir Humphrey's surprise visit and of his request.

'Oh dear, how very extraordinary. Did you believe him, about the designs being posted through his door late at night? It must have been after we saw him at the restaurant with that woman,' her grandmother said.

'It sounds strange but plausible.' Kitty frowned. 'This case doesn't seem to be very straightforward. How do you feel though, Grams? This is supposed to be a lovely holiday with you seeing Eliza and doing some of the things you've always wished to do. It seems rather unfair that Matt and I are being dragged along by Sir Humphrey to poke about in a murder.'

Her grandmother chuckled softly. 'Darling, I know you and Matthew too well. I can amuse myself in Paris you know. I'm quite certain if I telephone Eliza we can arrange our own amusements. In fact, it may do Eliza good to focus on something else. I don't think having Marie Dido burdening her with all her problems is very good for her.'

Kitty was relieved that her grandmother seemed to be taking her defection in good spirits. 'It may be that Inspector LeJeune has the case wrapped up by the time we are due to return home. We did warn Sir Humphrey that we really couldn't overstay our holiday.'

'Then you and Matthew had better get busy. Now don't worry about me, my dear. I'll organise an outing for today with Eliza. You two can go snooping around then to your heart's content. I do feel for Sir Humphrey, if he is innocent then his name should be cleared.' Her grandmother's tone sobered. 'False accusations are a dreadful thing.'

CHAPTER SIXTEEN

Matt was dressing when Kitty returned to their room to prepare for the day. She told him of her conversation with her grandmother.

'Are you all right about leaving her and Eliza to entertain themselves?' he asked as he buttoned his shirt.

Kitty opened the wardrobe to take out her dress. 'Grams does seem much stronger now than when we arrived, and she is very sensible.'

Matt smiled sympathetically. 'Exactly, she has run the Dolphin for many years so you know she won't get herself into trouble and she will be with your godmother.'

'I know, I just feel a little guilty,' Kitty admitted as she sorted out the rest of her garments.

'I agree it's not what we came here to do, but your grandmother does make a good point. If Sir Humphrey is innocent, then he needs to have his name cleared.' Matt dropped a tender kiss on her cheek.

'Yes, and I can't bear that Julian's name might somehow be tarnished too if Simone's killer is not caught,' Kitty agreed.

After a hearty breakfast of croissants with lashings of butter and apricot jam, Kitty was in a much better frame of mind. She kissed her grandmother goodbye and she and Matt set off to call at Nathalie Belliste's apartment.

They had agreed over breakfast that if the girl had returned home and had stayed there, then talking to her would be a good starting point.

'We don't know if she'll be here, of course. She may still be at the hospital or have decided to go elsewhere rather than return to the apartment,' Kitty said as their taxi dropped them off outside the model's apartment block.

'Very true, but we may as well start here. Eliza said that Julian will meet us later for lunch, so we have until then to follow up on your list of suspects.' Matt grinned at her.

Kitty's godmother had asked Julian to meet them at a café near his workplace in the business arrondissement of the city at one o'clock. She seemed to share Kitty's concerns that Julian's name should be cleared as well as Sir Humphrey's.

They walked up the steep flights of stairs to Patricia's apartment. When they reached the landing Kitty saw that the girl must have managed to get someone in quickly to make repairs to the door frame. She hoped that a new and more secure chain had been fitted to the door on the inside.

Matt pressed the bell, and they waited on the doorstep. Kitty listened out to try and hear if there was any sound from inside the apartment. She thought she detected a faint scuffling. If Nathalie was wary of opening the door after what had happened, then Kitty really couldn't blame her.

'*Allô? Qui est là?*' Nathalie called from inside.

'Kitty and Matt Bryant, Madame DeTourner's friends,' Kitty responded. 'It's quite safe.'

The door cracked open, and the girl peeped out to check their identities, before slipping off the new door chain and allowing them inside.

'My apologies, but I am still very shaken after what

happened yesterday. I heard that Sir Humphrey had been arrested but that seems *incroyable*.' Nathalie led the way into the small sitting room, before taking a seat on the sofa.

'When did you return from hospital?' Kitty asked.

'Yesterday afternoon. Patricia was here when I arrived. She had got someone to make the repairs to the door and to check all was secure. I wasn't sure if I was going to stay here last night but I knew if I didn't then I might never be able to face it. Then when we learned that Sir Humphrey had been arrested I thought perhaps it is over and I shall be all right,' the girl explained as she lit a tiny cigarette in a long black ebony holder.

'It must have been a very frightening ordeal for you,' Kitty said sympathetically.

The girl didn't seem to have been harmed physically, a small scratch on her jawline but no other signs of injury that she could see.

Nathalie shuddered. 'I was asleep in my room. I was disturbed by a noise at the door. I rose to see what was happening as it was early for the post. I was not properly awake you understand. As I reached the hall, the door flew open, and this masked man dived at me. I fought him but then I think I hit my head or I fainted and the next thing I knew I was lying injured in the hall. I called the police, and they sent for an ambulance.'

'Did this man say anything to you at all during the attack?' Kitty asked.

'No, nothing.' Nathalie tapped some ash from the end of her cigarette into an ashtray. 'He seemed intent on getting past me into the apartment. We do not have any money or valuable jewellery here so I don't know what he was after. I know some of Simone's ornaments were broken in the struggle. Patty told me you had helped her to clean up.'

'Have you had chance to check since if anything was stolen?' Matt asked.

The girl glanced up at him. 'I checked yesterday with Patty, and we couldn't see anything. I had a better look this morning once I felt a little better. I can't see anything that is gone.'

'Hmm, is there anyone at all that you can think of who may wish to harm you? Or who may have wanted to harm your sister?' Kitty asked.

Nathalie shrugged her elegant shoulders and extinguished her cigarette. '*Non*, Simone was very popular. Some models were jealous of her talent and success but not to harm her. As for me, I lead a quiet life outside of my work. You can ask Patty. I do not party like some of the girls do, or entertain gentlemen.'

'What did you think when you heard Sir Humphrey had been arrested? You seemed surprised?' Matt asked.

'But of course. Sir Humphrey is not the kind of man who would burst into my home and try to kill me. He certainly would not have hurt Simone. He was very fond of her, taking her out and looking at her designs,' Nathalie said.

'Could Sir Humphrey have been the man who attacked you?' Matt asked.

Nathalie looked confused. 'It's possible I suppose but my attacker wore a mask, and it all happened so quickly. I could not be at all certain.'

'Do you think Sir Humphrey was romantically interested in your sister?' Kitty asked.

'Is that what Madame Dido has told you? She was very jealous of Simone. I think she had hopes herself of Sir Humphrey in that way, but she is too old for him.' Nathalie gave a short, scornful laugh. 'I don't know if he liked Simone. I suspect he may have done; she was very beautiful. My sister was dating Julian DeTourner. I don't think she would have returned Sir Humphrey's interests.'

'Was your sister in love with Julian? I know he seemed to think it was a serious relationship. He was very keen that we meet her.' Kitty was curious about what Nathalie had thought of her sister's love affairs. Especially since Patty had thought Nathalie might have been jealous of Simone.

'I don't know. She seemed to see a lot of Julian. He often came here to our apartment and maybe he wanted to marry her. But Simone could be fickle. I tried to say this to Julian, he and I are friends. I knew she was seeing Sir Humphrey, but she had said it was purely business but maybe that wasn't so. I'm not sure.' Nathalie's gaze drifted away from Kitty's and Kitty wondered if the girl was being entirely honest.

'How did Julian react to the suggestion that Simone might not be as, well, interested in him as he was in her?' Matt asked.

Nathalie sighed. 'He wouldn't listen to me. Simone had told him I was jealous of her, and he was besotted with my sister. She could do no wrong in Julian's eyes.'

'And Simone? Did she object to you trying to tell her boyfriend that he had competition?' Matt continued.

Nathalie looked down and focused her attention on a loose thread on her pale-blue print skirt. 'She laughed. She said it was pitiful.' A red flush appeared on Nathalie's cheekbones. 'We argued and I told her she was not being fair to Julian. He is a good person. She said I should mind my own business. This was a week or so ago.'

'Julian knew about Simone's child?' Kitty said.

Nathalie looked startled, her eyes widening in surprise. '*Oui*, I think Simone must have told him. It is not common knowledge, not even Patricia knows about her. Perhaps he saw some of the photographs she had of the little girl. She kept them in her handbag and beside her bed. Simone was very young when she was born. It was just after our parents were killed. The girl is with the nuns at Nantes. Simone would send money and go to see her from time to time.'

'Who is the child's father?' Kitty asked. She wondered if perhaps there was someone they had not considered who may have had a motive for killing Simone.

Nathalie shrugged. 'I do not know. Simone never told me. It was something she would never talk about. I was young when the girl was born, and we had just lost our parents. I do not recollect a boyfriend.'

'Monsieur Mangan appeared to have quarrelled with your sister. We heard that he tried to get Marie Dido to turn down her designs.' Matt changed the subject.

'*Oui, c'est vrai.* He is stuck in his ways and was paranoid that Simone would take his position. He was, what is the English word, ah yes, snooty, that is it. He was snooty about her designs. I think he gave them back to her on the day of the show. Simone had argued with Marie and with Yves and I know she wanted them returned to her. Patty said they were in the changing room, I don't know.'

'And then they disappeared when your sister was killed.' Matt's tone was smooth and noncommittal. 'Would you be surprised to discover that someone delivered those designs anonymously to Sir Humphrey? Posting them through his letter box just before Inspector LeJeune searched people's apartments shortly after you were assaulted?'

Nathalie raised her gaze to look at Matt. Kitty thought she caught a flicker of something cross the girl's expression. Fear? Curiosity? Excitement?

'No, that is a very strange thing. I suppose I had thought to myself perhaps that was why someone broke into the apartment. To perhaps steal Simone's work. But, if they had some of the designs already why give them to Sir Humphrey?' Nathalie frowned as she replied.

'Indeed, that is an interesting question. Perhaps someone wanted to ensure Sir Humphrey was arrested,' Matt suggested.

'Who would do such a thing?' Kitty could see a pulse beating on Nathalie's temple as she asked the question. 'Who dislikes Sir Humphrey? Julian, perhaps, if he was jealous of the time Simone spent with him. Or Madame Dido. You know Sir

Humphrey has a large share in House of Dido and he might sell his shares to Marie's rival?' Kitty continued to look at Nathalie. 'That might also give Yves Mangan a motive if he was fearful of losing his position if the fashion houses merged in a potentially hostile takeover.'

'I suppose that is true of Yves Mangan. I had not thought of this. Julian, I think, believed Simone when she said her meetings with Sir Humphrey were just business,' Nathalie replied.

'Will you be all right staying here in the apartment alone now?' Kitty asked. 'I think Patricia will be away for a while staying with her great-aunt. She was very upset by your sister's death and now this attack on you.' Kitty could understand how Patricia felt.

'I think so. The apartment has been secured, and the police do not think the attacker is likely to return. Inspector LeJeune sounded most reassuring. Besides, I have nowhere else to go and no money to stay elsewhere.' Nathalie glanced around. 'Julian has been most kind too, checking that I am safe.'

'I'm glad you're feeling better. My godmother was very concerned when she heard that you had been assaulted.' Kitty thought it best to leave Nathalie with the impression that Eliza's concerns had been their primary reason for visiting.

'That is kind of her.' Nathalie gave a wan smile. 'She has always been very thoughtful.'

They declined the belated offer of coffee and said their goodbyes to the model. Kitty heard the chain slide back into place once the front door had closed behind them. They walked down the stairs and out into the street.

'We have time before we are due to meet Julian to go to House of Dido to see if Yves Mangan will see us,' Kitty suggested after consulting her watch.

'True. I expect the press attention on the business may have faded somewhat by now. Let's try our luck there and see if he is in,' Matt agreed.

The area around the front of House of Dido was deserted as they stepped out of the taxi. No journalists seemed to be lurking behind the elegant cast-iron street lamps or peering from behind the blinds and shutters of the neighbouring businesses. All seemed to be back to normal.

Matt strode up to the door of House of Dido and pressed the bell. After a few minutes a maid cracked the door open and peered out.

'*Bonjour*, we are friends of Madame Marie Dido, we are here to see Monsieur Yves Mangan.' Matt took a business card from his case and gave it to the girl.

'*Un moment, s'il vous plaît.*' She closed the door and left them to wait.

Presently she returned and opened the door to permit them to enter, all whilst looking around outside presumably in case anyone was lurking from the newspapers.

'Monsieur Mangan is in his studio.' The girl led them along the corridor in the direction of the workroom. She paused at a plain white-painted door near the workroom and knocked.

Yves Mangan opened his door and dismissed the girl as he invited them inside.

'*Bonjour*, Captain Bryant, Madame Bryant. If you are looking for Madame Dido I am afraid she is absent today,' he said.

'That's quite all right. We called to see you, actually, if you can spare us a few minutes,' Matt said as they took a seat on one of the plain wooden chairs inside Yves's office. The room was a large, square, well-lit space. Corkboards on the wall were covered with design concepts for garments and pinned samples of fabrics. A couple of mannequins were positioned near a large drawing board on a stand and rolls of fabric lay on a cutting table.

'Oh.' Yves Mangan instantly looked wary. 'I went to

Inspector LeJeune and confessed my part in taking the scissors to the backstage, if that is why you are here.'

'Not exactly. I take it you've heard of the assault on Nathalie Belliste?' Kitty asked.

'*Oui.*' Monsieur Mangan moved his shoulders in a dismissive gesture. 'Madame Dido told me that Sir Humphrey had been arrested. Is this true?' He looked first at Matt, then at Kitty.

'He was, but has now been released. Apparently someone posted some of Simone Belliste's missing designs through his door the night before Nathalie was attacked. The police found them when they searched his home,' Kitty said.

'*Pourquoi?* Who would do that? For what purpose? I don't understand.' Monsieur Mangan looked perplexed.

'We can only assume whoever did so wished to point the finger of suspicion towards Sir Humphrey. You know he is a shareholder of House of Dido, I presume?' Matt replied.

Yves sat down on his own chair in front of the drawing board. '*Oui*, I am well aware. He is purely a sleeping partner. He provides finance but until now takes no part in the commercial aspects of the business. He inherited the shares from his late wife.'

'He was taking a keen interest in Simone Belliste. He thought her designs had merit. Was he beginning to take more interest in the couture?' Kitty asked.

Yves Mangan's complexion turned an ugly shade of plum. 'It was *insupportable*. The man knows nothing of high fashion. He has no right meddling in the commercial decisions of what should be made. That is *my* role as chief designer. It is I and Marie who make those decisions, not Sir Humphrey. Always he seeks to undermine me.' He muttered the latter part of his statement in a low voice, almost to himself and Kitty had a job hearing his response.

'You clashed with him on the matter?' Matt asked.

'I made my feelings known to Marie. I discouraged her from taking on Simone as a designer. I felt it would be a mistake commercially. You must know this already.' Yves glared at him.

'We've heard that Sir Humphrey is considering disposing of his interests in House of Dido by selling his shares,' Kitty said.

The florid colour in Monsieur Mangan's cheeks ebbed away and he sank back against his chair. 'This I did not know. Who is he intending to sell them to?'

'A Madame Yvette Blanc's name has been mentioned. She owns a rival couture house?' Kitty could see that the couturier looked deeply disturbed by this news. He either was genuinely unaware of Sir Humphrey's plans, or he was a superb actor she thought.

'*Non, ce n'est pas possible.* This would be a disaster. Marie would surely not permit this. They are not of the quality of our work. He must at least offer her the chance to buy the shares herself first.' Yves gripped the edge of the drawing board as if to prevent himself from sliding from his chair.

'I don't believe that Marie has the money to buy him out. The business is not in good shape. I'm sure Sir Humphrey knows this,' Matt said. 'You must know this.'

Yves seemed to have shrunk down into himself as if each word Matt spoke was beating down on his head. 'It is true that Marie is having temporary problems. We have the new orders from the show if not too many of our customers have cancelled. She could go to the bank.' Hope flared briefly in his eyes.

'I suppose it's possible,' Kitty agreed as she glanced at Matt. 'I expect Inspector LeJeune will have more questions for everyone now that Sir Humphrey has been released. Sir Humphrey himself is keen to clear his reputation.'

'I expect so,' Monsieur Mangan agreed. 'Now, if you will excuse me, I have much to do. The problems caused by the press which forced us to close have created a backlog of work.'

'Of course, and thank you for seeing us. If you think of

anything, however small, which you feel might assist with the case please let us or Inspector LeJeune know,' Matt said.

Monsieur Mangan looked at them as they rose from their seats. 'You are investigating these matters? Madame DeTourner said that you are private investigators.'

Kitty inclined her head. '*Oui*, Sir Humphrey has engaged us to try to clear his name. *Au revoir*, monsieur.'

They left swiftly, leaving the couturier staring after them.

CHAPTER SEVENTEEN

As they closed the door to the fashion house behind them and stepped onto the pavement a black car pulled to a halt beside them.

Inspector LeJeune disembarked from the driver's seat of the car. 'Captain Bryant, Madame Bryant.'

'*Bonjour*, Inspector,' Matt greeted him cordially.

'You have been to call on Madame Dido?' the inspector asked, glancing at the nameplate above the doorbell.

'*Non*, Inspector, we dropped in to see Monsieur Mangan,' Matt said.

Kitty saw the inspector's brows rise slightly and a faint frown line appear on his brow. 'May I ask if it was for any particular reason?'

'Sir Humphrey has engaged us to clear his reputation of any involvement in the death of Simone Belliste and the assault on her sister. We wanted to find out if Monsieur Mangan knew of anything further that might help in the matter,' Matt said.

'I see. You should know that we have this investigation well in hand, Captain Bryant. I appreciate the assistance you and

Madame Bryant have provided so far, but I would prefer that you refrain from interfering in the case any further.' Inspector LeJeune looked at them and Kitty felt her cheeks grow slightly warm under the policeman's level scrutiny.

'You can be assured, Inspector, we shall not impede your work in any way. Should we stumble upon something which may assist you, we will inform you immediately. I would hope you have seen already that we can be trusted in that way.' Matt met the inspector's gaze.

'*Eh bien*, so long as we understand each other,' Inspector LeJeune replied after a moment's consideration of Matt's words.

Matt touched the brim of his hat in acknowledgement and the inspector returned the gesture. Kitty took Matt's arm as they walked away, while the inspector rang the bell for admission into the fashion house.

'We had better head for the café to meet Julian. It's almost lunchtime and I could do with a drink after this morning,' Kitty said as they went to take yet another taxi across Paris to the business arrondissement, where Julian's offices were based.

She couldn't help feeling a little disappointed that the inspector had not been more amenable to collaborating on the investigation. It was only to be expected really, she supposed, but frustrating nonetheless.

They arrived a little early at the café which was housed in a sleek modern building. They explained they were expecting a third person to join them and took their seats at a chic outdoor table beneath a stylish umbrella. The sun was pleasantly warm, and it was nice to be outside after a morning spent mostly indoors.

Kitty sipped her coffee and admired the fashions of the ladies walking past the restaurant. The French ladies all looked so smart she felt quite dowdy in comparison in her print dress.

Many of them wore small fitted jackets with beautiful buttons with intricate designs. She had sent some postcards already to Alice, but she knew her friend would have enjoyed seeing the sights for herself. Alice would love seeing the latest styles.

Julian arrived promptly and came to join them at their table. He greeted Matt with a firm handshake and Kitty with a kiss on her cheek. He looked tired and as if he had grown ten years older in the last few days.

The waiter brought them their menus, and they refrained from any meaningful conversation until after they had given their orders.

'I suppose you heard from *Maman* what happened to me yesterday?' Julian asked once a bottle of Chablis had been opened and approved.

'That you went to the police station to assist the inspector with his investigation?' Kitty asked after savouring a sip of the crisp wine.

Julian nodded glumly. 'That's right. He had telephoned my friend's house and asked me to meet him there. I don't know how he found the number, the directory I suppose. Then when I arrived at the station I was told I was not permitted to leave until certain matters had been examined. That was when I learned that Nathalie had been attacked and taken to hospital. I was very shocked and concerned. I didn't find out until later that he had been to *Maman*'s apartment and searched it.'

'Do you have any idea why someone might have broken into Nathalie's apartment?' Kitty asked. 'Did she or Simone have any enemies?'

Julian shook his head. 'The inspector asked me the same question. I have no idea why anyone would want to have harmed either of them. It's so incredible. I still can't believe that Simone is dead.'

Kitty glanced at Matt. She could see that Julian was deeply upset by the loss of his girlfriend.

'It seems so unfair. Simone was so vibrant, beautiful and talented. I intended to ask her to marry me. We had looked at apartments to make our first home. I had a ring ready. *Maman* was doubtful about my choice, but I knew once she knew Simone better she would approve.'

'Why was your mother so opposed to the match? She was a little vague when we asked her about it? Something to do with Simone's past?' Kitty asked, trying to be tactful.

Julian smiled ruefully. 'Ah, you have heard that Simone had a child? *Maman* will never admit it, but she is something of a snob. Simone's family are not the right social level to meet her approval. Simone also working as a model was something she found distasteful. That was partly why Simone wished to move into designing.'

The waiter arrived bearing their first course of *Coquilles Saint-Jacques*. Kitty eyed the delicate scallops appreciatively, her mouth watering in anticipation. Once the waiter had departed they resumed their conversation.

'Simone told you about her daughter?' Kitty asked.

Julian nodded. 'When we became more serious. She showed me pictures and said she hoped one day to have her daughter live with her. She was very open about it all to me.'

'Did she mention the child's father?' Kitty asked.

'She told me she was attacked when she was sixteen while walking home. She didn't know who the man was. It was all quite distressing for her. She lost her parents in an accident before the baby was born and Nathalie was only fifteen, so they were all alone. Despite that she loved her baby. She said the child was innocent and she was determined she should never know how her conception had come about. The nuns at her local convent helped her and her daughter lives there with them.'

Kitty thought if Simone had told Julian the truth, then that removed the possibility of a vengeful ex-lover being responsible for her death.

'That's so sad. It must have been very hard for Simone. Were she and Nathalie close? Obviously they shared an apartment and a profession, but did they have the same friends or move in the same circles outside of work?' Kitty was curious to discover what Julian thought of the girls' relationship.

Julian considered the question. 'Simone was outgoing and friendly. She had a small group of friends who enjoyed visiting galleries and seeing films. Nathalie was always quieter, more reclusive. She would often only go out when Simone prodded her into joining in with something. She often would tag along with us.'

'How did Nathalie feel about her sister moving more into designing? Simone was responsible for finding her sister most of her work we understand?' Matt asked.

'She wasn't pleased. They argued about it. Simone earned much more money than Nathalie. She had that star quality. You probably saw this at the show. Nathalie is a beautiful girl, but she lacks the *élan* that Simone had. I think Nathalie was concerned about money. The girls are from poor backgrounds. Simone said that they were fortunate to be lodging with Patricia since she only charged a small rent and it had helped them build up some savings. It also allowed Simone to send the nuns money to care for her child.' Julian wiped the corners of his mouth with his napkin as he finished his first course.

Conversation paused once more as the first course was cleared away and plates of bouillabaisse were set before them.

'These designs of Simone's seem to have stirred up a lot of problems,' Kitty observed as she speared a piece of white fish from the aromatic stew. 'Monsieur Mangan seemed to view her as a threat. Madame Dido appeared conflicted about the direction the couture house should take, and Sir Humphrey seemed to think they had merit.'

'Yes, you are right. Simone was excited about them. She had been working on her collection for some time, and she said if Madame Dido was not interested, then Sir Humphrey had told her he knew of other houses she could try. I believe he was even considering backing her himself to set up her own house.' Julian frowned. 'Do you think this is why she was killed? Because of those designs?'

'It certainly seems to be a strong possibility. The way some of them disappeared after she was killed. Then someone posted them through Sir Humphrey's door. That was why he was arrested,' Matt said. 'The police discovered them when they searched his house. He hadn't opened the envelope, thinking it contained papers from his solicitor.'

Julian looked shocked by this revelation. 'He was being led into the police station as my solicitor and I were on our way out. I was surprised to see him wearing handcuffs.'

'Sir Humphrey has since been released from custody. He has asked us to try to find evidence to exonerate him from any suspicion of being involved in either Simone's murder or the attack on Nathalie,' Kitty said.

'I see. I can understand his concerns. I must admit I have become worried about the effect of Simone's murder on my own reputation. The newspapers have not held back from naming people in the pieces they have published. Simone was quite well known and naturally they have been quick to print pictures of her and discuss how she was killed.' Julian shuddered. 'It's ghoulish and repulsive.'

'I can understand. Have the press been trying to contact you about your relationship with Simone?' Kitty asked sympathetically.

'I had to stay away from my office. My secretary has been fielding calls. Thankfully it has started to die down. Although if the papers discover this attack on Nathalie it may well set everything off again. I'm sure Nathalie too has been hounded by them,' Julian said.

'Have you spoken to Nathalie at all since the attack?' Matt set down his cutlery and picked up his wine.

Julian shook his head. 'Not really. A few words to make sure she was safe. I was going to call her again but, well, Nathalie has always been rather clingy. After I accompanied her and Patty back to the apartment after Simone's murder...' His voice tailed away and the frown line on his forehead deepened before he continued. 'She was naturally distraught. We all were, but she kept trying to persuade me to stay at the apartment. I knew Patty would be there with her and I needed space to come to terms with what had just happened. I checked on them both the next day and again she wanted me to stay with her. I feel bad for refusing but I just couldn't.' He looked at Kitty. 'Does that make me a bad person?'

Kitty smiled gently. 'No, it makes you human. You had just lost your intended fiancée and on top of that everyone there that afternoon was considered a suspect. Patricia was supporting Nathalie, and you needed support yourself.'

'Thank you. It's not that I am not concerned for Nathalie, she is Simone's sister after all.' Julian gave a small smile.

They finished the fish stew and waited once more for the plates to be cleared before ordering a dessert of *religieuse au chocolat*, which Julian assured them was a speciality of the restaurant.

'Did you believe Sir Humphrey might have killed Simone when you saw him at the police station?' Kitty asked as she admired the delicate cream and chocolate choux buns that arrived for her dessert.

'It seems impossible that any of the people that were there that afternoon or who knew Simone could have murdered her. I was very surprised to see Sir Humphrey in custody. He had always seemed supportive of Simone and her work.' Julian picked up his cutlery.

'Nathalie thought that perhaps Sir Humphrey had feelings for Simone.' Kitty phrased her sentence as delicately as she could.

Julian paused in the action of placing food on his spoon. 'Nathalie mentioned the possibility to me. Simone was beautiful. Sir Humphrey admired her. I knew this, she told me all about it. I never had any reason to doubt Simone.'

'Nathalie told us she thought her sister could be fickle,' Matt said.

Kitty thought he was being very diplomatic with his phrasing.

'That is not true at all, but if you mean did I think Simone was having an affair with Sir Humphrey then no, I know she wasn't.'

Julian sounded very definite in his response. Kitty wondered how he could be so certain. Marie Dido had suspected the relationship was not just business. So had Julian's own mother. Nathalie too had suggested there was more going on than mere generosity of spirit from the older man towards the attractive young model. Had Julian simply been blind to what was happening?

Kitty finished her dessert with a contented sigh. Whatever else Julian may have been mistaken about he had been entirely right about his recommendation for pudding. The *religieuse au chocolat* was truly delicious.

Julian declined to stay for coffee since he needed to return to his office. He insisted on paying for their lunch and left Kitty and Matt to enjoy their drinks in the sunshine.

'Well, what do you make of everything so far today?' Kitty asked as she added milk to her coffee.

'I don't know. I'm not certain that we are much further forward,' Matt said. 'I don't feel as if we have discovered anything that might exonerate any of them from murdering Simone.'

Kitty stirred her drink with a small silver-coloured teaspoon. 'If we think that whoever killed Simone also attacked Nathalie, then I suppose we could eliminate Marie Dido.'

'Unless she was working with someone else,' Matt pointed out.

'Julian said that living with Patricia had helped the Belliste sisters to save money. I wonder who was the saver, Simone or Nathalie? And who would inherit any money she may have had? Would it be her daughter?' Kitty looked at Matt. They had not until now considered the financial aspects of the model's death.

'I suppose unless she left a will, which would be unlikely given her age and circumstances, then Nathalie would inherit anything of Simone's.' Matt eyed her over the brim of his cup.

'I don't think the child would get anything unless Nathalie provided for her. I must confess, I don't know how things would stand under French law since the child is illegitimate. That would also include Simone's designs I assume. Nathalie would be free to sell them to anyone who was interested,' Kitty said.

'Would they be worth anything on their own? Nathalie doesn't have any ambitions in that direction, does she? So she couldn't produce more designs. I think all the houses employ or are owned by designers, like Coco Chanel for instance,' Matt pointed out.

'Then maybe Simone was killed to stop her designs from being made or sold elsewhere?' Kitty tried to work out what the murderer might have gained from Simone's death.

If the designs were rendered worthless in financial terms with no chance of more designs to come, then maybe it was to stop them being used at all. Why would that be important?

'We know Monsieur Mangan didn't want Marie to develop a ready-to-wear line. That would give him a motive. He admitted wishing to destroy Simone's work. Nathalie wanted Simone to drop the idea and continue modelling. Marie, I suppose, wouldn't wish to lose her favourite model and potentially a new line to a rival.' Matt took a sip from his cup.

'I suppose then that makes it less likely that Sir Humphrey was involved in Simone's murder since he supported her in trying to find someone interested in her ideas,' Kitty said.

'You understand that Julian is still also a suspect? He may have realised that Sir Humphrey and Simone were deceiving him, and he could have attacked her in a fit of jealous rage,' Matt warned.

Kitty raised an eyebrow at this. 'I think he was genuine when he was talking to us just now. He certainly seemed to believe Simone only had eyes for him. I know you can't dismiss him as a suspect, but I refuse to believe he would do such a thing, if only for Eliza's sake.'

She couldn't believe her godmother's son could be capable of murder and be able to lie to them so convincingly over lunch. Logically, she was forced to concede that Matt had a point, but she refused to believe it.

'I wonder where Marie Dido is today? Monsieur Mangan said she wasn't expected at House of Dido,' Matt mused before draining his coffee cup.

'Perhaps she's gone to see Sir Humphrey. She was very upset when she learned he had been meeting with Madame Blanc. They must have a lot to discuss,' Kitty said.

They strolled out of the restaurant and walked through the city streets to head back towards the hotel. They paused to browse in some of the elegant boutiques along the way and Kitty bought a pretty silk scarf in shades of green for Alice.

'I hope Grams and Eliza are having a lovely day,' Kitty said when they finally emerged onto the Champs-Élysées once more.

'I'm sure they are. I expect they have been taking a nice

nostalgic tour of the city to reminisce.' Matt smiled at her. 'Your grandmother looks much better than when we arrived, despite the murder.'

'Very true, or maybe that should be because of the murder. I get my inherent nosiness from her as well as my mother,' Kitty said with a chuckle.

CHAPTER EIGHTEEN

Matt was deep in thought as they continued to walk back to their hotel. It was pleasant spending time with Kitty out and about, enjoying the sights and sounds of the city. All the while though, his mind kept turning over what they had learned so far about possible motives for Simone's death. Then there was the added complication of the attack by a mysterious masked man on Nathalie Belliste.

They finally arrived at the hotel lobby in time for afternoon tea. He spotted Kitty's grandmother and Eliza DeTourner already sitting at their favourite table. Violette was at Eliza's feet as usual, a blue bow in her topknot. He pointed them out to Kitty, and they went over to join them.

As they grew nearer Matt could see there was an air of agitated excitement between the two women, and he wondered what was the cause this time.

'Kitty, Matthew, come and sit down. You will never guess what has happened now?' Eliza said as she leaned across the table towards them. Her eyes were bright with suppressed excitement.

Kitty set down her shopping bags as she sank gracefully onto a chair. 'Yes, what is it? What's happened?'

Matt took a chair next to Kitty and removed his panama hat. 'Has the inspector made another arrest?'

'You will never guess. Marie Dido has been arrested.' Eliza glanced around as if keen not to be overheard.

'Marie?' Kitty looked at Matt in bewilderment.

'Not for Simone's murder. No, for something else entirely,' Eliza announced.

'That sounds bad.' Kitty continued to look at her godmother for an explanation.

'She has assaulted Madame Blanc at her place of business in front of her staff. The gendarmes were called, and she has been arrested,' Kitty's grandmother said in a disapproving tone.

'I presume this must be something to do with Madame Blanc's meeting with Sir Humphrey?' Matt asked.

'I expect so. We only know because when we arrived back here this afternoon there was a message requesting one of us to telephone the police station.' Grams looked at Eliza. 'She expected one of us to stand surety for her.'

Matt guessed that it was probably Madame DeTourner who was expected to act as surety for the couturier.

'What did you do?' Kitty asked.

Madame DeTourner shrugged and continued to drink her tea before replying. 'What can one do? Marie is a dear friend. I can only think with this terrible murder she is losing her mind. I sent my solicitor to the police station to sort things out.'

Matt could see from Kitty's grandmother's demeanour that she had not been wholly in agreement with this course of action.

'Has she been released?' Kitty asked. 'Do we know exactly what she did?'

Grams sniffed. 'She poured a bottle of black ink over

Madame Blanc's head and tried to physically assault her. The solicitor reported back to us that Marie was also covered in ink and in a fine state when he arrived at the station. Madame Blanc is pressing charges and claiming damages.'

Kitty's eyes were wide, and she seemed lost for words at this latest incident.

'I shall have to call on her in a while when she has had a chance to go home, bathe and compose herself. I really need to speak to her. She cannot go around assaulting people. I don't know if Sir Humphrey is aware of what she's done, but I don't suppose he will be pleased when he learns of it,' Eliza said.

Violette gave a small yap as if to emphasise her mistress's disapproval of matters.

'I can't see that Sir Humphrey will wish to continue in business with Marie now. I doubt too that Madame Blanc will wish to buy the shares from him for House of Dido. I don't know if anyone would buy him out if this is how she behaved today,' Kitty said.

Matt agreed with his wife. Clearly Marie Dido had let her emotions get the better of her. Was this the case when Simone was stabbed? Did she act on impulse then too? But then who had attacked Nathalie? That had clearly been a planned and premeditated break-in but what had the man been hoping to find?

Had whoever had assaulted the girl thought the apartment would be empty? Had they assumed that both Patty and Nathalie wouldn't have wished to stay there after the murder? Nathalie was adamant that it had been a man who had broken in, so that couldn't have been Marie.

'Perhaps, Matthew, you and Kitty should accompany Eliza when she calls on Marie.' Grams looked at them. 'I don't think Eliza should go alone while Marie is so, well, volatile.'

Eliza immediately chimed in. 'Yes, that is a good idea. I am sure *chère* Marie would never harm me, but she is clearly in the grip of some strong emotions. She is usually so calm and poised. Please say you will go with me.'

Matt could see that Kitty clearly thought the suggestion a good one. 'Yes, I think you may be right. Kitty and I would be glad to accompany you.'

* * *

Kitty was keen to see Marie for herself to gain some insight into what might have provoked the woman's extraordinary behaviour. She wasn't sure how this linked to Simone's death, or even if it did. They had to follow it up though in case it provided them with the breakthrough they were looking for.

They finished their tea and Eliza and Violette left shortly afterwards promising to return in a few hours.

'That was terribly crafty of you, Grams,' Kitty said once her godmother had departed.

Grams put on an innocent expression. 'Really, Kitty, I have no idea what you mean. I was merely concerned for Eliza's safety.'

Kitty raised an eyebrow but refrained from answering. She knew her grandmother's scheming all too well. Not that she objected in this instance.

Eliza duly returned to collect them a few hours later, minus Violette.

'I've left her with Julian. She gets too excited when she senses people are emotional,' Eliza explained when Kitty asked her where the poodle was. 'He told me you had a nice lunch together. I'm so pleased. Different company is exactly what he needs right now after this business with the police and Simone's murder.' Eliza's lower lip trembled, and Kitty gave her godmother's arm a reassuring pat.

'I'm sure Inspector LeJeune is working hard to resolve the case,' she said. Privately she thought he would make faster progress if people didn't go about tossing bottles of ink around.

Marie's apartment was not far from House of Dido. Situated in a similar-looking block to the one which housed the fashion business. It was clearly a more affluent arrondissement than the one where Patricia and the Belliste sisters lived. The streets were wider and cleaner and trees lined the boulevard.

The light was just starting to fade, and the street lamps were coming to life as the car halted, and they disembarked.

'I called Marie and told her we were coming over. Indeed, after I stood surety for her she could hardly refuse to see me. She is expecting us,' Eliza informed them as she opened the door and led them into a spacious communal hallway.

Kitty and Matt followed her up the grand stone staircase with its ornate wrought-iron balustrades. Marie's apartment was on the second floor. Eliza adjusted her summer wrap and pressed a gloved forefinger firmly on the bell.

At first Kitty thought Marie was not going to answer. However, just as Eliza was poised to press once more the door cracked open and Marie peered out at them. She stood aside to allow them in, and she led them along an elegant hall to a spacious drawing room.

Marie took a seat on one end of a damask-silk upholstered sofa and opened a carved-ivory cigarette box. She selected one for herself before offering them around. Kitty could see there were still faint black blotches of ink on the backs of her hands and fingertips.

Her blonde hair had been pulled back in an untidy loose chignon and she looked weary and defeated. The others refused the offer of cigarettes and took their seats, Eliza on the other end of the sofa and Kitty and Matt in the matching gilt-framed armchairs.

Matt produced a silver cigarette lighter and politely offered Marie a light. She murmured her thanks as she accepted.

'*Chère* Marie, whatever happened today? We, all of your friends, we are so worried for you!' Eliza began, a look of concern on her face as she studied her friend.

Marie drew on her cigarette and exhaled, blowing a thin plume of pale-blue smoke into the air. 'I do not know, Eliza. That is the truth. After I learned of Sir Humphrey's betrayal, it stewed in my heart all night long, festering. This is so typical of Yvette. It has always been this way. All of our lives from when we were children. If I had something she would have to copy it. To do it better or to destroy what I had. I cannot explain. It was like a great wave broke something inside me.' Marie's hand trembled as she tapped the ash from her cigarette into a Lalique ashtray.

'You have known Madame Blanc for a long time then?' Kitty asked, puzzled by the woman's choice of words.

Marie's lips twisted into a bitter smile. 'All my life. It is not known but Yvette and I are sisters.'

Kitty could see that Matt and Eliza were as shocked by this revelation as she was. 'You and Madame Blanc?' Kitty asked, unsure if she had heard correctly.

'*Oui*. She is younger than me by eight years. She was always spoiled as a child. The golden one. The precious one. What Yvette wanted, Yvette got, and usually at my expense,' Marie confirmed.

'Why have you never said anything about her being your sister?' Eliza asked.

'I wanted to put distance between us. I have avoided her as much as possible. We hadn't spoken more than ten words in the last ten years until today. The last full conversation we had was at our mother's funeral.'

'*Tiens*, Marie!' Eliza pressed her hand to her bosom.

'All my life since the day she was born she has been a thorn in my side. *Maman et Papa* indulged her. She had the toys she wanted. I had to give her my things as she was younger, and I should learn to share with her. I wanted piano lessons, but Yvette wanted to do ballet. There wasn't money for both so she learned to dance. She wanted a new dress for a party but, of course, she should have it. I got my cousin from Reims's hand-me-downs,' Marie said bitterly.

'She started her couture house after you started yours?' Kitty asked.

Marie stubbed her cigarette out in the ashtray. '*Oui*, as soon as she discovered what I was doing she had to try to make her business bigger, better, more successful.'

'I knew you were rivals, but this...' Eliza shook her head in disbelief.

'House of Dido was doing well but then Yvette began to target my customers. She offered them incentives to go to her. She made all these promises and put down my creations. I have worked hard on my business. After I divorced my husband I threw everything into my work. Then my eyesight began to cause me problems. I employed Yves to take some of the strain of designing from me. Yvette told people I was going blind. I don't know how she heard of my health issues.' Marie rose from her seat and crossed the room to a small trolley containing glasses and bottles of wine and spirits.

Kitty watched as she poured herself a cognac in a large balloon-shaped glass before resuming her seat. She didn't offer anything to her guests.

'Was that when House of Dido began to have problems?' Kitty asked.

'*Oui*, Sir Humphrey's wife, Gilda, who had been my business partner, became ill and died. It was the most terrible time.' Marie stared into her brandy.

'What happened then?' Kitty was fascinated by Marie's story.

'Sir Humphrey assured me that he would continue to support the business. I was relieved. For a while all has been smooth sailing. Then in the last eighteen months the orders have been less. I hear more stories of Yvette stealing my clients. The younger ones defecting to her label. Always she seemed to be one step ahead of me. I looked at Simone's designs as I thought maybe since Sir Humphrey was keen on them, despite Yves's reservations, this might be the way forward. *Prêt-à-porter* for a youthful market.' Marie shook her head slowly.

'Then you learned Sir Humphrey was holding business meetings with your sister. You heard he was thinking of selling his shares,' Matt said.

'*Oui*, that thought lay on me so heavily. It was such a betrayal from a man I had begun to have feelings for.' Marie looked at him with anguished eyes. 'I was not thinking. I was like a woman possessed.'

'So, you arrived at your sister's design house armed with a bottle of black ink?' Kitty said.

Marie nodded, her gaze now downcast and a faint flush visible on her cheeks. 'I knocked on the door and barged my way inside demanding to see my sister.' Her voice faltered for a moment, and she set down her glass so she could retrieve her handkerchief from her belt. 'She was in her studio. She didn't even seem surprised that I was there. I think she must have known that I would discover her bid to buy Sir Humphrey's shares.'

'*Pauvre* Marie, how dreadful,' Eliza said.

'She laughed at me. She stood behind her drawing board and laughed in my face. She said she would soon own the shares and would close down House of Dido. My workers would work for her. I was so angry. I pulled the ink from my bag, took off the stopper and poured it all over her head. Ah! It was a glorious moment!' Marie's eyes now flashed fire. 'Then she dived at me and one of her staff I think had telephoned the gendarmes as soon as I had arrived. They were there very quickly. I was arrested, wrapped in a towel and bundled off to the police station like a common criminal.' The glow in her eyes disappeared. 'It was then that I realised how foolish I had been to act so rashly. I had given her my business on a platter.'

'Have you spoken to Sir Humphrey since you returned home?' Eliza asked.

'*Non*. I tried to telephone him early today before I went to see Yvette but there was no reply. I tried again this evening after I had attempted to remove all of the ink but again there was no answer. I doubt he will wish to speak to me again. His shares and mine will not be worth the paper they are written on when this gets out. Yvette will get them for a song and then I might as well just burn mine. Over twenty years of hard work gone, pouf! In a flash.' Marie picked up her drink once more and took a large gulp.

She gave a little shudder as she swallowed, before draining the remainder of the drink with a second gulp.

'Do you think there is any connection between your sister and Simone's death or the attack on Nathalie?' Matt asked the question Kitty had at the forefront of her own mind. It seemed to her that if Yvette could sabotage her sister and steal Simone's work, either to use herself or to stop Marie from using them, then they had another suspect in the mix.

Marie set down her glass. 'I don't know. I mean I don't see how she could be responsible for Simone's murder. She herself could not have come into the salon. At least I don't know that she could. The guest list was strictly monitored. I knew everyone there. *Non, ce n'est pas possible.*'

'Do you think any of your staff may have been assisting your sister? You said she always seemed to be a step ahead of you. Was someone tipping her off about your designs or your plans?' Kitty asked.

Marie looked as if she was about to reject Kitty's suggestion but then she paused. 'I had not thought. My staff are loyal. Elise, my forewoman in the cutting room, and Ginny and Babette, they too have all been with me for years.'

'And Monsieur Mangan? Are you certain of his loyalty?' Eliza asked.

CHAPTER NINETEEN

'He is my head of design. He's worked with me for years. I give him free rein much of the time since I can only work for short periods. I approve all of the designs obviously, but he has a lot of creative freedom.' Marie looked confused.

'I take it he also doesn't know that you and Yvette Blanc are sisters?' Kitty said.

'*Non*, no one does. Eliza here is one of my closest friends and she did not know.' Marie took hold of Eliza's hand.

'That is true. I am very shocked. I cannot believe you did not confide in me,' Eliza agreed.

'I know, I am so sorry.' Marie looked imploringly at Eliza. 'Please forgive me.'

'You didn't tell anyone of your connection. Do you think your sister also kept the fact that you are sisters to herself?' Matt asked.

'I don't see why she would want it to be known. It would not benefit her in any way. Believe me, *ma sœur* only does things which are of benefit to her. She even stole my inheritance from my parents. When the will was read I learned she had convinced my mother that I did not need her support. Yvette got the house, the savings and all of my mother's jewellery. I received the bill for the funeral.' Marie threw up her hands. 'This is how she is. Now she will make sure that I go to court, and she will make ridiculous claims for damages and spread lies about me in the papers.'

'What will you do?' Eliza asked.

Marie shrugged. 'I do not know. I think I may have to dissolve my business. No doubt Yvette will hope that I will go to her and beg her to withdraw the charges. She will wait a long time for that. Hell will freeze over first. I will not beg to her. I would rather starve on the streets. If my business is gone then there will be little she can do. She can have her day in court. It will be *fini*.'

'Will you try to speak to Sir Humphrey again? Perhaps he may be able to do something to help you?' Kitty suggested.

Marie shook her head. 'Thank you, Kitty, you and your husband have been very kind to me.' She patted Eliza's hand. 'So has my *chère* Eliza. *Non*, this is a mess mostly of my own making. At least I have had the glorious satisfaction of seeing that black ink dripping down her face and ruining those shoes she is so proud of. Childish I know, but still it is something.'

'Shall you be all right here alone tonight? Where is Zelle, your maid?' Eliza asked.

The room had grown darker while they had been talking, and Marie moved to turn on one of the pale-peach silk-shaded lamps. 'She is visiting her mother. She will be back at ten. Do not worry, *chérie*. I shall survive.'

They talked for a little longer while Eliza telephoned for a taxi to collect them. At least Marie seemed to be in a more settled frame of mind by the time the car arrived.

'*Pauvre* Marie, I didn't know Yvette Blanc was her sister,' Eliza said, once they were seated inside the taxi. 'It explains so much. I hope she will be all right.'

The taxi took Eliza home first, before turning to take Kitty and Matt back to the hotel. They were almost at their destination when Matt requested the driver to take them to a different spot in the city.

'Where are we going?' Kitty asked, looking at her husband.

The car halted and they got out. '*Un moment, monsieur, s'il vous plaît,*' Matt asked the driver as he led Kitty forward to a small terrace just off the main street. The area was a place above the city bordered by a low stone wall.

The evening air was cooler now after the heat of the day and fresh green plants growing in pots nearby scented the air. Kitty gasped as she looked out across the darkened city to see hundreds of lights twinkling below her with the Eiffel Tower gently illuminated against the skyline.

'We will be leaving soon, and I thought we shouldn't go without you seeing this.' Matt placed his arm around her waist, and she leaned her head on his shoulder.

'Thank you, it is quite magical.' She reached up to kiss his cheek. 'After the last few days this will give us a nice memory to take away.'

They lingered for a few more seconds then returned to the waiting cab and headed back to their hotel.

Kitty's grandmother was seated on the sofa in their suite, a large cup of hot chocolate in her hand and a fashion magazine open on her lap. It was clear she had been waiting for them to return.

'Now, my dears, tell me what happened? Is Madame Dido recovered? Is Eliza all right?' Grams asked as she removed her wire-framed reading glasses.

'It seems there is a lot that Eliza didn't know about Marie and this Yvette Blanc,' Kitty said as she took a seat beside her grandmother.

Matt sat on one of the armchairs and between them they told Kitty's grandmother everything they had learned at Marie's apartment.

'My goodness.' Grams appeared suitably shocked as she sipped her drink and listened to the story. 'Sisters, how extraordinary. Then it seems I may have stumbled on something tonight that might interest you both.'

She set aside her now empty cup and slipped her glasses back on. Picking up the discarded magazine, she flipped through until she reached the page she wanted.

'Now then, Matthew, my ability to read French is even rustier than my speech but can you look at that advertising feature and see if it says what I think it says.' Grams pointed to an article on the page with her finger.

Kitty leaned over to look at the feature while Matt studied the print below the illustration. The image accompanying the feature showed a drawing of a beautiful young woman wearing winter clothing, her head turned to look back over her shoulder. The picture seemed strangely familiar.

'What does it say?' Kitty could only pick out a few of the words.

'It's an advertorial for Madame Blanc's fashion house about their upcoming autumn ready-to-wear collection for the stylish young lady about town,' Matt said.

'Does that picture look familiar to you?' Kitty asked.

'Yes, it does. I would swear it was almost identical to one of the drawings we saw in Simone's design file.' Matt studied the image closely.

'How did Yvette get this design and presumably enough of them that she could create an entire fashion line and advertise it?' Kitty asked. 'What's the date of this magazine?'

Matt flipped back to the cover. 'It's current, out yesterday.'

'I bought it from a newsstand while I was with Eliza this morning,' Grams said.

Kitty peered at the cover. 'It's a weekly magazine too so they must have had this placed recently. Alice says the monthly magazines are planned months ahead.'

'I think we need to try and speak to Madame Blanc,' Matt said.

'It's too late now, but perhaps after breakfast we can try and find her.' Kitty took the magazine and turned the page back to the advertisement. 'At least there is an address and a telephone number here.'

'Yes, that's helpful. I think we may need to have another word with our client, Sir Humphrey, again too,' Matt said.

'Hmm, it all seems very interesting if you ask me. Not that I condone violence but perhaps Marie may have been justified in dumping ink all over her sister after all,' Grams said. She got up from the sofa. 'Well, I am retiring to bed. You two have a lot to do tomorrow. Eliza and I have a lovely day out planned so I expect I shall see you both for dinner, if we don't meet at breakfast.'

Kitty kissed her grandmother goodnight, then she and Matt followed her example and decided an early night would be very sensible.

* * *

Matt had a poor night's sleep. He woke early and rose quietly so as not to disturb Kitty. He wasn't certain what had been the reason for the nightmarish dreams that had plagued him. The trip back to Plymouth might still have been on his mind and could have triggered his nightmares. He was only thankful that he had not gone sleepwalking and hadn't damaged anything in the room.

He dressed and left Kitty a note so she wouldn't be alarmed if she woke up and found him missing. He decided a walk outside the hotel in the cool early morning air might help to clear his mind.

The lobby was deserted as he went outside and started to stroll along the virtually empty street towards the Seine. It was too early even for the shopkeepers to be preparing for their opening. Instead, there were the street cleaners, cigarettes clamped between their lips, flat-capped and armed with carts and brooms. Newspaper sellers were at their stands cutting open the bundles of newspapers and arranging them on the racks for sale.

Matt took his time as he walked, enjoying seeing the city slowly coming to life. The florists were setting up their carts by the side of the river, placing beautiful blooms in buckets of water. He stopped to buy a small posy for Kitty.

He sat for a time on a bench overlooking the river while his head cleared of the final fragments of his dreams of men calling for help, the sound of shelling and the neighing of terrified horses. He sniffed the posy, the fragrance of the flowers removing the last vestiges of the odour of burnt flesh from his memory. Once he felt better he set off back to the hotel, picking up a newspaper on the way.

Kitty was up and dressed when he arrived back at their suite. Her eyes lit up when he presented her with the posy and she promptly went to find a glass to put the flowers in water. He sat down and looked at the newspaper he had bought from the stand. Simone's murder was no longer on the front page. However, as he opened the paper he could see the second page was filled with more on the model's death. It also reported on a burglary at Nathalie's apartment.

It seemed clear that the story was not going to go away soon and there was some criticism of the police for having not yet made an arrest. He knew Inspector LeJeune would not be pleased by the article.

Kitty's grandmother was not yet awake, so he and Kitty dined alone in the hotel restaurant.

'Who shall we try first today?' Kitty asked as she brushed a few pastry crumbs from the corners of her lips.

'I think perhaps, Sir Humphrey. Then since he is

acquainted with Madame Blanc he may be able to persuade her to talk to us,' Matt suggested. He had been giving the question some thought while on his walk and it seemed to him to be the most sensible route to take.

Kitty nodded. 'Good thinking. Perhaps if we just set off and try the element of surprise. You have his address on his card, I think?'

Matt swallowed the last of his coffee and they went out to try to find Sir Humphrey at home.

* * *

'We know he can't flee the country as Inspector LeJeune has his passport, but I'd like to know why he isn't answering Marie's telephone calls,' Kitty said as they arrived outside the smart Parisian townhouse where Sir Humphrey resided.

Kitty raised the black doorknocker on the dark-blue painted door and rapped loudly. After a moment a rather surprised-looking Sir Humphrey opened the door.

'Captain Bryant, Mrs Bryant, I wasn't expecting you. Do come in. I hope you have good news for me.' Sir Humphrey led them through to a large square drawing room tastefully furnished in shades of ivory and gold.

'Take a seat. Can I get you a drink? Coffee? Tea? It's too early for anything stronger.' He smiled genially at them as they refused and took a seat on the cream-coloured couch.

'We wondered if you had heard what happened yesterday between Madame Dido and Madame Blanc?' Kitty said as she drew off her cotton gloves and rested them on top of her handbag.

'Ah.' Sir Humphrey took a seat. 'Um, Yvette did call me after she had returned from the police station.'

'Did she explain what had happened?' Kitty asked. She wondered what Yvette's version of the incident had been.

'She told me that Marie had forced her way into her premises and had assaulted her by throwing a bottle of black ink over her head.' Sir Humphrey's brows rose. 'I know Marie can be somewhat volatile, but I had never anticipated she would act in such a disgraceful way.'

'We saw Marie last night. She said she had tried to call you, but you were not answering the telephone,' Matt said.

Sir Humphrey looked a little shamefaced. 'I must admit I guessed that she would try and I had no desire to speak to her. I had already taken one call from the police asking me if I would stand surety for her. I refused.'

'You didn't trust that she would return for any hearings?' Kitty asked. 'She is your business partner after all. I would have thought you might have been willing to pay her bond.'

Sir Humphrey looked even more uncomfortable. 'Alas, I have decided I wanted to place some distance between myself and Marie. She seems to have developed a few, well, romantic ideas about our relationship lately. Then with Simone's murder and my decision to separate myself from House of Dido, well, acting as her bond might send the wrong signals. The police might also think that my support of her actions could indicate some sort of involvement in Simone's murder and Nathalie's assault.'

'Madame DeTourner has agreed to stand as surety for Marie, so the police released her yesterday afternoon. Madame Blanc, however, has said that she wishes to press charges and claim damages from Marie,' Matt said.

'I see.' Sir Humphrey looked at Matt and then at Kitty. 'Do you think Marie could be responsible for Simone's death?'

'We can't rule her out completely, but it seems unlikely. Do you know of any personal connection between Marie Dido and Yvette Blanc?' Kitty asked.

Sir Humphrey's expression remained puzzled. 'No, only

that they are business rivals and don't really speak to one another.'

'Would it surprise you to learn they are sisters?' Matt asked.

The look of astonishment on Sir Humphrey's face seemed to Kitty to be entirely genuine. He stared at Matt for a moment before looking back at Kitty. 'Sisters? Are you sure?'

'We are very sure. There is a long history between them of bad feelings it seems. Sir Humphrey, did you at any point in your conversations with Yvette Blanc talk about Simone Belliste's designs or did you show her them at all?' Kitty asked.

Sir Humphrey shook his head. 'No. I mentioned the girl wanted to become a designer and she was working on some things. That was as far as it went. My conversations with Yvette were about her potentially purchasing my shares in House of Dido.'

Kitty picked up her handbag and moved her gloves to one side before pulling out her grandmother's magazine. She had folded it open to the page with the advert for Yvette Blanc's fashion house.

'Is there anything in this advertisement that seems familiar to you?' she asked.

Sir Humphrey frowned at her and took the magazine. He peered carefully at the page. 'Good Lord, is that one of Simone's designs?'

'We found this last night. Are you certain you didn't show the designs to Yvette?' Matt asked in a firm tone.

'I'm absolutely certain. Simone had shown them to me and, obviously, Marie and Yves Mangan, but she was very careful about who she let see them. I know that Monsieur Mangan had them. I never showed them to Yvette. Simone didn't give them to me.'

CHAPTER TWENTY

There was a ring of sincerity in Sir Humphrey's voice.

'I think we need to speak to Madame Blanc. Could you telephone her and arrange for us to call in the next hour? Please don't mention anything about these designs or the advertisement,' Kitty said.

'Yes, of course. I'll do it now. I have her private number.' Sir Humphrey rose and went to the modern ivory Bakelite telephone on the far side of the room. He still looked shaken by what they had just told him.

'Yvette, *bonjour*, how are you, my dear? Have you quite recovered from yesterday?' Sir Humphrey glanced over to Matt and Kitty while he listened to the couturier's response.

'I'm pleased to hear it, Yvette. Listen, I wonder if you might do me a small favour. I have some friends here. They are English private investigators and are trying to help me clear my name over what happened at House of Dido.' There was another pause, presumably while Yvette expressed her feelings about her sister's business and Simone's murder.

'Could they call on you in the next hour or so? Are you at home? They don't have much longer left in Paris and I should like to clear things up so I can retrieve my passport from Inspector LeJeune.' Sir Humphrey twirled the cord of the telephone between the fingers of his free hand as he listened to Yvette.

'Thank you, my dear. I am most grateful to you. They'll be with you shortly.' He replaced the receiver. 'She's expecting you at her home. I'll write the address down for you. She says she is still shaken by the assault so asks that you forgive her appearance.'

'Of course, thank you, Sir Humphrey,' Kitty said as he took a fountain pen and scribbled the address down on a sheet of notepaper, blotting the ink carefully before passing it across.

'You will let me know what you discover? This business about Simone's designs affects me deeply. Someone tried to frame me by posting those images through my door,' he asked as Kitty placed the address and the magazine with the advertisement back into her bag.

'We understand and if there is anything relevant we will of course be in touch,' Matt assured him.

The address on the notepaper was not far away. Matt had a small visitors' guide with a map in his pocket and once they were out of the apartment he consulted it for directions. It was pleasant to stroll along the streets admiring the scenery as they walked.

Kitty was glad to be outside again. The bill for taxi fares would be quite substantial for their trip. Matt, however, was unable to take the metro which ran beneath the city streets. His fear of enclosed spaces after his time in the war made it impossible. Still, on a lovely day it was much nicer to be above ground.

Madame Blanc had a smart townhouse in a very upmarket street. The houses had black-painted wrought-iron railings outside the frontages separating them from the pavement. Everything appeared well kept, discreet and spoke of affluence. Clearly Yvette Blanc was doing better than her sister.

A youthful maid dressed in a grey uniform with a white cap and apron answered the door. They gave their names, and she instructed them to follow her saying her mistress expected them. Kitty's heels clicked against the black-and-white marble floor tiles as they walked down a short corridor and into a large drawing room at the rear of the house.

Madame Blanc was seated on one end of a long black leather and silver chrome couch. Clad entirely in black with a small black veil pinned to her hair which covered the top half of her face, she looked as if she were in mourning.

The maid announced them and Madame Blanc instructed the girl to bring coffee. Kitty and Matt took a seat each at their hostesses's invitation.

'Please forgive my appearance. I realise it is somewhat unconventional. After Marie Dido's assault on me yesterday the ink is taking some time to come off my skin. I had not intended to receive any visitors today,' Yvette explained.

Yvette Blanc had a pleasant, well-modulated voice and spoke English well with only a faint trace of an accent.

'Thank you for seeing us, madame. We appreciate that yesterday must have been a most distressing day for you,' Matt said.

The maid returned and placed a brass-bound wooden tray containing coffee things on the chrome and glass table beside the couch. Madame Blanc dismissed the girl and set about serving them coffee and a small Italian-style biscuit.

'Sir Humphrey seemed to believe that I might be able to assist you in some way to clear him of involvement in Simone Belliste's death. I am not sure how,' Yvette said as she handed Kitty her cup and saucer.

'We have been tasked by Sir Humphrey with examining the events surrounding Simone Belliste's murder and the subsequent attack on her sister, Nathalie. Sir Humphrey is most concerned that his reputation may have been compromised by these events. Inspector LeJeune is currently holding his passport,' Kitty said as she settled back in her seat and stirred her coffee with a small silver spoon.

Yvette passed a cup to Matt and shrugged her elegant shoulders. 'So he said. I am not sure how I can help you with any of this but please feel free to ask any question you choose.'

'Sir Humphrey has said that he was negotiating with you to sell his portion of the shares he inherited in House of Dido,' Matt said.

'*Oui, c'est vrai*. We had conducted a few meetings. The last one was a couple of evenings ago after Simone Belliste's death. We went to dinner to finalise the figures ready to notify our legal people.' Yvette added sugar to her cup.

'Later that evening Sir Humphrey received an envelope through his door. He didn't open it, leaving it till morning since he expected some papers from his solicitor on another matter. The next day Inspector LeJeune and a gendarme arrived to search his home. The gendarme opened the envelope and discovered it contained some design sketches which had gone missing at the time of Simone Belliste's death,' Matt said.

Kitty watched Yvette Blanc closely while Matt was speaking. She was keen to observe anything that might reveal what the couturier knew of this. She wished Yvette wasn't wearing the veil since she would have liked to have seen her eyes.

'*Eh bien*, and what has this to do with me?' Yvette asked.

'Did you know Simone Belliste wished to move from modelling into design? Had Sir Humphrey or Simone herself approached you and shared any of her sketches with you?' Kitty asked.

Yvette took a sip of her coffee before replying. 'Sir Humphrey had told me the girl had plans to become a designer. He said Marie Dido was considering her ideas. It was to develop a ready-to-wear collection for a younger clientele. Not that it would help Marie's fashion house, of course. Most of her clientele are tottering towards the grave.'

Kitty opened her handbag and took out the magazine which was still folded open to show Madame Blanc's own advertisement. 'A line like this one which your couture house is advertising?' she asked.

Yvette looked at the magazine. 'I suppose so. I have not seen Simone Belliste's designs, and I don't know of Marie Dido's plans apart from what I learned from Sir Humphrey.'

'Who is the designer for your new ready-to-wear collection?' Matt asked.

'That is confidential.' Yvette's tone sharpened.

'Has it been designed in-house? Did you design it?' Kitty persisted.

'Why do you ask? What does it matter?' Yvette asked.

'It matters because we have seen this design before. It forms part of a folder full of similar designs all completed by Simone Belliste before her death. So, you see, madame, we need to know. Where did you get this design from and when?' Matt's voice was cold and grave as he looked at the couturier.

'I bought the designs in good faith. We had been considering such a line, but I was not satisfied with what my own head of design had produced. They were too old and high end. I only work with my exclusive clients these days taking special commissions. Then I was offered these designs with a promise of more to come. They were exactly what we were looking for,' Yvette said.

'Who sold you these designs?' Kitty asked.

'It was done via my solicitor. The designs were sent to me a few weeks ago and a letter accompanied them saying if I was interested in purchasing them then I could make arrangements with my solicitor and it gave the details of another law firm. Here, I have the letter in my bureau.' Yvette rose and crossed over to a small regency-style bureau, heavily ornamented in gilt.

She opened a drawer and took out a letter which she passed to Matt.

He read it while she retook her seat on the couch and added more coffee to her cup.

'May I retain this letter, madame?' Matt asked as he refolded it and returned it to its envelope.

'*Oui*. You see I only dealt with the designer through our solicitors.' Yvette added more sugar to her coffee.

Kitty could see splashes of faded ink on the woman's wrist when her cuff moved as she stirred her drink.

'None of this struck you as odd at all?' Matt asked. 'This cloak-and-dagger way of doing business?'

'Captain Bryant, the world of couture is often bizarre to those who are not a part of this world. There is much secrecy and rivalry. I was looking to add a ready-to-wear line to my fashion house. I was not going to...' Yvette paused. 'What do you say, look a gifted donkey in its mouth.'

'Would your solicitor know or be able to discover who was offering the designs for sale?' Kitty asked. 'Or have you tried to find out already?'

'I did not ask too many questions. The price the designer was asking was reasonable and we wanted to get started quickly on this project. Since my solicitor was handling things it seemed that everything was in order,' Yvette said. 'You can telephone my solicitor if you wish. The number is there on the bureau beside the telephone.'

Matt rose and dialled. He spoke to the person on the other end and hung up. 'They will contact the other solicitors and call back in a moment.'

'Why did you want to buy Sir Humphrey's shares in House of Dido?' Kitty asked as Matt loitered beside the telephone.

'I knew House of Dido was struggling. My own business is at capacity, and I wish to expand. Marie employs some good workers. Sir Humphrey wished to offload the shares, but I think he felt an obligation to Marie to sell them personally, rather than place them on the open market,' Yvette explained.

'You didn't think to tell him that you and Marie are sisters, even though you are estranged?' Kitty said.

Yvette's head jerked up at this and Kitty felt as if the woman was scrutinising her through the black lace mesh of her veil.

'*Non*. It is no one's business that Marie and I are related. She does not talk of it and neither do I. Can you blame me when she is so irrational. Look at what she did yesterday.'

'And yet you wanted to buy shares in her business. To what end? To force her out? A hostile takeover?' Kitty asked.

'It would be up to Marie what she wished to do with her shares. I would be pushing for our businesses to merge so she would have a smaller stake in a much more successful and profitable enterprise. I know she does not really do any designing herself now, or very little. Yves Mangan does all the work. I was doing her a favour,' Yvette said.

The telephone rang and Matt picked up the receiver. He spoke a few words and listened intently to the voice on the other end.

'*D'accord, merci beaucoup, au revoir.*' He replaced the receiver.

'Did they know who was selling the designs?' Kitty asked, looking at her husband.

'The solicitors said the other company were very reluctant to disclose the person's identity. They had to threaten that this was connected to Simone Belliste's murder.'

'And who did they say it was?' Yvette asked.

'Monsieur Yves Mangan.' Matt retook his seat.

'Yves Mangan stole Simone's designs and then sold them to me. *Pour quoi?* He could have just said they were his own, why go through all of this rigamarole? I think that is the word.' Yvette sounded astonished.

'He must have felt he could replicate more of the designs

and make money without having his name associated with a *prêt-à-porter* collection. He has always prided himself on his couture reputation. At least that is what we've heard,' Kitty said.

Yvette nodded. '*Oui*, that is true. He is a proud man and guards his reputation jealously.'

A shiver ran down Kitty's spine. It seemed that Yves Mangan definitely had a strong motive for killing Simone. If she had discovered that he had stolen her designs and sold them behind her back, then things could have been very sticky indeed for the designer. His reputation would have been in ruins if she had gone to the police.

It would also give him a motive for attacking Nathalie if he had been trying to get hold of the rest of Simone's work. She looked at Matt. It seemed to her that they needed to speak to Inspector LeJeune and give him this information as quickly as possible.

Matt was obviously of the same opinion as he asked Yvette if he might use her telephone once more.

'*Oui, bien sûr*,' Yvette agreed.

Kitty finished her coffee as Matt placed the call and was soon speaking to someone at the police station. Her French was not as good as her husband's, but she heard Yvette's name and Monsieur Mangan's name mentioned, along with that of Nathalie and Simone Belliste.

'Well?' Kitty asked as soon as he hung up. 'What did he say?'

'He listened to what we had discovered, and he was going to go straight out to pick up Yves Mangan,' Matt said.

'You think he killed Simone?' Yvette asked.

'He has a strong motive, and he has already admitted to being the person who placed the scissors that were used in her murder in the backstage area,' Kitty said.

'*Mon Dieu*, I cannot believe it. I hope he is captured swiftly,' Yvette said.

CHAPTER TWENTY-ONE

They left Yvette Blanc's house shortly afterwards to return to the hotel. There seemed little more they could do at this point. Matt told Kitty the inspector had said he would telephone them at the Ritz and let them know when Monsieur Mangan had been safely apprehended.

'I don't think we should speak to Sir Humphrey until we are certain that Monsieur Mangan has been arrested and that he has been charged with Simone's murder,' Matt said as they entered the hotel lobby.

'No, I agree. It would be unwise to start rumours going around. If they reach Monsieur Mangan before the inspector gets to him then he could flee,' Kitty agreed.

He hoped Madame Blanc would keep her word not to say anything until Monsieur Mangan was in custody.

It was almost lunchtime now but neither Matt or Kitty felt particularly hungry. Instead, they opted to sit in the lobby for a while in case the telephone call came through from Inspector LeJeune.

Kitty's grandmother had obviously departed earlier for a day of sightseeing with Eliza DeTourner. He hoped they were having a good time. He and Kitty found a pleasant spot where they could watch the world go by and stay in sight of the desk.

They had not been there for very long when Matt saw the receptionist answer the telephone and look around the lobby. His gaze met Matt's, and he signalled for Matt to approach the desk.

'An Inspector LeJeune *pour vous*, Captain.' He passed the receiver to Matt and discreetly moved down the desk to assist another guest.

'Inspector, what news?' Matt asked.

'Monsieur Mangan *est mort*. We have discovered him dead with severe head injuries at his apartment. It seems he let his attacker inside and they bludgeoned him to death with a bronze figure he had on his hall table.' The inspector's voice was grave.

'I see. That's dreadful. It seems the killer is still at large and the one person who may have helped to identify them is now dead.' Matt was shaken by the news. He had been convinced after talking to Madame Blanc that Yves Mangan was their man. He had been certain that this was the breakthrough to solving Simone's murder.

'It does indeed. I ask you and Madame Bryant to say nothing of this for now. I shall be in touch if we discover anything more. Oh, and, Captain Bryant, please take care. There is still a murderer at large.' The inspector hung up and Matt replaced the receiver before going back to Kitty.

'What is it? Have they arrested him?' Kitty asked almost before he sat down. He guessed his expression must have alerted her that things hadn't gone as they had thought.

'Yves Mangan is dead. Murdered in his apartment. The inspector thinks he let the killer in, and they hit him over the head with a bronze he had in his hallway,' Matt said.

Kitty gasped. 'Oh no, that's dreadful. That would mean that he and whoever killed Simone must have been in cahoots. It's the only possible explanation that makes any sense.'

'The question is who could that person be? Is it someone we've already spoken to or someone else entirely who has been outside of this enquiry all along?' Matt said.

'Marie is the obvious choice,' Kitty said slowly, a frown puckered her forehead as she spoke.

'I expect that is what Inspector LeJeune will think too,' Matt agreed. This news about the murder of Yves Mangan had shocked him and he could see that Kitty felt the same way. After visiting Yvette Blanc it had all seemed so clear that Yves must have been Simone's murderer and the person who had attacked Nathalie.

'What shall we do now? We can't just sit here and wait for the inspector to call again. He will be very busy,' Kitty said, as she gazed out at the people sauntering past the windows of the hotel.

'Let's go out for a few hours. We could go to the gardens at the Tuileries or back to Montmartre to explore. The weather is so glorious, and we will be leaving soon. There is nothing else we can do at the moment and perhaps inspiration might strike while we are out,' Matt suggested.

He knew Kitty would be restless and unsettled after hearing about Yves Mangan. He was sure she would have liked to have seen the latest crime scene for herself, but they had to let Inspector LeJeune and the gendarmes do their job.

'Yes, you're right. Let's go to Montmartre. We didn't visit the market when we were there before and it might provide a good distraction until we hear something more.' Kitty gathered up her belongings.

* * *

The trip to Montmartre proved to be a good choice. Kitty relaxed a little more as she and Matt browsed the colourful stalls between the iron pillars of the market. The area was bright with many flower stalls and the warm air softly perfumed. Her mind kept returning, however, to the puzzle of Yves Mangan's death. Surely, it had to be Marie who he had been working with. Who else could it have been?

She couldn't see it being Sir Humphrey. Why would he have used a go-between? That made no sense. Julian too didn't seem to have any connection to Yvette Blanc, and he wasn't short of money. So, she didn't see how he could have worked with Yves.

Unless, she shivered as she picked up a plump, juicy lemon to examine it, Julian had killed Yves to avenge Simone's death if he had discovered somehow that the couturier had stolen Simone's designs and murdered her.

Kitty continued to hold the lemon in her hand. Then there was Nathalie, she could have sold her sister's designs and murdered Simone if her sister had discovered what she'd done. But then Nathalie had been attacked. Had that been Yves, her partner in crime? Had he come to try and get something from her?

Patricia too knew both sisters. She lived with them, and she worked with them and with Monsieur Mangan. What if Patty had stolen the designs or killed Simone?

'Darling, I think you need to purchase that piece of fruit or return it to the stall,' Matt murmured in her ear.

'Oh.' Kitty realised the stallholder was watching her closely, so she fumbled in her purse to find a few francs to purchase the lemon and a small bag of cherries.

'You were miles away there,' Matt remarked with a smile as she retook his arm and offered him a cherry from the brown paper bag.

'I know, I keep thinking about the case. I can't help it,' Kitty apologised as he took a cherry and popped it into his mouth.

'I understand. I feel the same way,' Matt confessed as they made their way out of the market and back into the bright, afternoon sunshine. He disposed of the cherry stone in a nearby bin and they walked along to a small pavement café.

A red-and-white-striped canvas stall had been set up nearby where a puppeteer was entertaining a small group of children. They paused to watch for a moment before choosing a table in the shade of a large umbrella. After ordering a lemonade each they continued to sit back and enjoy the sights and sounds of Montmartre.

'Are you going to tell me what you were thinking while you were fondling that lemon?' Matt leaned back in his chair and grinned at her.

Kitty blushed. 'I really was lost in thought, wasn't I? No wonder the poor stallholder gave me such a funny look.' Kitty returned his smile and went over the ideas she'd had about who may have been working with Yves Mangan.

She hated bringing Julian's name up since it seemed so disloyal to Eliza, but she had to put her personal feelings to one side. Matt listened carefully.

'I can see your ideas match mine. I expect Inspector LeJeune's thought processes will also be running along similar lines.' He traced a finger down the outside of his lemonade glass, following the condensation where it had formed.

Kitty smiled. 'I wish he would make an arrest so we could enjoy this last little bit of our holiday. That sounds dreadfully selfish with two people dead, and Nathalie attacked.'

'No, it's understandable, I think, especially when we know Eliza and Julian and have no desire to see them entangled in all of this.' Matt gave her a sympathetic glance.

Kitty sipped her drink and continued to idly look around at the people passing by.

'Look, isn't that Patty over there?' Kitty sat up straighter in her seat and waved her arm vigorously in the air.

Patricia seemed to notice her and murmured something to the girl who was walking with her, before leaving her companion and coming over to their table. She was carrying a large leather satchel, and her pretty face was flushed almost as red as the curls peeping out from under her straw summer hat.

'Gosh, you do look hot. Come and sit down, we'll get you a drink.' Kitty pulled out the vacant chair beside her and patted the cane seat invitingly.

Patty sank down on the seat. 'That sounds divine. I've just come from a job, and I feel completely exhausted.'

Matt caught the attention of one of the waiters and ordered Patty a lemonade.

'This is so kind. I've been doing a shoot for a department store modelling winter fashions for their catalogue. I mean, wearing furs on a day like today under hot lights. I thought I was gonna get a heatstroke.' Patty pounced on her drink when it arrived and downed half the glass straight off.

'I don't envy you,' Kitty said.

'And all everyone could talk about was what Marie Dido did yesterday to Yvette Blanc. Did you know about it?' Patty asked, her eyes wide.

'About Marie hurling ink over Yvette? Yes, we saw Marie last night and visited Yvette this morning,' Matt said.

'I think Marie must have lost her mind. It's so unlike her. No one cares much for Yvette Blanc, she's kinda a cold fish. Very businesslike, if you know what I mean. Why would Marie do that though?' Patty asked as she took another gulp of her drink.

'You know Sir Humphrey has shares in House of Dido? Well, he was negotiating to sell them to Yvette Blanc behind Marie's back,' Kitty explained.

'Wow! Well I guess that would have set the cat among the pigeons.' Patty's delicately pencilled eyebrows lifted in astonishment. 'Nathalie was supposed to be booked for the shoot this morning too, but she didn't show up. I hope she's all right. I spoke to her last night, and she seemed fine. I felt kinda guilty you know about leaving her in the apartment by herself.'

'Does she often not turn up for jobs?' Kitty asked.

'She is kinda unreliable. It's one of the reasons I think she used to get booked at the same time as Simone. Simone would always make sure they were on time. Nathalie on her own is sometimes late and things,' Patty said as she wafted her free hand in front of her face to cool herself down. 'I was thinking I should drop in on her just in case she's not well or something. I do need to talk to her.'

'She may just be resting,' Kitty suggested, looking at Matt. She hoped that was the case and that no harm had befallen the girl. After what had happened to Yves Mangan it was rather worrying to hear of the girl's failure to turn up for work.

'True. It seems to be kinda the day for strange stuff. The girl they got to replace her at the last minute came from House of Dido. She said that Marie obviously wasn't there and that Monsieur Mangan hadn't gone in either. The woman running the workshop wasn't very happy at all,' Patty said.

'Oh, dear.' Kitty hoped Patty wasn't going to ask them anything about Monsieur Mangan. Matt had given his word to Inspector LeJeune that they would refrain from letting the news out for the time being.

'I suppose I should go to the apartment to see Nathalie. My father telephoned me last night and he's flying in from London again tomorrow. He wants me to return to the States with him. This whole business of Simone being killed and Nathalie being attacked has bothered him no end. He wants me to sell the apartment. I guess I should let Nathalie know so she can figure out what she wants to do.' Patty looked less flushed now than when she had arrived.

'Do you want us to come with you?' Kitty offered. 'I was just thinking that if Nathalie is unwell when you get there or if she is upset when you tell her about the apartment, it might be good to have some moral support.'

'That's awful sweet of you. I guess you've figured out that I'm kind of a wimp about this kind of stuff. My pop says I'm a people pleaser. I hate upsetting anyone, but truthfully I don't think I would want to carry on living with just Nathalie. I mean, she's nice and all, but Simone was more my friend than Nathalie. We used to have such fun together.' Patty looked sad. 'I miss her.'

'I don't blame your father for being worried about you. A lot has happened in a short space of time,' Matt said. 'Kitty and I are happy to give you some support. Nathalie too. She must be feeling very alone after losing Simone in such a dreadful way.'

'You're both so kind. I really do appreciate it.' Patricia seemed relieved that she didn't have to return to her apartment alone. They finished their drinks and hailed a taxi together to go over to the apartment.

'This feels so much nicer than battling the Métro. It's so hot and stuffy down there right now,' Patty said as she enjoyed the breeze flowing in through the partly opened window of the taxi. 'No wonder everyone is heading for the coast or the mountains with this heat.'

Matt paid for the cab as the girls got out. Kitty glanced up at the front of the building.

'The windows are open,' she said. The fine voile curtains were blowing in the faint breeze above the stone ledge.

'Great, I guess that means she must be home. I hope she's all right.' Patty looked anxious as she led the way inside and up to the apartment.

'Nathalie, it's me, Patty,' the American girl called out as she unlocked her front door. 'Captain and Mrs Bryant are with me. Are you okay?'

Nathalie suddenly appeared in the doorway of the sitting room. She was elegantly dressed in a soft crêpe de chine summer dress in shades of lemon and pale green. Her hair was styled and she was nicely made up.

'Oh, I was expecting Julian to call. He said he'd drop by this afternoon.' Nathalie looked first at her flatmate and then at Kitty and Matt.

'That's kind of him,' Kitty said as they entered the compact room.

She noticed it had been swept and the place tidied up. Fresh flowers were in a couple of crystal vases and the air smelt of roses and violets. In fact, it looked to her almost as if Nathalie had been setting the scene for romance rather than a visit from her late sister's recently bereaved boyfriend.

'I was concerned when you didn't arrive for the catalogue photographs this morning. I tried to telephone at lunchtime but there was no answer,' Patty said.

Kitty could see that Nathalie's flatmate had also noticed the changes in the room and appeared slightly bewildered. The small knick-knacks which Patty had said had been Simone's were all missing. Kitty knew she had swept some up that had been broken in the attack, but she wondered where the rest had gone.

'I expect that was when I had gone out to get some groceries. I didn't feel well this morning so thought I should take a little time to rest and to make myself feel better,' Nathalie said. 'You really shouldn't worry so, Patty.'

'I ran into Kitty and Matt as I was on my way here. They were concerned about you too. You heard what happened yesterday I suppose between Marie Dido and Yvette Blanc?' Patty said.

'*Oui*, I was shocked. I heard about it from Julian when he telephoned. His mother had told him about it. She visited Marie yesterday evening he said. She is standing surety for her.' Nathalie busied herself rearranging the velvet and silk covered cushions on the sofa as she spoke.

'Monsieur Mangan also didn't turn up to open House of Dido this morning,' Patty said.

'That is very odd. Perhaps he is looking for a new job. I mean if Marie is so unpredictable then who can blame him.' Nathalie's tone was dismissive.

Matt's gaze met Kitty's. She could tell he was baffled by Nathalie's odd behaviour too.

CHAPTER TWENTY-TWO

'Anyway, Nathalie, I wanted to see you to talk about the apartment. It's just that my father wants me to go back home to the States with him. Simone's murder and the break-in here has him worried. That means that I shall probably have to sell this place.' Patty followed Nathalie around the room as the girl continued to tweak and tidy the already immaculate apartment.

'Then that is what you must do. You can tell me when you wish me to go and I shall make arrangements to vacate the apartment.' Nathalie sounded unconcerned.

'I really wish I could stay on here, but Pops is worried about my safety and well, he holds the purse strings. Are you sure you'll be okay with it?' Patty persisted.

The doorbell rang and Nathalie virtually pushed Patty over in her haste to get to the hall. 'That will be Julian now. I am perfectly fine, Patty. I am not an *enfant*. I can find a new place to live.' She paused to fluff her hair in the hallway mirror before opening the door with a beaming smile.

'Julian, come in. Patty is here at the moment with Captain and Madame Bryant, but I am sure they are soon leaving.'

Nathalie ushered Julian into the now quite crowded sitting room.

Julian shook hands with Matt and greeted Kitty and Patty warmly with kisses on their cheeks.

'You all need not rush away on my account. I merely came to see if Nathalie was recovered. She still sounded shaken when she telephoned me,' Julian said as he settled down on the sofa next to Kitty.

She frowned, surely Nathalie had said Julian had telephoned her.

'Would anyone like a drink?' Patty asked, ignoring Nathalie's pointed looks.

'No, thank you, Patty.' Kitty declined the offer, as did Matt.

'I'm sure you both must have lots to see in Paris before your vacation ends.' Nathalie looked at Kitty.

'Actually, it's Kitty's grandmother who is the real tourist. She and my mother are having a wonderful time, despite everything that has happened. They are reminiscing and revisiting the places of their younger days. I think my mother wants to take it all in one last time before she leaves,' Julian answered Nathalie before Kitty could speak.

'Your mother is very kind. Grams was so ill just before we came away. Being with Eliza again has done her a power of good. I know she's looking forward to having her move back to England.' Kitty smiled gratefully at Julian who appeared oblivious to Nathalie's barely concealed desire to get rid of them from the apartment.

Nathalie didn't appear pleased by the conversation and looked even less happy when Patty poured herself a large glass of cold water infused with slices of lemon and lime, before perching on the arm of the sofa next to Julian.

'How are you feeling now, Julian?' Patty asked. 'Simone's death was such a dreadful shock to all of us, but I know it has been especially hard for you.' Her tone was gentle and concerned.

'I'm bearing up, as they say. I still don't think it's really sunk in yet. Until the police say a funeral can go ahead it feels unreal. As if she'll walk through the door at any minute, laughing and chatting as usual.' He glanced at the door leading to the hallway, a deep sadness evident in his eyes.

'I don't suppose you have heard anything yet about when the funeral can be arranged?' Matt looked at Nathalie.

'*Non*, I suppose the inspector will let me know.' Nathalie's tone was abrupt.

'I'm sorry, Nathalie, *chérie*. This is so difficult for you too. I'm really bringing everyone's spirits down,' Patty apologised.

'No, it's all right, Patty. It's good to talk of Simone. It makes her alive again to know she was loved and is missed,' Julian reassured her and placed his hand on the model's arm in a gesture of gratitude.

Kitty noticed Nathalie's eyes narrow as he did so.

Julian glanced around the room. 'It looks different in here. Was anything stolen when that man broke in?'

'Some of Simone's ornaments were broken. The ones she had collected from that little stall she liked on the market that sells the second-hand things.' Patty looked around as if she too were suddenly realising that more things were gone than just the ones that Kitty had swept up after the attack.

'I have packed some of them away, the ones that were left. I could not bear to see them knowing how much Simone had loved them,' Nathalie said.

Patty made sympathetic noises at this admission, but Kitty was not so convinced by the girl's story. She thought she had detected a calculating expression that had flitted across Nathalie's face before she had given her explanation.

'Do you have the little glass ornament of the two lovebirds?' Julian asked Nathalie. 'I was wondering, if you still had it, if I might have it as a memento of Simone. She always said it reminded her of the two of us.'

Nathalie looked sad. 'I'm afraid that was one of the ones that was shattered when the man attacked me.'

Julian looked downcast at this. Kitty remembered just how smashed and broken some of the ornaments had been when she'd swept them up. How had so many things been damaged? She was sure most of Simone's collection had been away from the door on the windowsill.

Some of the things had been in tiny fragments. At the time she hadn't questioned it, thinking it was because the things were old. Now she came to think of it, some of the glass fragments had seemed almost ground into the rug. As if someone had deliberately pressed their heel on them.

'It's shocking really how much damage was done. It must have been quite a struggle, Nathalie?' Kitty tried to look and sound sympathetic as she probed.

'*Mais oui*, he flew into this room like a madman. I tried to escape but I was pursued around the furniture as I tried to evade his clutches. If it had not been for something disturbing him I do not think I would have survived,' Nathalie said.

'You were fortunate to escape with relatively few injuries.' Matt joined in the conversation as if sensing that Kitty was following a line of enquiry.

'Yes, indeed. What an ordeal,' Julian agreed.

Nathalie shifted uncomfortably on her seat as everyone looked at her.

'Perhaps there is something else of Simone's that you could have, Julian? I'm sure Nathalie would be pleased to give you something,' Patty suggested. 'There were still a few of her things that were unbroken. Those china Siamese cats perhaps that used to be on the sideboard? I know you never cared for them.' She smiled at Nathalie.

'I'll have to look later. I've packed everything away for now.' Nathalie glared at the hapless Patty.

'Of course, forgive me. I shall have packing of my own here to do soon enough,' Patty said.

'Oh, why's that?' Julian looked up at the model as she continued to drink her water.

'I'm returning to the States with my father. He is concerned about my safety staying here in Paris. I'm sure my great-aunt has fuelled his fears telling him tales about what's gone on. I just told Nathalie that I shall probably be selling this apartment,' Patty explained.

'I can understand his concerns. My mother probably has some extra packing cases. I think she over ordered the amount if that would help you,' Julian said.

'That's real kind. Thank you,' Patty said, before taking another gulp of her water.

'You will miss your *maman* very much when she is gone to England I suppose. Still, you have many friends here.' Nathalie looked at Julian.

'I think she and Kitty's grandmother have found her a potential house to rent in Devon. I was going to stay here in Paris but now with Simone gone, I think I'm going to join her there, at least for a while. My job has said I can transfer,' Julian said.

'You are leaving Paris? Going to England? For good?' Nathalie stared at him.

'I'm not certain if it will be permanent but I need to get out of Paris, a least for a while. I can help Mother to get settled too,' Julian explained.

Nathalie rose from her seat and disappeared into the kitchen. 'I think perhaps I too need a drink,' she said.

'Everyone deserts Paris in the summer. At least that's what your mother said, Julian. It seems it's true, but I wish it was for happier reasons.' Kitty smiled gently at him.

Nathalie returned from the kitchen with a glass of water like Patty's.

'What will you do, Nathalie? Will you stay in Paris, or will you move elsewhere?' Julian asked.

The girl looked dazed, Kitty thought, as if she was still processing what Julian had said a moment ago about returning to England with his mother.

'I do not know. I hadn't thought. I imagined that you would still be here. You said you had found an apartment. My sister said you had gone together to see it.' Her voice was low, and Kitty could see she was gripping the glass so tightly her knuckles had whitened.

Julian sighed, sadness returning to his expression. 'That's true. We did. It was going to be our first home together after we were married. It was perfect, everything we had dreamed of. Now though, with Simone gone, I'm glad we hadn't signed the lease. I don't think I could face going there again.'

'But you could find a new apartment, make new memories here,' Nathalie suggested. 'Why would you all go and leave me behind?'

Her voice had risen slightly, and Julian and Patty stared at her.

'Perhaps you too should go away from Paris, at least for a while,' Patty suggested. 'Do you have friends or family where you could visit?'

Nathalie's eyes were flinty as she looked at her flatmate. 'Simone and I have no family, not here. I know you have said I may stay here for a while until the apartment is sold but I shall need to find a room somewhere. If House of Dido closes, then I shall also need a job. I don't have anywhere to go.'

'Oh, Nathalie, you know I'm not throwing you out on the streets. It will take a while to get this place up on the market and sold. I won't rush you at all. I just wanted to give you plenty of time to find somewhere nice,' Patty tried to comfort her.

'I thought that perhaps with Julian here, he could assist me.' Nathalie looked at him. 'But if you are going to England, then I don't know what I shall do. I have never visited there,' she said. 'I have heard it is very nice, with many opportunities.'

Kitty could recognise a hint when she heard it.

'You and your mother will have quite a lot to do when you relocate. I suppose it will be quite sometime before you are in a position to invite guests,' Kitty said, looking at Julian.

Julian appeared relieved by her comment. It seemed that he had also picked up on Nathalie's hint. 'Yes, Mother said she had found a small place to rent for three months and then she intends to purchase a house. Your grandmother and her friends will assist her. I shall have a lot to do with settling into the Exeter office. It's much smaller than the one here, of course, and I shall need to get used to speaking English more than French again.'

'When do you think you will leave?' Patty asked as she finished her drink.

'Probably not long after Kitty and Matt here have gone. Mother is keen to get going now she's almost packed and her place has been decorated for sale. She thinks she may have a buyer already. I presume that the inspector will grant me permission to go. Hopefully he'll catch Simone's murderer before much longer.' Julian leaned back on the sofa.

'So soon.' Nathalie looked horrified.

'I'll be here until after Simone's funeral obviously, but then, yes, the sooner I can go the better I think,' Julian said.

'Poor Julian.' Patty touched his arm in sympathy as she rose to place her empty water glass back in the kitchen.

'It's such a pity that you didn't get a better look at the man who attacked you. Any clue may have helped Inspector LeJeune to identify him, even if it was something small,' Kitty mused as she looked at Nathalie.

'He wore a mask, and it all happened so fast. I was taken by surprise,' Nathalie said.

'You said he never spoke either?' Kitty continued.

'*Non*, not one word. I cracked open the door and in he flew. He almost knocked me from my feet down the hall and into this room.' Nathalie waved her free hand in a dismissive gesture.

'Was he tall, short, skinny, plump? Dressed in conventional clothing?' Julian asked.

'It was quick. He was average I would say in height and build. He had a dark coat and trousers and this black mask over his face so only his eyes were showing.' Nathalie shifted uncomfortably as they all began to ask questions.

'What colour were his eyes?' Patty asked as she emerged from the kitchen.

'Greyish blue, I think. I don't know.' Nathalie's voice rose slightly.

'The police found a mask discarded on the pavement outside the front of the building,' Matt said.

'The man must have ripped it off and discarded it as he ran away.' Nathalie looked at Julian.

'He must have been after something very specific, this burglar.' Julian's brow creased. 'He passed the apartments downstairs and came straight for this one.'

'Perhaps he thought it was empty. Although, then why wear a mask?' Patty looked puzzled.

'Who knows what these criminals have in their minds,' Nathalie snapped.

'I wonder why none of the neighbours came out to see what was happening? He must have made quite a racket. Monsieur Poitier usually comes out to complain if there is so much as a squeak on the stairs,' Patty said.

'I don't know. I was unconscious and do not know what happened.' Nathalie's tone was quite shrill now. 'It was all very fast. There was so much crashing about. I fought for my life.'

'Inspector LeJeune interviewed all the neighbours, and no one mentioned the noise until they said they heard you scream for help,' Kitty said.

Nathalie banged her almost-empty glass down so hard on the table that some of the liquid jumped up and splashed over the top leaving a small puddle on the polished wooden surface.

'Why are you asking me all these things?' Nathalie leapt up from her seat and whirled around to glare first at Kitty and then at Patty. 'It was a most terrible ordeal. I could have died.'

'We are just trying to see if there is something that could help in finding Simone's killer.' Patty stared wide-eyed at her flatmate. 'I'm sorry, Nathalie. We didn't mean to upset you.'

'Mother was still worried about Marie this morning. She telephoned her first thing before breakfast. That business with Madame Blanc is very strange. And Sir Humphrey receiving Simone's designs through his door late at night.' Julian shook his head in faint disbelief as he changed the subject.

Kitty reached into her bag and pulled out the magazine. 'I forgot to show this to you, Patty. You had better take a look too, Nathalie. You may recognise the design in the advertisement.' She showed the picture to the two girls.

Julian stared at it too. 'That's one of Simone's designs. It was one she was very proud of. You must recognise it, Nathalie. It was in the bundle she gave to Monsieur Mangan to show Marie. The ones that went missing when she was killed.'

'Was it in the package that the gendarme discovered at Sir Humphrey's apartment?' Kitty asked. 'Does anyone know? Nathalie, did the inspector ask you about the designs they found? Or show you them?'

'I don't know. Simone had made a lot, and I think some of them are still missing.' The girl ran her tongue nervously over her lips as she answered. 'Maybe Sir Humphrey had it.'

'Oh, let's go get the folder and take another look. Maybe we can figure it out,' Patty suggested. 'After all, the police did arrest Sir Humphrey at one point. Perhaps he is guilty after all.'

CHAPTER TWENTY-THREE

'*Non, ce n'est pas possible.* I have put them all away.' Nathalie glared at Patty, her hands were balled into fists at her side.

'Why not? You have Simone's designs. Surely you can get the folder out again. I mean, this could be important,' Patty said.

'Yes, Patty's right. Sir Humphrey could be the murderer. Where are they, Nathalie? We should take a look and see if we can work it out,' Julian agreed.

He moved forward in his seat as if eager to go and collect the file himself.

'*Non.* I have said no. I do not wish to revisit them. I cannot bear it,' Nathalie said.

'Why not? Surely you want to try and help the police to find who killed your sister. If Sir Humphrey is guilty then we need to try and assist the inspector to capture him.' Kitty had a sudden horrifying feeling that she knew why Nathalie was trying to throw obstacles in their path. She thought it was very unlikely that Sir Humphrey was the killer. It seemed to her that perhaps Simone's murderer was present in the room right now.

'It is too distressing for me. Like I said, I have packed away all of Simone's things.' Nathalie looked imploringly at Julian. 'You understand my feelings?'

'I don't know, Nathalie. It seems very odd to me,' Kitty spoke out again before Julian could reply. 'Do you even have the folder still? Or were you the person who worked with Yves Mangan to steal your sister's work to sell to Madame Blanc?'

Her accusation seemed to hang in the silence for a moment as everyone turned to stare at Nathalie.

The girl shook her head, her dark hair tumbling around cheeks that had suddenly grown pale. '*Non*. Julian, do not listen to her. I beg of you. She is trying to cause trouble. She is working for Sir Humphrey. That is why she says such terrible things.'

'Then where is the folder, Nathalie? Tell me and I'll fetch it if you don't wish to get it. That will soon clear the matter up,' Julian said.

'I can find it. I know where Nathalie has probably put it,' Patty offered and slid off the arm of the sofa as if about to go to Simone's room to try and retrieve the designs.

'No, it is not there. I forbid you to go in my room. It is gone.' Nathalie moved as if she were about to physically prevent Patty or Julian from trying to leave the room.

'What do you mean gone? Gone where? You mean you *have* sold the designs? All of Simone's work?' Julian asked.

He looked at Nathalie as if he were suddenly seeing her for the first time. An expression of dawning horror on his face.

Nathalie's gaze skittered around the room as if weighing up her chances of how to escape from her predicament. The incriminating magazine still lay open on the table where she had dropped it.

'You stole the designs and sold them to Madame Blanc behind Simone's back?' Patty glared at her flatmate.

'Monsieur Mangan, he arranged things. He did everything. I knew about it, that is all. It was not my idea,' Nathalie said.

'Julian, I agreed for Simone. So her work would have a buyer.' She looked imploringly at Julian. 'You must believe me. I thought it would be a good thing for her.'

'A good thing to steal her work. A good thing to sell it behind her back to a buyer you carefully chose not to tell her about. How could you? You knew Simone had her own plans for her work. You knew what it meant to her, the plans she had,' Julian said.

'I was going to surprise her. Yves, he said it would be good. It could lead to more work for her, give her the break into designing that she wanted.' Nathalie looked pleadingly at Julian as if desperate to convince him that she was telling the truth.

'When did Simone find out what you'd done?' Kitty asked.

'She didn't know. She didn't find out. Monsieur Mangan, he had the designs. He took them from the envelope. I swear, Julian, you must believe me.' Nathalie broke into a torrent of French.

Julian had his head between his hands as if trying to shut out her pleas. 'I cannot believe what I'm hearing. This is awful, just awful. You betrayed your own sister.'

'It was Yves, he persuaded me that it would be good for Simone,' Nathalie persisted.

'Was it Yves Mangan who broke into this apartment? Or did you just stage the whole thing yourself to throw suspicion about what happened to your sister away from you?' Kitty asked, looking at Nathalie.

Julian raised his head and stared at Kitty. 'What are you saying? That she faked the break-in?'

'That's exactly what I'm saying. That there was no masked man who broke in here and assaulted Nathalie. I think she staged the whole thing herself and faked her injuries. She smashed Simone's things on purpose out of spite. Then she dropped a mask out of the window before calling out for help.

That's why the neighbours didn't hear anything until then,' Kitty said.

'Oh my gosh, I think you're right.' Patty looked at Kitty, her eyes wide. 'Everything that was broken was Simone's. All of her little ornaments, even the Tiffany lamp in the hall that she was so proud of. Nothing of mine or Nathalie's was damaged. It all makes sense. It was you, wasn't it? Everything? Oh, dear heaven, you killed her too, didn't you? It was you!' She turned to Nathalie.

'When we found you holding those scissors, you hadn't just picked them up like you claimed. You were the one who'd used them.' Julian's face was stern.

Patty was shaking and she moved closer to Julian as if seeking protection from her flatmate.

'*Non*, it was not me! It was Yves Mangan. He was the one. He took those scissors backstage. He had a fake envelope which he pretended had Simone's designs that he was returning.' Nathalie lunged forward and grasped Julian's arm. 'I didn't do it.'

Julian tried to shake her off as he shielded Patty. 'I don't understand. How could you do something so terrible? What had Simone ever done to you? She was your sister. She loved you.'

'*Non*, Julian!' Nathalie begged.

'I think I should call the police station.' Patty made a move towards the telephone as Matt and Kitty leapt up from their seats.

Nathalie instantly released Julian's arm and flew across to Patty. Before anyone could prevent her she tugged the telephone cable free from the wall, effectively cutting off the line. Everyone seemed frozen in place, too stunned to move by the scene that was unfolding right in front of them. Nathalie herself clutched the wire, staring at it almost blankly.

'Simone had found out what you had done. You and

Monsieur Mangan. I presume he needed some money, and he was jealous of Simone. She was a threat to his job so if Madame Blanc had her designs she would be out of his way, and he would benefit financially,' Matt said.

Nathalie rounded on him, the telephone cable still dangling from her hand. 'Yves was the one responsible. Simone could never have had her own label at House of Dido. Yves would have made certain of that. I did what I could to try to help my sister. He used me.'

'That's not true. You were jealous of Simone and worried she was going to leave modelling behind her. It was you who used Monsieur Mangan. You saw your chance when you found the scissors backstage. Yves had told you he intended to destroy the envelope so that Simone would believe the contents were gone. You knew though that it was only a matter of time before she discovered you were involved,' Kitty said.

'Why though? I don't understand. Why would anyone want to kill Simone over a few designs? She would have forgiven you.' Julian looked broken and bewildered.

'Was it just the money?' Patty asked.

'Madame Blanc paid well. Simone was a fool. She was planning to throw everything away to pursue a dream. It was all right for her. She was the beautiful one, the one everyone wanted on the catwalk. She had Julian and his money to back her up. He had even forgiven her for the child. All the plans for a wedding, a new apartment. I was to be left behind with nothing. Yes, the money was nice, but it wasn't everything.' Nathalie threw the telephone cable down as if suddenly realising that she was still holding on to it. 'Julian, *mon cher*, you must understand.' She stretched out her hand as if to touch him once more.

Julian physically recoiled away from her, shrinking back against the leather sofa as if trying to climb inside it.

'You hated Simone. You were jealous of her. Jealous of her

talent and her success and most of all you were jealous of her because of Julian,' Kitty said.

'Me?' Julian stared at Kitty.

'Nathalie is in love with you. You must have realised. She thought with Simone out of the way she could take her place. That was why Simone had to die. It wasn't just the theft of the designs. It was everything. Nathalie wanted what Simone had. The jobs, the success, money, her fiancé.' Kitty could see Matt out of the corner of her eye, edging very slowly around the room towards the door.

She guessed he intended to block Nathalie's exit should the girl try to escape.

A look of revulsion crossed Julian's face as he looked at Nathalie. 'That would never happen. I have no idea why you would ever think that way. I loved Simone and only Simone. I could never be with you, never.'

Nathalie shook her head vigorously. Angry red spots of colour flashed onto her pale cheeks. '*Non, non, non.* This is not what is supposed to happen. This cannot be. With Simone gone there is nothing now to keep us apart. We should be together like I planned.' She dived towards him and he moved out of her way.

'No, get away from me. How could you even think like that? I could never be with you. Never love you.' Julian pushed her away.

'*Non, mon amour*, it was just Simone that blinded you. She was untrue to you. She was seeing Sir Humphrey trying to get him to back her. She didn't deserve to be your wife. She would never have loved you as I love you,' Nathalie wailed.

'Her meetings with Sir Humphrey were simply business meetings. She told us that,' Patty rounded on her flatmate. 'There was no reason not to believe her. You're just plumb crazy to think otherwise.'

'It was probably you that kept dropping sly hints to my

mother, poisoning her against Simone by suggesting she was two-timing me. You told her you thought Simone was seeing Sir Humphrey.' Realisation seemed to dawn on Julian's face. 'Did you tip her off about Simone's daughter too?'

Patty stared at Julian as this news sank in. 'Daughter?'

'Simone had a child in Nantes. I knew all about it and understood,' Julian explained.

'I would be a much better daughter-in-law. I am respectable. I would happily keep your home and cook and clean. Simone was too busy with her big ideas. She would never have made you happy,' Nathalie retorted.

'I could never marry you if you were the last woman on earth. You're a monster,' Julian snapped.

He plunged towards her without warning. Nathalie screamed and skipped out of his way before producing a small, sharp knife from the pocket of her dress. The steel blade glinted in the sunlight through the open window as she waved it around in the air in front of her.

'You will all stay where you are,' she warned.

'Put the knife down. This is ridiculous, you've done enough damage already by killing Simone.' Julian eyed her warily.

Nathalie smiled, a grim smirk highlighting the coldness in her eyes. 'We could be together you and I, leave these idiots behind. We could go to England together. Yes, that is how it will be. We can make a new plan. I will look after you. You will forget Simone ever existed.'

Kitty saw Matt edge closer to the door. She wasn't certain now if he intended to block the girl's escape, go for help, or try to get around to disarm her. She could only think that his plans had changed when Nathalie had produced her knife.

'I don't think so,' Julian said. 'You're insane.'

Patty was pressed back against the wall, her gaze fixed on the blade her flatmate was brandishing in the air. 'Nathalie, please, don't do this.'

'*Pour quoi?* You do not care. No, you are going to go away and live in America with your rich father. You would leave me here, not even with a home. You were always Simone's friend more than mine. You and your coffees out in the city and your silly jokes that did not include me. Going to parties and events leaving me behind without a care. Always left behind like an afterthought.' The corners of Nathalie's dark-red lipsticked mouth lifted into a cruel smile as she brought the blade closer to Patty. 'Did you think I didn't know? Even when Simone was dead you couldn't wait to leave me here alone.'

'My great-aunt needed me, and I had work,' Patty protested, fear showing in her bright-blue eyes.

'How convenient for you,' Nathalie sneered.

Matt moved and Nathalie turned sharply. 'Not so fast, Captain Bryant. You and your wife think you are so clever, *n'est ce pas?* You have it all worked out. Well, you are mistaken. Julian will come around. He just needs time to realise his mistake. Then he and I will be together. We will marry and live in England.' She looked at Julian. 'I had hoped we would move in together into that nice apartment you found with Simone. I went to see it, you know. The agent was most kind and showed me around. I had it all planned. Our furniture, the curtains, where we would place our bed. *Eh bien*, I can do that again in an English cottage.'

It was clear to Kitty that Nathalie's narrow grasp on reality was growing ever thinner. Her blind belief that Julian secretly returned her feelings was divorcing her from the truth. Her heart thumped against her ribs as Nathalie refocused her attention on Matt.

With the telephone out of action there had to be a way to disarm the girl and raise the alarm before someone got hurt. She wished Julian would humour the girl and play along. He might be able to sweet talk her into giving up her weapon before someone got hurt.

It was plain, however, that either Julian didn't agree or was too shocked to think of pretending to cooperate. 'You got the agent to show you the apartment Simone and I intended to lease?'

Nathalie shrugged. 'I told her my sister had asked me to take a look and measure up for some things to make certain the furniture would fit. She was *très agreeable*. She told me all of your plans.'

'And what was your plan if Simone had discovered the theft of her work? Did Monsieur Mangan intend to assist you to kill your sister? Or were you gonna murder her anyway?' Patty asked, wincing as Nathalie flashed the tip of the blade near her face.

'Sir Humphrey was perfectly placed to be the scapegoat. Obviously he has been seen with Simone. She has shown him her work, and he has offered to make the introduction to Madame Blanc if Marie doesn't buy her designs. It was easy to slip some of the designs through his door late at night. Then to imply to Inspector LeJeune that perhaps it might have been Sir Humphrey who was my attacker. Although I was careful not to be too specific in case it didn't work.'

'And Monsieur Mangan? Where did he fit into all of this scheming?' Matt asked.

'He was feeling guilty about taking the scissors from the workshop. I think he thought perhaps the gendarmes might discover fingerprints or that Patty might have seen him with them. He knew that it must have been me who killed Simone, but he could not say so without implicating himself. His conscience was becoming annoying.' Nathalie scowled as she spoke.

'So, you dealt with him too?' Matt asked.

There was a horrified gasp from Patty and Julian as the implication of what Matt had just let slip sank in.

'You mean she has attacked Monsieur Mangan? Is that why

he didn't go into work this morning?' Patty asked, looking first at Matt then at Kitty.

'It would be most foolish of me to leave any loose ends lying around. Yves had served his purpose, and he was of no more use to me.' Nathalie sounded almost bored by the conversation. 'As indeed the three of you are of no use. Julian and I will be leaving, so I suggest you move aside.' She moved the blade from Patty to Matt forcing him to raise his hands where she could see them and to sidle away from the door.

'You must have lost your mind if you think I would wish to accompany you anywhere. The only place for you is prison,' Julian said.

'It would be simpler if you came willingly but you will come with me.' Nathalie took the knife and traced it along Julian's cheekbone just breaking the skin sufficiently for it to bleed. 'You love me.'

Patty emitted a terrified squeak. 'Please go with her, Julian. Do as she says.'

Julian rose reluctantly from the sofa. Nathalie kept the blade at his throat.

'Now, Julian and Captain Bryant, you will both remove your ties, *s'il vous plaît*,' she instructed.

'What are you doing?' Patty asked.

'You don't think I shall leave the three of you here to alert Inspector LeJeune? Not without giving my beloved and I time to get away from here,' Nathalie scoffed.

Once both men had complied, Nathalie gestured to Kitty and Patty to sit back-to-back on the floor, before requesting that Matt tied the girls' hands behind their backs with his tie. Since Nathalie could clearly kill Julian if he didn't comply, Kitty saw Matt had no choice but to reluctantly obey. She winced as he was compelled to pull the silk material tight around their wrists.

'Now you, Captain Bryant, sit with your back to the radiator. Julian fasten your mother's friend to the heater. Make sure the knot is tight.' Nathalie watched to make certain Julian obeyed her orders and then got him to test the knot both on Kitty and Patty's bonds and on Matt's to make certain she was satisfied.

'Now, *mon amour*, we shall go. Remember that I can end you in seconds. So, I suggest you do whatever I tell you.' Nathalie bestowed a kiss on Julian's cheek just below the cut whilst keeping the knife at his throat. He flinched as she did so.

'Nathalie, I beg you, don't do this,' Patty implored as Julian was forced towards the door.

The sofa blocked Kitty's view as Nathalie propelled Julian from the room. A moment later the door to the apartment banged shut and they were gone.

CHAPTER TWENTY-FOUR

'We have to hurry and try and get out of these ties,' Kitty instructed Patty. 'Try and manoeuvre the knot round a little.'

'We need to get after them and alert Inspector LeJeune as quickly as possible. Julian's life could depend on it,' Matt agreed.

'I've managed to turn it. I think this is coming looser,' Patty said hopefully as she struggled with the bonds fastening her to Kitty. 'It's so darn tight.'

'Where do you think they could be going?' Kitty asked as she attempted to wriggle the knot round to Patty so that her fingers could work it loose.

'She won't risk taking public transport. Too difficult, especially if Julian is not cooperating. So that rules out buses and the Métro,' Matt said.

'Taxi perhaps?' Kitty suggested. 'No, I don't think that would work either. Patty, is there anywhere not too far away that perhaps was special to Julian and Simone? Somewhere quiet?'

Patty paused in her efforts for a fraction of a second. 'There's a little park, not too far away, just down the next street. There's a small wooden summer house where no one really goes as it's tucked away in the trees. Simone used to call it their love nest. It's by a little lake with water lilies. They would take a bottle of wine and some bread and cheese there for a picnic. Why? Do you think that's where she might go?'

'It's possible. She desperately wants to erase Julian's memories of Simone. To take everything that was Simone's and make it hers. So, she could well go there to start with, while she works out her next move.' Kitty's wrists were sore and chafed now but she was sure she felt the knot loosen.

'Phew, my wrists are so sore. I think it's moving though.' Patty wriggled a little more as she worked on the knot holding them together.

'I just hope Julian comes to his senses and plays along with her until he gets the opportunity to escape,' Matt muttered darkly.

Kitty shuddered. She couldn't bear to think of what an increasingly desperate Nathalie might do if he didn't cooperate.

'Oh, I think I'm almost there. Kitty, can you just move more toward me?' Patty asked excitedly.

Kitty did her best to comply and hitched closer. She suddenly felt the fabric bonds slacken as Patty managed to release the knot.

'That's it! We're free!' Kitty slid her hands out of the bonds at the same time as Patty.

'Patty, can you go to one of the neighbours who has a telephone and let the police know what's happened? Tell them where you think Nathalie may have taken Julian. I'll untie Matt and we'll head for this park.' Kitty suited her actions to her words, grabbing another knife from the kitchen to cut Matt free while Patty quickly gave them instructions on how to find the spot where she thought Nathalie might have gone.

Kitty used the serrated blade of a steak knife to saw through the last remnants of fabric binding Matt to the radiator. Patty hurried out of the apartment to alert her neighbours.

'Come on, at least we can see if Nathalie and Julian have gone to the park.' Matt winced as he rubbed his chafed and sore wrists before heading out with Kitty hard on his heels behind him.

'I just hope that we're not too late,' Kitty said.

She was forced to place a hand on her hat to stop it from blowing off her head as she ran along the deserted Parisian streets after Matt. Patty's directions proved to be accurate. Within a couple of minutes they arrived at a narrow gate in a set of wrought-iron railings bounding a green space filled with trees and flowers.

'The gate's open,' Kitty gasped as she peered into the park looking for any sign that Nathalie and Julian might have passed that way. 'I hope Julian has recovered his wits and is trying to cooperate with her.'

'I do too. I think he was just in complete shock over what she'd done. Now, Patty said to take the path towards the lake on the left-hand side. We had better be careful. If the place she suggested has a good view over the water then they could see us approach,' Matt said.

'Then we had better see if we can find some cover and avoid the main path.' Kitty's breathing had started to settle, and she was glad they were going to head toward the lake at a slower pace.

They followed the path for a few yards until they caught a brief glimpse of water ahead of them.

'This way,' Matt suggested, and they turned off the path and behind a belt of flowering shrubs.

Kitty could see the lake between the branches as they made their way as quietly and swiftly as possible along the side parallel to the path. Branches snagged at her clothes and a disgruntled squirrel chittered at them from a nearby tree.

As they drew closer to what Kitty assumed must be the head of the lake, Matt stopped suddenly. A small wooden structure in the style of a Chinese pagoda was in view. Painted in shades of faded blue-and-green with an ornate pantile roof, it was mostly hidden by flowering rhododendron bushes. The front was open and overlooked the lake, so it was a good thing they hadn't gone along the path.

'That must be it. It looks like the place Patty described,' Kitty said quietly in Matt's ear. 'Can you see them?'

She hoped the girl's suggestion for where they might have gone was correct.

'I think I can see Nathalie's dress. They must be sitting on a bench inside the summer house.' Matt inched forwards slowly and moved a branch aside so he could take a better look. 'Yes, it's definitely them. Nathalie seems to still have the knife at Julian's throat and she's talking.'

Kitty felt sick at the thought that anything bad might happen to Julian. Eliza would never recover. After losing her husband she doted on Julian. 'At least it seems calm at the moment.'

'We need to get closer if we can. We need to try and see or hear what's happening,' Matt murmured.

Kitty followed as he crept further round the strand of bushes. Their view of the couple was not quite so good but now at least they could hear what was being said. The park was quiet with just the faint sound of birdsong. There was the gentle burble of a small fountain in the centre of the water which made the large green lily pads with their creamy-white flowers bob to and fro on the surface.

It was an idyllic spot for lovers to come with a picnic and Kitty could see why Julian and Simone must have enjoyed coming there. How Julian must be feeling now she simply couldn't imagine.

'See how *très jolie* this is? We can bring our children here to feed the ducks when we return to Paris. Two children would be perfect, *un garçon et une fille*. After all you wouldn't wish to always live in England.' Nathalie appeared to still be convincing herself that she could take Simone's place in Julian's life.

'Nathalie, you must understand this is not easy for me,' Julian said.

Kitty breathed a small sigh of relief that it sounded as if he were trying to play along with her delusion.

'*Bien sûr*, but we have the rest of our lives together. You will soon forget Simone and any of this unpleasantness,' Nathalie said.

'I wish you would move the knife. It is difficult to think when you are holding me captive,' Julian suggested.

'When you are more composed, then of course I shall move it,' Nathalie agreed. 'But for now, it is best you think carefully about my proposal of marriage.' Her tone hardened and Kitty swallowed. It seemed Julian had no choice but to at least pretend to go along with her plans.

'You know it was all Yves's fault really. If he had not pushed me into selling Madame Blanc those designs then none of this would have happened. You do see that, don't you?' Nathalie continued.

'Why didn't you just leave Yves Mangan out of it and tell Simone what you had planned? She may have gone along with it and split the money with you,' Julian said.

'You think she would have stood aside for me? *Non*, I told her, you know, just before the show, that you were in love with me. She laughed in my face. I said then that she should just walk away so you and I could have our happiness. I told her I had seen the apartment and planned all the furniture that you and I would have.' Nathalie's voice rose a little as she spoke. 'She thought I was making a joke on her, a prank.'

'Why did you kill her?' Julian's voice was so soft that Kitty struggled to hear his question.

'Because she wouldn't give you up of course. She was the block to our happiness, our future,' Nathalie said. 'It's been so much nicer not having that old rubbish she collected all over the apartment. No more talk about how she would go to Nantes to see the child and bring her back. Now it's just you and I. Our life together will be perfect.'

There was the sound of a commotion further down the path near to the entrance of the park. Kitty placed her hand on Matt's arm as Nathalie sprang to her feet and urged Julian up.

'Come, we must leave.' Nathalie's tone was urgent and she pressed the knife closer to Julian's throat once more.

'That must be the gendarmes. This could cause a real problem,' Matt said. 'They may well be armed.'

'We need to get out of here.' Kitty tightened her hold on her husband's jacket sleeve. 'If anything goes wrong we could be in the line of fire.'

Nathalie had hustled Julian out of the summer house and was heading away from the lake along an informal track in the grass beyond the building. Matt set off in pursuit with Kitty beside him. 'Matt!' Kitty warned.

She could hear men shouting in French now on the path and the sound of running feet behind them. She could only guess that the police were going to the summer house.

'*Arrêtez! C'est la police. Jetez votre arme.*' The shouted instruction from the gendarmes was clear but Nathalie ignored them. She continued to try to coerce Julian along the track.

Kitty could only assume there must be another exit from the park which the girl intended to take. Matt was clearly using the skills he had learned during the Great War to track Nathalie whilst keeping them out of any immediate danger.

'Kitty, stay here. I'm going to try and cut her off.' Matt had moved again before she could stop him.

Kitty was torn between obeying Matt's instructions or following after him. Two uniformed gendarmes ran past where she was hiding.

'Mademoiselle Belliste, *arrêtez ou nous serons obligés de tirer.*'

Kitty gasped. Matt had been correct in his assumption that the police were armed and would shoot to prevent Nathalie from escaping. Now it seemed Nathalie, Julian and Matt could be injured or killed if the police opened fire.

Nathalie halted and Kitty could see she had Julian in front of her like a shield, the knife still glittering dangerously in the sunlight. She held it at his throat, now exposed since he had used his tie to fasten Matt to the radiator in the apartment.

The blood from the cut on his cheek had dried and she could see he was trying to break her hold on him without her cutting his throat.

'*Restez-là!*' Nathalie warned the gendarmes, and they were forced to obey her command to remain where they were.

'Nathalie, you can't run away. The park is surrounded by gendarmes. Throw down the knife.' Matt emerged into the open behind the girl, effectively blocking her escape. He had his hands in the air so the police could see he hadn't a weapon and he had placed himself carefully so should the police fire he was not impeding their line of fire.

Kitty gasped and bit her lip, tears forming in her eyes at her husband's bravery.

'Tell them all to go away or I shall kill Julian,' Nathalie said.

Kitty saw the gendarmes' hands were resting on top of their gun holsters. One wrong word or false move could prove fatal.

'You know that won't happen. If you leave the park then where will you go?' Matt asked.

'*Oui*, listen to Captain Bryant.' Inspector LeJeune strode up to join his gendarmes and Kitty allowed herself to breathe a small sigh of relief. The inspector always struck her as a sensible man, surely he could help persuade the girl to surrender.

'Julian and I will be together, just like I planned. We are going to live in England in a cottage,' Nathalie called back.

'Julian has obligations here first. His mother needs his help to pack up. You need to pack too. You need a passport,' Matt said.

Kitty knew it was a gamble to pander to the girl's delusions, but it seemed they had little choice in this stand-off. One false move and Julian would be dead. Nathalie seemed to hesitate.

'You said you would be a better daughter-in-law than Simone. Now you can prove it. Eliza would give you and Julian her blessing then,' Matt said.

Kitty saw him exchange a glance with Inspector LeJeune and she saw they were clearly going to try to work together.

Nathalie paused, the knife blade dropped down a fraction.

'*Maman* would help you to plan our wedding. All of this misunderstanding can be sorted out. Is that not so, Inspector?' Julian managed to say. It seemed he had finally realised he would do better to agree with the girl.

'We can have a church wedding, with bridesmaids and orange blossom?' Nathalie asked as she scrutinised the men watching her every move.

'With church bells and lilies at the altar,' Matt said.

Kitty heard her husband forcing himself to sound calm and authoritative as if this madcap fantasy could be real.

'Then we would live in England for a while before coming home to Paris with our children?' Nathalie looked at Julian.

'*Oui, c'est vrai. Une fille et un garçon,*' he assured her.

Nathalie scanned Julian's face as if to assure herself that he was telling the truth.

Kitty's shoulders sagged in relief as Nathalie finally removed the knife from Julian's throat.

'*Mon amour*, let us sort out this misunderstanding with

Inspector LeJeune, and then we can give *Maman* our happy news,' Julian suggested to Nathalie.

Inspector LeJeune gave a discreet signal to the gendarmes that they were to stand down from drawing their guns as he approached the couple.

'Perhaps, I should look after the knife for you, Mademoiselle Belliste,' he suggested when he reached them.

'*Merci*, Inspector.' Nathalie handed it over meekly as Julian moved to support her with his arm around her waist.

'*On y va*.' Julian guided the girl forwards, and she smiled happily up at him.

'Monsieur DeTourner, may I trouble you to accompany Mademoiselle Belliste with the gendarmes to the exit of the park. I shall be there in a moment to assist,' Inspector LeJeune said.

'Of course.' Julian walked Nathalie back along the path accompanied by the police.

Kitty rushed forwards to Matt as soon as the couple had gone. She flung her arms around her husband and hugged him. 'Oh, Matt, that was so frightening.'

'My thanks to you, Captain Bryant, Madame Bryant. Both of you were very brave. I will need to speak to you both to complete statements but now I must go and deal with Mademoiselle Belliste. I think she will require medical aid. Monsieur DeTourner will then be free to join you,' the inspector said.

'Of course, thank you. She has made a full confession in front of witnesses to her part in murdering her sister and Monsieur Mangan,' Matt said.

'She is clearly deeply troubled,' Kitty added.

The inspector nodded. 'Yes, she has definitely suffered from some loss of her mind. Do not worry, she will be well cared for. Thank you again.' He hurried away to part Julian from Nathalie so they could arrest the girl and ensure she was seen by a doctor.

'I was so scared. I didn't know if she would cut Julian's

throat or if the police would draw their guns.' Kitty shuddered as Matt placed his arm firmly around her shoulders. 'I'm just so thankful no one else was hurt.'

CHAPTER TWENTY-FIVE

They walked slowly back along the path together to the gate where they had entered the park. Kitty was glad of Matt's support as she still felt shaken by what had just happened. The police cars were driving away, with Nathalie seated in a car between two gendarmes. Julian was standing holding a distraught-looking Patty in his arms.

'I ran down here as soon as I could. The police obviously wouldn't let me or anyone else enter the park. I can't believe it was Nathalie who killed Simone. Poor Monsieur Mangan too. It's awful, just awful. I was so scared.' Patty drew out her handkerchief and blew her nose. Her eyes were red around the rims where she had been crying.

'At least it's all over now. I had no idea that she felt that way about me or was so jealous of Simone. Nathalie needs help, it's clear her mind has gone,' Julian said.

'It's terrible, so frightening to think I was living with her. I shall sure be glad to see Pops and get on that ship back to the US.' Patty shivered.

Kitty understood how the girl felt. It was a good thing the

model had been staying away from the apartment at her great-aunt's home. Kitty would be quite glad to return home herself now. She wasn't looking forward to telling her godmother and her grandmother all that had happened.

They stayed for a few more minutes to make sure Patty was all right before taking a taxi back to their hotel. Julian went with Patty to lock up the apartment and then to see her safely back to her great-aunt's. Then he planned on going home to see his mother.

* * *

Grams was waiting for them in their suite when they returned to the hotel.

'Matthew, you seem most dishevelled. Where is your tie?' she asked as they entered the room.

'It's a long story,' Matt said as they took a seat on the sofa.

'It sounds as if tea is in order,' Grams remarked, looking at Kitty's expression and she telephoned reception.

Once room service had delivered their drinks they told her everything that had happened.

'Monsieur Mangan is dead? Oh dear, how dreadful. You say Nathalie killed him and her sister because she was in love with Julian?' Grams was horrified. 'Eliza will be distraught. Thank heavens Julian was unharmed. He could have been her next victim, as could either of you and that nice young American girl.'

It took a concerted effort from both Kitty and Matt and copious amounts of tea with a splash of brandy to soothe her grandmother.

'And all the time Eliza and I were having such a wonderful day oblivious to everything. My goodness me, I must say I had no idea that our restful little holiday would turn out to be so calamitous,' Grams said.

'Inspector LeJeune will require statements from Matt and I and then we will be free to leave. At least we should be able to return home as planned,' Kitty said as she examined the bruises now starting to appear on her wrists.

'Dear me, I must say I think even I have seen quite enough of Paris for the time being after hearing all this. Eliza is following us to Devon soon. She has settled on a house to rent, and it will do her and Julian good to be away from France for a while. Perhaps you can help him to settle into a quieter life in England. But please, for mine and Eliza's sake, do not drag him into any more murders,' Grams said.

Kitty wasn't entirely certain that she and Matt could avoid any more murder cases, but she was hopeful that Julian at least would be safe. She wondered what would happen once they were home.

There was still Redvers Palmerston to track down. A shiver ran along her spine, and she glanced at Matt who was calmly discussing packing with her grandmother. At least Grams looked much healthier now despite everything. She wondered if Chief Inspector Greville had uncovered any more information in the last few days. The fire at Plymouth was a serious matter and it was unclear how it had started or why the unknown man had Redvers's ring.

She was also quite certain their services would be in demand as usual over the summer on other cases. Although, with any luck, perhaps Inspector Lewis might finally get his promotion and stay in Exeter. That would be one less thorn in their side. Although she expected that Mrs Craven was probably home from Dartmoor by now and would be waiting to annoy her as usual.

There was also a much pleasanter task to look forward to. That of helping Alice to plan her wedding to Robert Potter. Kitty smiled to herself, at least hopefully that was one thing that should now go smoothly. She finished her tea and set her cup and saucer back down. Perhaps by the time they were home, Alice and Robert might even have set their wedding date. A wedding was always a cause for celebration in Kitty's book.

A LETTER FROM HELENA

Dear reader,

I want to say a huge thank you for choosing to read *Murder in Paris*. If you enjoyed it and would like to keep up to date with all my latest releases, just sign up at the following link. Your email address will never be shared, and you can unsubscribe at any time. There is also a free story – 'The Mysterious Guest', starring Kitty's friend, Alice.

www.bookouture.com/helena-dixon

Writing *Murder in Paris* bought back many happy memories of previous travels to the magical city of light. It was made even more special by the safe arrival of my second grandson whilst I was writing the book.

I do hope you loved *Murder in Paris* and if you did, I would be very grateful if you could write a review. I'd love to hear what you think, and it makes such a difference helping new readers to discover one of my books for the first time.

I love hearing from my readers – you can get in touch through social media or my website.

Thanks,

Helena Dixon

KEEP IN TOUCH WITH HELENA

www.nelldixon.com

facebook.com/nelldixonauthor
x.com/NellDixon

ACKNOWLEDGEMENTS

My thanks to my Torbay friends for all their help, support and knowledge including my museum contacts who assist me to get my facts as accurate as possible for my stories. Special love to the Tuesday zoomers and the fabulous Coffee Crew who help support me in so many ways. Thank you to my incredible, hard-working agent, Kate Nash. My fabulous family too, who are always there for me. Finally, much love and thanks to everyone at Bookouture on team Kitty who all work incredibly hard to make the books the best that they can be. I appreciate each and every one of you.

PUBLISHING TEAM

Turning a manuscript into a book requires the efforts of many people. The publishing team at Bookouture would like to acknowledge everyone who contributed to this publication.

Audio
Alba Proko
Sinead O'Connor
Melissa Tran

Commercial
Lauren Morrissette
Hannah Richmond
Imogen Allport

Cover design
Debbie Clement

Data and analysis
Mark Alder
Mohamed Bussuri

Editorial
Cerys Hadwin-Owen
Charlotte Hegley

Copyeditor
Jane Eastgate

Proofreader
Shirley Khan

Marketing
Alex Crow
Melanie Price
Occy Carr
Cíara Rosney
Martyna Młynarska

Operations and distribution
Marina Valles
Stephanie Straub
Joe Morris

Production
Hannah Snetsinger
Mandy Kullar
Nadia Michael
Ria Clare

Publicity
Kim Nash
Noelle Holten
Jess Readett
Sarah Hardy

Rights and contracts
Peta Nightingale
Richard King
Saidah Graham

RAISING READERS
Books Build Bright Futures

Dear Reader,

We'd love your attention for one more page to tell you about the crisis in children's reading, and what we can all do.

Studies have shown that reading for fun is the **single biggest predictor of a child's future life chances** – more than family circumstance, parents' educational background or income. It improves academic results, mental health, wealth, communication skills, ambition and happiness.

The number of children reading for fun is in rapid decline. Young people have a lot of competition for their time, and a worryingly high number do not have a single book at home.

Hachette works extensively with schools, libraries and literacy charities, but here are some ways we can all raise more readers:

- Reading to children for just 10 minutes a day makes a difference
- Don't give up if children aren't regular readers – there will be books for them!

- Visit bookshops and libraries to get recommendations
- Encourage them to listen to audiobooks
- Support school libraries
- Give books as gifts

There's a lot more information about how to encourage children to read on our websites: **www.RaisingReaders.co.uk** and **www.JoinRaisingReaders.com**.

Thank you for reading.

Printed in Dunstable, United Kingdom